By Camille Pagán

Dog Person

Good for You

Everything Must Go

It's a Wonderful Wife

Don't Make Me Turn This Life Around

This Won't End Well

I'm Fine and Neither Are You

Woman Last Seen in Her Thirties

Forever Is the Worst Long Time

Life and Other Near-Death Experiences

The Art of Forgetting

DOG PERSON

DOG PERSON

A Novel

CAMILLE PAGÁN

DELACORTE PRESS | NEW YORK

Delacorte Press
An imprint of Random House
A division of Penguin Random House LLC
1745 Broadway, New York, NY 10019
randomhousebooks.com
penguinrandomhouse.com

Hardcover ISBN 979-8-217-09205-5
Ebook ISBN 979-8-217-09206-2

Printed in the United States of America on acid-free paper

1st Printing

First Edition

BOOK TEAM: Production editor: Michelle Daniel • Managing editor: Saige Francis • Production manager: Richard Elman • Copy editor: Laura Dragonette • Proofreaders: Amy Brosey, Melissa Churchill, Claire Maby, Catherine Mallette

Book design by Kim Henze Walker

For my many pets, past and present—
but especially D.L., who made me a dog person

AUTHOR'S NOTE

I like to know what I'm getting into when I begin a novel. If you do, too, *Dog Person* includes scenes that depict grief over the loss of a partner and a pet nearing the end of its life. Even so, this is a hopeful story about love, second chances—and, of course, dogs.

Thank you for reading my work.

—Camille

DOG
PERSON

One

There are two kinds of people in this world: dog people, and people who still need to meet the right dog. That's what Amelia said when she brought me home to Miguel. "That may be, but I'm happiest being a *you* person," he replied. Then he kissed her and went back to reading a novel.

Amelia, of course, was a dog person. She spotted me in the shelter and saw something other than a yippy mutt who'd licked the fur clean off his belly. I was nervous, nervous, nervous. Even though the shelter gave me a nice big space to pace in, those metal bars were too much like my crate. My first owner bought the crate for training, but an hour usually turned into all day. When he wasn't busy working at a place where I couldn't be, he and his friends hollered at the television and ignored the sound of my barking from the basement. And still it took him a whole year to realize I wasn't going to be the dog to make him a better man.

I feel sad when I think about all that time I spent alone.

But then along came Amelia. She didn't look me in the eye.

She just sidled up next to the pen so I could sniff her, all espresso and ink and old books.

It was like inhaling heaven.

I was not cool about meeting her. When the shelter woman let me out, I jumped on Amelia. She was a small human, so it wouldn't have taken much to knock her over. But she just laughed and squatted down in front of me.

"Don't worry, you silly beast. I'll come to you," she said, gazing over my head so I wouldn't feel threatened. Not that I would have been, not by her. "I hear you go by Harold. Do you like that name?"

I licked her cheek, and she laughed again. "Well, that's a funny thing to call a dog, but you're a funny dog, aren't you? All right, Harold," she said as I tried to burrow my way into her heart through her armpit. "I'm Amelia. I'm going to be your person."

And oh, was she ever. She gave me a soft, fluffy bed that reminded me of my mother. She found a dog park, too, and although I'm not much of a dog's dog, I do love that leashless freedom. She even took up running for me, because she knew I needed more exercise to be my best self. I'm sorry to say that despite the miles we covered, I remained a creature of habit; I'd catch a breeze and dart out the door like I was trying to escape my crate. Then I'd sprint through the streets like a greyhound at the track (poor things). Amelia never yelled at me when I came back. She'd just hug me and press her wet cheek against my head and say, "I'm not ready to lose you, Harold. Please stop doing that."

I did try. I ran away less and less, until one day Miguel left the back gate open while he was hauling in groceries, and I was just so sad that I didn't have it in me. I'll be honest: That was a rough afternoon.

But not nearly as bad as the ones that he and I had recently been through.

Now it's just me and Miguel. Amelia's been gone for almost six seasons, and Miguel's still intent on staying holed up in our house. He doesn't return calls and hasn't flown home to Puerto Rico once, even though his sister warned him that their Aunt Ceci doesn't have much longer to live. Worst of all, he barely goes into Lakeside Books, which he and Amelia opened right before she rescued me. Miguel's an obsessive reader—or at least he was—who'd dreamed of owning a bookstore; Amelia claimed he'd sleep in the stockroom if she let him. These days, he heads back there if he doesn't feel like talking to customers, which is pretty much any rare occasion we're at the store. "Harold, the fewer people I have to interact with, the less life sucks," he tells me.

I miss the way things used to be.

Of course, Miguel does, too. Maybe that's why we both sleep in most days. On this particular morning, however, I'm startled awake by him clapping his hands over my head.

"There you are!" he exclaims, peering down at me. "Welcome to Tuesday, Harold! Now, up and at 'em—we've got things to do."

Do we? If memory serves, said things will be walking around the block and me watching him bicker with bill collectors at the kitchen table. The prospect's so enticing that I cover my eyes with a paw to block the light streaming in through the window.

But then my brain turns all the way on, and I remember

that I have a duty to fulfill. I promised Amelia I'd take care of Miguel, and I can't exactly do that while I'm unconscious.

"You good, dog?" Miguel asks, frowning at me.

I raise my head in his direction, hoping to convey that I'm *fine.*

If only it didn't take so much effort to scramble onto all fours. I can still tear through the backyard like I did in my prime, pretending that I fully intend to dispatch a squirrel. Afterward, though, I have to walk slowly; sometimes I need an extra nap. Customers no longer ask if I'm a puppy or try to figure out if I'm more of a Brittany or a setter. Now they pet me softly and laugh at the light patches over my eyes, which they say look like eyebrows. Just last month, the vet had to take out two of my teeth. These are not the problems of a young dog. That's what's troubling me.

Still—another day is another chance, and I'll be darned if I'll let this one pass me by.

"Good boy," says Miguel, ruffling my fur as we head into the hallway.

His praise is almost enough to make me forget that I really, really need to pee. When he starts for the bathroom, I whimper and look pointedly in the direction of the staircase.

"Right," he says quickly. "Sorry, Harold. Showering can wait."

Can it, though? I don't want to tell Miguel how to live his life, but he really should have bathed and tended to the rug on his face days ago. Still, my bladder's ready to burst, so I clamber down the stairs behind him, trying to mask how difficult it is to do so. When we reach the kitchen, he opens the back door and steps onto the deck. He's yet to put on pants, and

Raina, our next-door neighbor, is on her patio watering her flowers.

"Go run," he commands, pointing at the yard. Raina's looking at him now, and he lifts his chin to acknowledge her instead of acknowledging that, you know, there's one thin layer of cotton between his jiggly bits and our neighborhood. Is there an acceptable window for random acts of grief? If so, I worry Miguel has exceeded it. "Do your business," he adds before stepping into the house and leaving the door ajar.

I do as I'm told, naturally, then come trotting back inside. Miguel has made no indication he intends to fully clothe the bottom half of his body, but he's smiling into a bowl of cereal at the counter.

The smile's a rare sight, one that's probably owing to the upcoming event with Jonathan Middleton-Biggs. JMB, as he's known, is Miguel's favorite novelist, and he's been trying to get him into the store for as long as I can remember. Jonathan is a very important author, and Lakeside is just a random bookstore in a small tourist town in Southwest Michigan. So, Jonathan's answer was always the same: no.

But Amelia used to say that the universe delivered gifts at the most unlikely times. Maybe so, because a few months ago, Jonathan's assistant called to say he'd like to do a ticketed signing at Lakeside. I heard Riley, our book buyer, tell Dane, who's a clerk, that JMB's event will help offset the margins and keep our doors open a little longer. Now, I don't know a margin from margarine, but I can't imagine life without the bookstore.

Then again, I couldn't imagine either without Amelia.

Mostly I'm happy that Miguel's excited about *something*. He sets his bowl on the floor for me, and he's even left a few marshmallows floating in the milk! I wag what's left of my tail in gratitude and slurp down his leftovers.

"Don't overdo it," he warns, squatting to wipe my splatter with a paper towel. Then he pats my back and says the same thing he tells me nearly every day: "I need you, Harold. You're all I have now."

Listen, I'm no dolphin. But even *I* know this isn't the kind of dog person Amelia wanted Miguel to be.

I wish I could believe Lakeside will keep him going once I'm gone. After all, it wasn't just his dream; it was theirs. But a bookstore, no matter how splendid, is not a companion.

"Help Miguel find someone to love," Amelia murmured to me at the end. She was the only one who understood what was happening; I couldn't comprehend it myself, and everyone says that dogs can sense these things. She was too weak to scratch my ears, so she stroked the top of my head gently. "He won't want to, but love's the only thing that can heal a broken heart. You're such a good dog, Harold, and while I've asked the impossible of you, I know you'll find a way. I love you."

I look at Miguel, who's heading for the stairs. But in my mind, I only see Amelia. *I love you, too,* I think, just as I did on that terrible morning. *And I will do everything I possibly can to help your person find another person.*

I just hope I figure out how—and soon. Because forget new tricks.

What this old dog's really worried about is time.

Two

We're at the store—we're at the store! No wonder Miguel woke me up. He knows this is my very favorite place other than his and Amelia's bed, except I'm actually allowed here. I go round and round the aisles and their miles of books. People sit. They stay. Sometimes they even bring their dogs. It smells like adventure.

The front doors are deep green, or so everyone says; I can only really see blue and yellow. And Dane painted a rainbow across the picture window facing the street, right below the LAKESIDE BOOKS sign. I've just barely bounded inside when Riley greets me. "Good morning, Harold! How are we feeling?" she asks.

Her long braids make a curtain around us as she bends to scratch behind my ears. If Miguel and Amelia had ever had a daughter, she'd have been just like Riley, whose nose is always in a novel. She's a walking card catalog, says Miguel, though I don't actually know what that means. I'm guessing it has something to do with the fact that you can tell Riley "grieving travel writer" and "dog trainer" and she'll think for a moment, then exclaim, "*The Accidental Tourist!*" and fetch you a copy. Customers love her. So do I, and not just because she slips me bites of her donuts, knowing full well they'll turn me into a stink bomb. Riley's the best.

I push my head into her hand to show her that although I did feel a tad stiff in the hips after the car ride over, I'm better already.

"Excellent," she says. "Me, too. I'm going to try to sell a lot of books today."

Yes, I'd like that. Amelia would be so pleased to know the bookstore's holding on. It was more important to her than anything aside from me and Miguel and her own books. Amelia wrote romance novels, one after another; I heard Dane tell Riley that she sold a series about a bunch of sexy siblings and used that money to start the store. Her parents called her books "smut," and even some of our customers think romance is cheesy. But Amelia's readers adored her stories—and like she used to say, what kind of monster doesn't love love?

"Harold, come get some water," says Miguel, trying to guide me to the back of the store. "You've got to stay hydrated." When I push my paws against the tile, trying to resist, he frowns and examines me. "*¿Qué te pasa? ¿Te sientes bien?*"

I raise my head to indicate that I am feeling perfectly normal. Mildly wonderful, even!

It wasn't always like this. We had a nice understanding, Miguel and I: We shared a person, and for her alone, we were content to coexist while staying out of each other's way. Now he's under the impression that I can't make it down the block without his assistance when I'm the one who's supposed to be taking care of *him*.

Dane's at the register. Unlike Riley, who's been at Lakeside only a few years, he was one of the first people Amelia hired. He's got hair like a molting dandelion and a summer-day smile. Miguel may claim I'm his only friend, but Dane's determined to prove him wrong, especially now that Amelia's gone. "Hey, chief," he says to Miguel. "Looking bright-eyed and bushy-tailed today! You get my message about Kathy?" Kathy owns our building. She's also Riley's aunt, which is how Riley ended up working here. "She's been trying to get in touch with you."

Miguel sighs. "I'd have to listen to my answering machine to get the message. But I already paid the rent, and the plumbing seems to be working, at least for now. Whatever she needs can wait until after I'm done checking our JMB inventory."

"I already did that."

"You trying to take my job?"

"I'm trying to be helpful. Also, you're welcome."

"Thank you. Also, you're fired."

Dane smirks. "Nice try. You can't fire me—customers like me too much. Or at least I like them, which is basically the same thing."

"I assure you it's not."

"You want Jeannie back here? Suit yourself."

Jeannie was always wagging her finger at kids and telling them that Lakeside's a bookstore, not a library. Amelia rehomed her at a gift shop the next town over. "Books are replaceable," she explained to Miguel when he protested because finding year-round employees in a tourist town isn't easy. "Our customers aren't."

"The longer you keep talking, the more I'm considering selling Jeannie this business so she can manage you," Miguel tells Dane, but he's looking at a couple of teens near the comic book racks. Then he glances at me and frowns. "I'm aware that you don't want to do inventory with me, Harold. How about you hang out here?"

"He can stock with me," says Riley, who's just wheeled over a big metal cart loaded with books.

"Okay," Miguel agrees. "But please make sure he doesn't overexert himself."

Riley winks at me. "I promise to make him go nap on the rug the minute he looks pooped."

I'm happy to trail after her, even if fresh ink doesn't smell nearly as nice as the kind that's had a chance to settle. Miguel says publishers care most about selling books right after they're published. But the ones that are no longer new—like dogs, those need a home most of all. This is where Riley comes in. Read all of Jude Deveraux's backlist? You're overdue for some Beverly Jenkins. Dug *Dalva*? *Love Medicine*'s the real deal. She sells as many books as all our other employees combined. Miguel says that if she ever left, we'd be sunk.

Today, we're stocking adult fiction. We start with Sci-Fi and Historical before moving to Stabby Peeps, as Dane named the Mysteries and Thrillers section. Then we fill regular Fiction, and don't ask me how that's different from the rest. Last, there's Romance, which is located at the back of the store because some people are sheepish about buying what they like—or maybe it's because of that one shirtless guy with the flowing hair on so many of the covers. Either way, it's the section we end up restocking most frequently.

Riley and I are just wrapping up when Kathy comes flying into the bookstore, her flowered tent of a dress billowing behind her.

Amelia adored Kathy but admitted privately that she could

be a wee bit flaky. Now, flaky is just the thing when it comes to baked goods. But since Miguel often wanted the toilet fixed the same week it stopped working, she's not his type of treat. Still, she never raised the rent more than inflation, and although I'm not clear on what that means, Lakeside has been able to stay in the same location all this time. Meanwhile, the psychic who told Dane he'd already met the love of his life has moved up and down the block a bunch of times, and the falafel place has switched spots twice.

"Miguel! We need to talk!" Kathy calls, even though Miguel's nowhere to be seen. "Riley, where is he? I saw his car. I know he's here."

"Hi, Auntie," Riley says, grimacing at Dane.

"I'll go get him, Kathy," says Dane, giving Riley bug eyes from the register. "You make yourself comfortable."

"Child, it's 2003. I haven't been comfortable since 1979." She grabs her tortoiseshell eyeglasses, which are hanging from one of the many necklaces around her neck, and sets them on her nose. "But I'll look for the new Nora while I wait."

On Riley's recommendation, Kathy ends up with a Nora Roberts novel and two from Connie Briscoe. She's just cracked one open when Miguel finally emerges from the stockroom. He tries to force a smile, but it's no use. "Kathy, what brings you in?" he asks.

"Well," she says, peering at him over the top of her glasses. "What brings me in is you not returning my calls, not to mention running out the back door when you spotted me last week."

So . . . she did see that.

"Sorry," he says, and while I'm not excited to see him sheepish, at least he cares—even two or three seasons ago, that wouldn't have been true. "I haven't been in the chattiest mood lately."

"Miguel, I'd love to hear about a single day in your life you were chatty. All the same, apology accepted. Is there a good place for us to talk shop?"

He gestures to the reading nook, which is tucked into one of the front corners of the store, and the three of us amble over there. Kathy plops down in the yellow armchair, but Miguel stands next to the sofa with his arms crossed over his chest.

"You got July's rent, right?" he asks her. "I dropped it off almost a week ago."

She leans back. "I know you did—and in the spirit of 'better late than never,' thank you. But this isn't about that."

He frowns and waits for her to continue.

"Mr. Rivera, I feel like we've been in business together long enough for me to be frank with you."

He nods.

"I appreciate that. Long story short, I received an offer to buy the building."

"This one?" he says, retracting his head like a turtle. "Are you evicting us?"

"No, no, no," Kathy says quickly. "The offer's good. Better than I expected, if I'm being honest. But you know I'm fond of Lakeside, and I don't want to put my own niece out of the job that suits her so well. Besides, this isn't the first time someone's tried to buy—it's just the first time I had to consider selling."

The air-conditioning's on, but Miguel's face is starting to drip. "I'm not sure I follow."

"Well, the upkeep on this fossil is more expensive by the

hour. The bigger issue is, I'm getting old, and money's tighter than it should be—my investments have taken a huge hit because of this whole Iraq War mess. I refuse to ask my kids to pay for my care once I'm drooling on myself. Which means I need to make some difficult decisions."

Miguel, still as a stone, says nothing.

"I'm not going to kick you out, but I do have to raise the rent. You've been through a lot over the past two years, so I've been holding out on telling you as long as I can. Unfortunately, I can't afford to wait any longer."

"How much?"

"Another grand a month starting in September when the lease renews. I'm sorry," she says, and she does sound like she means it. "That's the lowest I can go with the property taxes going up again, not to mention the plumbing repairs that we both know I need to make. That's going to take extra cash. Try as I might, I can't keep pretending I've got all the time in the world."

I know the feeling.

She gets up from the chair and puts a hand on his arm. I wonder if she hasn't noticed he's wincing or is simply pretending not to. "Thank you for understanding. I've got my fingers crossed that this'll work out, because I'd like the bookstore to stay put—I've always thought of it as the heart of West Haven. But I understand if you decide it's time to find a new space, too."

"Thanks," he says quietly. "I'll be in touch."

Once Kathy's gone, Miguel crouches beside me on the floor and runs his hand down my back. After a moment, he says, "September's five weeks away, Harold. The revenue from JMB's event that isn't already earmarked for staffing can help with the first month or two—but I'm not sure we can pull it off all year long when the postholiday season's so slow and I'm already draining my savings to make payroll. I guess we could move, but that'll probably be even more expensive. We're screwed."

He's staring at me with big eyes, but instead of staring back, I gaze around the store. I want him to see what I see, to remember the story he and Amelia used to tell people when they asked how Lakeside came to be.

"Many years ago, in a land before email," he'd begin, "a beautiful sprite of a woman was browsing at the original Borders bookstore in Ann Arbor when a man spotted her through the window . . ."

And something about the woman—perhaps her halo of curls, or the constellation of stars dotted across her nose and cheeks, or maybe just her sparkling self—made the man stop in his tracks and go inside, even though it meant he would be late for the meeting he was heading to.

Now, this woman didn't usually trust random men. After all, most men give no reason to be trusted. Yet something about this one was different. So, she was willing to humor him when he asked if she'd read *Alaska* by James Michener, which happened to be on the table she was standing in front of.

She held up another novel with a bright red cover and large gold script and told him that was more her style.

He laughed and asked her if he could have her number.

She said that she didn't give her number out to strangers. Also, she had a boyfriend. But she smiled at him in a way that made him feel an entirely different sort of strange, and in that moment, he knew he'd met his match.

So, he plucked a copy of the red novel off the table and jogged over to the checkout counter, where he purchased it and borrowed a pen from the cashier. He returned with a paper bag and told her his number was on the inside cover, if she ever wanted to talk books—and by the way, his name was Miguel Rivera.

Three months later, she called him to say that while she hadn't liked *Zoya* as much as she'd hoped to, she was single now. Oh, and her name was Amelia May, and she was a romance novelist who wanted to open a bookstore one day.

"Which was exactly what I wanted, too," Miguel explained, slipping his arm around her waist when he said this part. "Spotting you through the window was the happiest coincidence of my life."

"There are no coincidences," Amelia would respond, then kiss him. "Everything lines up as it's supposed to, even if it takes a while to see how and why."

I believe that. After all, if I hadn't lived with the other man first, I wouldn't have ended up at the shelter, where Amelia happened to drop in on a whim and decided to make me hers. Which led to the most magical sixty-some dog years of my life. Sometimes I wish I'd gone with her to wherever she is now—but if I had, I wouldn't be here to help Miguel. I guess that worked out the way it was supposed to, too.

I just wish it hurt a little less.

Miguel must've just remembered their origin story because he stands, puts his fists on his hips, and says, "Harold, we're going to have to find a way to fix this. Losing Lakeside would be like losing Amelia all over again—only this time, I can do something about it. From here on out, my only focus is to make money and keep the store afloat. I owe her that."

I'm glad to see him worked up about *something*. Except . . . Amelia didn't task me with saving Lakeside.

Given how stubborn he is, I'm more likely to grow another tail than convince the man to change his mind about his new-found purpose. Which means my job just became twice as hard.

Because somehow, some way, I'm going to have to make him see that love's the key to his next chapter.

Three

"We're going to meet JMB, Harold," Miguel says, opening the car door so I can hop into the back seat. "After all this time! I can hardly believe it."

Me neither. Miguel's been a wee bit obsessed with Jonathan ever since he read his first novel, *Missing Person*. Oh, how he can go on about that book—how lyrical the prose, how clever the narrator! But most of all, he loves the story, which is about two siblings who lose their parents and have to make their way in the world by relying on each other. It's fiction, but it's based on Jonathan's life—and it's what happened to Miguel and his sister, Miriam, too. Their dad left them and started another family, and their mom died soon after of a broken heart. He told Amelia that *Missing Person* is the only book he's ever read that made him feel someone understood what that was like for him.

And now he's finally—*finally*—going to get a chance to tell JMB that himself.

As he and I make the short drive to the bookstore, I hear a strange yet familiar sound that makes my ears perk up. It's been so long since I heard it that it takes me a moment to recognize it as something other than an amorous cicada. He's humming!

Oh, this will be a good night indeed.

There's a crowd gathering in front of the store, which has closed early for the event, so Miguel and I go through the back entrance.

"Boss," Riley greets Miguel from the register. "You look sharp."

"Um, thanks," he says, glancing down at himself. He finally shaved, and he's wearing pants and a pair of shoes that cover his toes. "Ready to sell as many books as possible?"

Across the room, the long, rectangular display tables have been moved to make space for rows of folding chairs.

"You know I am. Might be the first and last time we have more than a hundred people in here at once," says Riley. "Speaking of people, Zara Aboah will be here tonight. She drove in from Detroit to hear JMB, of course, but she'd also like to say hi. Can I grab you for a minute before he speaks?"

"Mmmm," Miguel says. From another person, this noise might imply a willingness to be persuaded. From him, it means *absolutely not.*

Riley, dog bless her, won't be turned away so easily.

"Zara was a friend of Amelia's. Remember, Amelia helped her find a literary agent? So, she'd like to say hello and talk about maybe doing a launch event for her debut novel here."

"Maybe some other time—I need to give JMB my full attention. You can introduce her to Brenna." Brenna does the store's events and bookkeeping.

"Miguel." Funny how a name can mean different things

depending on how you say it. Right now Riley's commanding him to listen. "Amelia really liked Zara."

His face twists up all strange, so I scooch closer to him and lean against his calf. "Sorry, Riley. Maybe next time."

She eyes him, then sighs quietly. "Not a problem. I'll take care of it."

"Sorry," he says again. "I'm going to test the mic and see if Jonathan's here yet."

She looks down at me. "Come on, Harold. Let's go get a few more of JMB's books to put out."

I trot behind her to the stockroom. I peed in here once. Miguel said I wasn't going to be allowed in the store anymore. No one believed him—he loved Amelia too much to deny her anything, even her excitable mutt—but I never did it again. Amelia used one of those natural cleaners on my mess. Even all these years later, I still catch the occasional whiff of my youthful indiscretion.

Riley uses a knife to carefully cut the seam of a box of books. "What are we going to do, boy? It's been well over a year, and he still seems so depressed. I mean, believe me—I get that grief takes time. But I really think he should see a therapist."

Over a year was a very, very long time ago to me. Though sometimes not. Every now and then, I wake and immediately put my paws on Amelia's side of the bed—*let's go, let's go, let's go!*

And then I realize she isn't there; she never will be again.

That's when I understand Miguel most of all—why he still reaches for her before his eyes open in the morning, the way his whole body seems to collapse into itself after he calls across the house for her, only for reality to come crashing down on him all over again.

I respond by lying at Riley's feet. If I'm honest, I have no idea what we're going to do, since I seem to be unable to find so much as a single person for him to date, let alone share his life with. I'm counting on JMB to reinvigorate Miguel, or at least remind him that it's important to connect with people you won't find on a page. I'm a first-rate companion if I do say so myself. But humans need humans; even I know that.

We leave the stockroom to set even more of JMB's books on the tables in front of the window. Brenna has placed a big poster with a picture of Jonathan beside the display tables, and another one outside the store. He's wearing a jacket and wire-rimmed glasses and seems very serious. Miguel claims he's a literary genius, but I'm not so sure about that. What kind of genius writes stories about people falling out of love instead of into it?

The crowd outside the building is even larger now. Some people are clutching hardcovers under their arms; others are flipping through their copies. A few are peering in the window to see if they can catch a glimpse of the famous JMB.

Dane, who's come in through the employee entrance, joins us at the front of the store. His hair's sticking up even more than usual, and I'm pretty sure he was wearing the same T-shirt and shorts when I last saw him. He directs a big grin at Riley. He's as wild about her as I am, except he wants to mate with her. He gestures toward the street and whistles. "That's a mob! We're going to bring in some serious moola tonight."

Riley grins back at him. "From your lips to the cash register's drawer." She turns to Miguel. "Should we start letting people in? It's almost six-thirty, and we want to give them time to get settled."

"Not yet." He glances at his watch with a troubled expression. "Jonathan should be here by now."

Dane shrugs. "Train's probably delayed. The one from Chicago's never on time."

"Maybe, but I told him to take the earlier one just in case."

"You talked to JMB? Sweet," says Dane.

"Not technically—I told his assistant that. He's famously reclusive, which I can understand."

"Maybe a little too well, huh, chief?"

Miguel arches an eyebrow in warning.

"Eyes on the prize, big guy," Dane tells him. He looks down at me. "Wanna go find that author, Harold? Don't worry," he assures Miguel. "I'll be careful with him."

Careful? Pshaw. I'm in fine form tonight, so Dane and I head outside to see if Jonathan's getting accosted by overzealous fans. There are a ton of those, but no author. When we return, Miguel's squinting at the computer on the counter. It's a big box, even deeper than our television, and he keeps leaning toward the screen and then away from it. He used to use reading glasses, but I haven't seen him with a pair . . . well, come to think of it, since the last time I saw him reading a book, which was around when Amelia first got sick. He did peek at *I, Edward* before we drove over, but that doesn't really count. Like with *Missing Person,* he can probably recite half the novel from memory.

"No email from Jonathan. Not from his publicist or agent, either," he tells Brenna.

"That may be, but the crowd's getting restless," she responds. "We should let them get settled."

"I guess we don't have a choice," says Miguel, looking at the doors. "I just hope he gets here soon."

There's a buzz in the air as people stream in and take their seats. I can tell Miguel's too nervous to attempt to socialize, so I work the room for him, letting customers rub my head and pat my back and tell me what a sweet, well-behaved dog I am. As I mingle, I try to see if anyone smells like they could use a Puerto Rican pal. There are lots of nice people, yet no one seems right for Miguel.

The store grows quiet, but JMB still hasn't appeared. Finally, Miguel goes up to the podium. A bead of sweat rolls down one side of his face; another immediately appears on the other side. He doesn't bother wiping them away. "Thank you all for being here tonight. I apologize that we're running late, but I'm sure Jonathan will arrive shortly."

"I hope so. At fifty bucks a pop, I could've gone to see the Rolling Stones," an older man calls from the back row.

"Um, I assure you that would have cost more—and it definitely wouldn't have come with a signature from Jonathan Middleton-Biggs," Miguel tells him.

"Apparently neither does this," the man volleys back.

Miguel attempts to smile, but it's no use. "He should be here," he says, and though he's not addressing the crowd, the microphone picks it up and sends his voice echoing through the room.

"What happens if he *doesn't* show?" asks a teenager with raccoon rings around his eyes.

"I just cannot imagine that happening. Jonathan offered to do this event," Miguel tells him. "So, he'll be here. It's simply a question of when."

"I have to get home to my sitter soon," says one woman.

"My shift starts in an hour," says a man a few seats over from her.

"Everyone, hold tight," Brenna calls from behind the seating area. "I'll grab some wine from the back."

"Is that even legal?" Dane asks Riley in a low voice.

"Private event—as long as she doesn't serve anyone underage, it's fine," she tells him quietly. "Let's just hope there's enough for this crowd. Where *is* JMB, anyway?"

"Please do your best to stay comfortable," Miguel says into the mic. "We should begin any minute now."

We do not begin.

Soon the wine's gone and people get up from their seats to mill around. No one's buying books, though, or even browsing; they're just complaining. Some are even speculating that JMB never planned to come to the store in the first place.

Now, of course he did—I heard that conversation myself. Jonathan's been super famous ever since some woman named Oprah told everyone to read his second book. So, it did take his assistant some time to convince Miguel he wasn't being pranked, that Jonathan really did plan to visit the store and sign every last ticket holder's novel. The assistant swore he wanted to help and get readers to buy more books at Lakeside. Which is even more important to Miguel than getting a chance to shake his favorite author's hand.

Riley pulls him away from the podium. "Boss, he's an hour late. Something must have happened," she whispers.

"*¡Claro!* But I'm not sure what I can do. I can't refund everyone right here and now," he whispers back.

Dane's slunk over to the register where they're standing.

"Dude, don't refund yet—rain check. Tell them you'll have a do-over in the very near future, and that you'll throw in a free book at that event."

Miguel gives him the same look he gives me when I try to steal food off the counter. "I can't afford that. I'll . . . offer a discount on anything they buy tonight."

"No one's buying," says Riley glumly. "I actually had someone ask for their money back for *I, Edward.*"

"The next time they come in, then."

She nods. "Okay."

But it isn't okay at all. Miguel's practically lifeless as he tells them about the discount and vows to be in touch soon with a rain date.

The customers stream out. Then Miguel sends the staff home, even though Riley offers to close up shop for him. Once the store's empty, Miguel sits beside me on the tile and runs his hand down my back again and again, which means he's really trying to soothe himself, not me.

"I can't refund all those tickets—I already spent some of that money on July's rent, and the rest is earmarked for August payroll," he tells me.

I'm about to start getting worried about him giving up the hope he's barely got in the first place when he narrows his eyes. "Looks like we're going to have to find JMB, Harold. Because the only way he's not coming into Lakeside and doing this event like he promised is if he's dead."

Four

When we get to Lakeside the next morning, Miguel quickly greets Riley and Dane, then disappears into the stockroom.

"Think he's okay?" Dane asks later. I'm wondering if he means me when he adds, "He's been in there for a while."

"I mean, no," she whispers back. "He hasn't been okay for a long time."

"Right, but now with JMB not showing . . . I mean, it sounds like we might be in trouble, money-wise. And the last thing the guy needs is more stress."

"Trust me, we all know Miguel's been through enough already—and that we can't afford to issue refunds." Riley glances toward the back of the store. "I wish he'd listen to me about e-books. I mean, it's the twenty-first century. If Stephen King's doing it and half the romance author community's already on board, it's only a matter of time before the rest of publishing catches up. We could get out ahead and start making some real money to keep this place open. At the very least, we could start taking online orders and shipping books across the country. If anyone can figure out the digital stuff, it's you."

Dane runs a hand through his hair, which makes it stand at attention. "Thanks, Riles. I like to think I know my way around the interwebs, but we can't push him. Remember the memorial?"

Miguel held Amelia's memorial at the bookstore, and lots of her writer friends came into town for it. Some of them wanted him to feature her novels. He said no—that it wasn't the right time to sell them. But one author took it upon herself to pull Amelia's books from the Romance section and place them on the first table customers saw when they walked in the door. "The point of being a novelist is to create something that lives on," she told Miguel when he asked her what compelled her to rearrange their bookstore.

He didn't respond. In fact, he didn't look at her or speak to anyone—even *me*—for the rest of the day.

Riley exhales. "That was awful."

"Hey," says Dane, eyeing her. "I hope I'm not stressing you out."

I don't know all the details because Riley never mentions it. But something called 9/11 happened the year Amelia first started fainting. That's when Riley moved from New York to Michigan to live with her Aunt Kathy, who told Miguel he'd be an idiot not to hire her. She's been at Lakeside since right before Amelia got sick.

"I'm good," she tells Dane. "Promise."

"Well, you know, let me know if that changes."

"I will."

A few minutes later, Miguel wanders out of the stockroom and takes Dane's place behind the register. "Since I'm here, I'm going to contact JMB's team," he tells him. "Then I'm going to head home. If anyone comes in asking for a refund, tell them we're still working on a rain date."

"You upset?"

"I'm perfectly fine."

Dane shoots me a knowing look. People may call him dense, but he's one of the rare humans who gives me the credit I deserve. "No feelings—just facts," he says to Miguel. "Got it. What are you going to say?"

Miguel frowns. "I'm going to email his agent and assistant and tell them I'll be out eight thousand dollars if he doesn't reschedule. Since I haven't heard otherwise, I assume JMB didn't have an emergency. Which means he's a terrible person." He shakes his head, then mutters, "So much for helping an independent bookstore survive. What a crock."

Dane claps his hands several times, startling me and Miguel. "Email? *Email?* If the store's in danger, you need a show of *force*. We should storm the publisher's office—and his agent's, too. New York's, what, an eleven-hour drive? We could be there by tonight. If all goes well, we could have JMB tied up and in the trunk by tomorrow morning."

"Jonathan lives in Chicago, Dane." Miguel snorts. "And according to, say, any map, New York's the wrong direction if we're planning on kidnapping him. Which, for the record, we are not, because I cannot run a bookstore from prison."

"Touché."

"You know what? You're right about one thing," says Miguel, whose eyes have just brightened.

Dane flashes him a crooked grin. "I love it when you talk dirty to me. Go on."

"Email isn't enough. No, I'm going to call them." Miguel's

already stepping behind the counter. He pushes a button on the computer, and it makes a chiming noise. "I have their info."

"That's it?" Dane's eyes bulge. "*That's* your big idea?"

Admittedly, a parrot could probably plan more than a phone call—but at least Miguel's looking for a solution. It's better than him slinking off into the bushes and waiting for the bitter end.

"Shhhh," says Miguel.

Dane watches expectantly as Miguel grabs the little plastic thing attached to the computer and moves it around as he leans close to the screen. After a moment, he picks up the phone and dials. "Yes, I'd like to speak with Bunny Lê. Um, this is Miguel Rivera . . . I'm the co-owner of Lakeside Books." His face twists in pain as he registers his mistake. "Um, owner. My—never mind. This is about Jonathan Middleton-Biggs. He was supposed to be here last night for a reading and book signing and he didn't show . . . right. Well, can you give Bunny my contact information? It's important. As in, eight thousand dollars' worth of important." Miguel rattles off his number, then hangs up.

"No dice?" says Dane. "That blows."

"Why are you still here? Go sell some books," Miguel growls. "Or, better yet, dress up like a chicken and stand on the side of the highway with a sign telling people we exist."

"I don't hate it. But first I'm gonna go check and see if the guy in the back needs help."

Miguel waits for Dane to leave. Then he gets back on the phone, and this time, he sounds like he knows what he's doing. "Yes, this is Miguel Rivera, the owner of Lakeside Books in Michigan. It's regarding Jonathan Middleton-Biggs and the event he was supposed to attend last night at our store."

Across the store, Dane gives him a thumbs-up, and Miguel responds with a tight smile.

"Um, hi. Thanks for taking my call." He sounds surprised. Optimistic, even, which makes me think our luck's finally about to change.

But then his face falls. "What? Oh no. No, I had no idea . . . *Dios mío.* Right—well, please let me know if you find out more. Thanks."

Dane, who's mistaken Miguel's gaping mouth for delight, lopes over. "Well, boss? What'd the agent say? Is she going to get the future Mr. Pulitzer to do the right thing?"

"That was his assistant, not his agent. And . . . not exactly." Miguel rubs his forehead for a moment, then says, "Turns out she hasn't been able to get ahold of Jonathan, either—and worse, no one seems to have any idea where he is."

Five

When we get home, Miguel strips down to his underwear and pours himself a bowl of Lucky Charms. It was Amelia's favorite cereal, but she never would've had it for dinner. Miguel used to cook all sorts of things for her—Japanese curry, empanadillas, spaghetti squash with shrimp, and whatever else he felt like whipping up. It wasn't all good (there was a particularly unfortunate incident with sea scallops and maple syrup), but they were real meals, effort, love.

Now it's just marshmallows and milk, day after night after day.

I stare up at Miguel, hoping to remind him that I, too, need to be fed, and more than just his leftovers. When that doesn't work, I push my metal bowl to make it bang against the wall.

"Sorry, Harold," he says wearily as he gives me a scoop. Moments later, it's gone. This is the drill: I inhale the contents of my bowl, then we go for a walk. Otherwise, my stomach does weird things; sometimes I even upchuck whole kibble onto the rug, which every dog knows is the best place to barf.

But there will be no walking tonight. Instead, he sends me into the yard to speed my digestion, then turns off the lights and crawls into bed. I hate to see him like this, so I lie on the floor next to him, just in case.

I let him sleep in the next morning, too, because I know he needs a break. But his snoring goes on so long that eventually I nose him to tell him the sun's been up for a good long time—as have I—and it's his turn to rise.

"Go away," he mumbles.

I most certainly will not. I whimper, and when he pulls a pillow over his head, I have no choice but to jump onto the bed.

"Harold!" he grouses, but I won't be dissuaded. While I may not know how to help him find a new partner or keep the bookstore open, I'm certain he'll accomplish neither feat between filthy sheets. So I stand over him, and when he doesn't move, I bark—just once, but sharply.

"All right, Cujo, I'll feed you," he says, tossing the pillow at me. "After all, it's not your fault humans are the worst."

Woof.

He stops in the bathroom briefly, then lets me out. When I trot back inside, I find him in the living room—curtains drawn, thank goodness, as he's clearly in no rush to get dressed. He's hunched over the coffee table, muttering at his computer. It's wired to the wall but is still much smaller than the one at the store and somehow folds in half. He jiggles it, then smacks it with his palm because this, apparently, is how machines do their best work.

After a moment, the thing starts to hum and glow. Miguel leans in toward the screen and types frantically, pausing to shake his head every so often. Eventually he looks at me. "Nothing. Not a peep from JMB *or* his agent, and no updates from his assistant, either. I'm not sure what to do next. You have any ideas, Harold?"

He never used to talk to me like this; I was just a dog to him. I almost miss his blissfully ignorant days. I cock my head to indicate I'm thinking, which gets a tiny smile out of him. But then his lips tighten into a straight line. "I'll have to keep brainstorming, and in the meantime come up with some cash. At this point, I doubt I could get a banker to lend me so much as a pen, but maybe I can sell the house," he says, glancing around. "But then I'd have to find a rental that'd take you. Besides, I wouldn't be able to sell by September—and how would I box up Amelia's things when I can barely make myself go into her office?"

We both sigh.

Now, I like our house. I do. It's a lovely little place with tiger-striped wood trim and a narrow staircase on the second floor that leads up to the attic, which Amelia turned into her writing space. Miguel joked it was a jungle because she had so many plants. But . . . like him, I don't go up there anymore. I can't. And the rest of the place feels cold and empty with her gone.

I swear I'm not trying to, but I must be giving him puppy dog eyes because he leans down and hugs me. "Sorry, Harold, I didn't mean to upset you. I'll always take care of you—promise."

He's going to take care of *me*? That's cute.

Before I can come up with some way to make it clear that his worries are misdirected, the phone rings from the kitchen.

I don't expect him to answer, but he clearly thinks it's JMB because he sprints across the house to get it.

"*¡Ay, bendito!* You finally picked up!" Miguel's hit a button on the phone that sends his sister's voice fluttering into the air. Miriam lives in Bayamón, which is apparently somewhere in Puerto Rico and not a place a dog can get to easily. She flew in for the funeral and wanted to bring him back with her for a couple weeks. But Miguel refused—told her he couldn't visit anytime soon because he needed to stay home to take care of me.

For beings with such big brains, humans can be awfully dumb.

"What's this 'finally'?" he scoffs. "I didn't know you called."

"Which time? I've tried you three times in the past two days!"

"*Lo siento*. I haven't been listening to my messages."

"Listening to what? Your voicemail's been full since last year. Welcome to the twenty-first century, Miguelito—turn on your cellphone and take it with you like the rest of the world. No answering machine required."

"I only got that stupid thing because Amelia made me. *Y sabes que yo lo odio*."

"Love it or loathe it, it might be useful when I have an emergency and need to contact you."

Miguel straightens his spine. "*¿Qué pasó? ¿Es Titi Ceci?*" Their aunt raised them after their mom died when Miriam was nine and he was twelve, but now she's in a nursing home and doesn't always remember them.

"No, she's fine. I just wanted to see how you were doing."

"Hmph," he says, but I know he's happy to hear from her.

Then he tells her about the event. “Between the rent increase and Jonathan not showing up, I’m out of cash and almost out of options.”

“Listen, this is just a setback—not the end. You remember what happened after Mami passed?”

“Not really. Which is probably my brain trying to save me from myself.”

Miriam snorts. “Lucky for you, your sister has a mind like a steel trap. Remember how we didn’t want to ask Titi for cash because we felt bad that she was already grieving about Mami?”

“Hmm.”

“And you knew my sneakers had holes in them. So instead of telling her, you marched over to the comic book place and somehow convinced the owner to let you sell copies outside of school for however much you wanted to charge. Remember?”

Miguel’s expression is slowly changing, but I can’t tell if he’s about to smile or cry.

“And damned if you didn’t convince every other kid at St. Mary’s to spend their lunch money on the latest *New Mutants*. It was like, what, a week before I had a brand-new pair of kicks? But instead of pocketing the leftover money, you gave it to Titi for groceries. I’ve never seen anyone with more hustle and heart.”

“That was then, Miriam. I’m not that person anymore,” he says gruffly.

“Sure you are,” she coos. “I know it doesn’t feel like it right now, but that fighter’s still in there, Miguelito. If anyone can figure this out, it’s you.”

He sniffs. “What if I don’t *want* to figure it out?”

Her voice lowers. “That’s okay, too—just keep putting one

foot in front of the other. And if you can't, you call me, and I'll pull you along until you can walk again."

He wipes his eyes and swallows hard. "Thanks, but I'll be okay—promise. *Te quiero.*"

"Te quiero también. Besito."

After he hangs up, he rubs his lids with his knuckles, then turns to me. "My sister should be a motivational speaker, Harold. I have no idea how we're going to pull this off—but somehow, you and I are going to have to find a way."

Six

Miguel peers into the bathroom mirror. "I can't believe I'm doing this," he tells me as he attempts to get his curls to submit to his demands.

Then don't! I think from my spot beside his feet. *Use that enormous noggin of yours to think of something else!*

"You know I've been brainstorming for hours, and this is the only thing I've been able to come up with," he says defensively, as though he's heard me—although maybe my pointed stare implies that I believe he's about to throw himself to the wolves. He spent hours muttering and pacing the living room after talking to Miriam yesterday. But by the time he fed me dinner, he'd decided he had one decent idea: He'd ask Amelia's parents for money.

Now, the money in question isn't theirs; it's Amelia's. She used some of the royalties from her novels to keep the bookstore up and running. Miguel felt bad about it, but she insisted. "It's our business, sweetheart. We decided to open it together, remember? I know you hate to accept help, but this is our dream," she'd said the last time he protested. She stood on her tiptoes to kiss him. "Now I have a new dream," he growled, making her giggle. Then he scooped her up in his arms and closed the bedroom door so I couldn't bother them while they were mating.

Based on what I heard Miguel tell Miriam a while back, Amelia's books are still selling well. But since she and Miguel never married, her parents get that money now that she's gone. And at the funeral, they made it clear they didn't intend to share it with Miguel or the store.

I follow him out of the bathroom, down the stairs, and into the kitchen. "You can't come with me," he says, slipping into his sandals.

Can't I? I circle around him to demonstrate my enthusiasm because according to Amelia, that's the third most attractive characteristic a creature can exhibit—the first being kindness, obviously, followed by curiosity.

"Not a chance," he says. "Besides, I'm doing you a favor. You know how awful Bob and Becky are."

Do I ever. Amelia took me to their house once. It was summer, and they made me wait in their backyard where there are no trees; I had to huddle beside the scorching aluminum siding of the garage to get a spot of shade. That wasn't even the worst part. A few minutes after I was banished, I heard loud voices, mean ones, and then I heard Amelia's sad voice. Though I put my paws up on the back door and scratched and scratched, no one would let me in, and there was nothing I could do to help her. When we finally left, Amelia's mother told her I'd ruined their door, and Amelia choked out that she would send a check to cover it. When we got home, Miguel asked her if her parents were going to send a check for therapy. She managed to laugh and held him even tighter.

But she can't do that for Miguel now the way he did for her. And while I can't pull him along like Miriam offered to, I could still be there for him—even if it means waiting next to the garage or, *shudder,* in the car.

Alas, he jabs his finger toward the living room. "Go take a snooze, Harold," he tells me. My snaggleteeth must have slipped out because he snorts and says, "I can see that you're upset, but don't even think of doing something naughty while I'm away. I'll put the TV on for you."

Unlike some of my species, shoes and underwear are safe with me; even my toys get cradled ever so gently in my mouth, as I'm not wired to destroy things. But now? I can make no promises. I tilt my head and give him one more chance.

He does not take the bait.

Well, fine. *Fine.* I glare at him through the back window as he leaves, then run to the front windows and watch his car disappear down the road.

I almost don't have it in me to begin my circuit, but it occurs to me that if I let myself go, I may not have the stamina to help Miguel find a new mate. Admittedly, I remain murky as to how to accomplish that—but it will likely involve some degree of agility and speed on my part.

So, I begin.

Every room gets a good sniff and a thorough examination. Though I find the living room livable, the downstairs bathroom has more odors than even a bathroom should. The kitchen gets most of my attention, with no crack or corner ignored. I gobble up a withered almond under the edge of the stove but leave last night's soggy cereal leftovers on the floor because I have recently decided that anything consumed so frequently ceases to be charming.

Then I head upstairs. First, I roll around on the rug in the guest bedroom. It appears I'm part goldfish, because I've somehow forgotten that, just like the last several times I did this, it brings me no joy. I head to Miguel and Amelia's bedroom and leap on the bed, knowing full well that my shedding will betray me. Then again, Miguel doesn't seem to care about the cleanliness of his bedding these days, so I may just get away with it. I twist from my back onto my belly and back again. Then I stick my face in the pillows for good measure. One of them smells ever so faintly like Amelia's shampoo. Though I have more ground to cover, I let myself linger. It's not easy to breathe with all that fluff covering my snout, so I pull my head out and rest it on top of the pillow. Then I let my eyes close, just for a moment.

"You're a good dog, Harold. The very best," I can hear her say, and it could have been at the very beginning of our time together or right before the end. I stay still, very still, because I nearly feel her hand on my head, and that phantom touch is almost enough.

The next thing I know, Miguel is hollering and I'm scrambling to my paws and hoping I don't pee all over the covers. Although honestly, he's lucky I didn't nip him—even a cat person knows to let sleeping dogs lie.

"How long were you on the bed?" he demands.

I stare at him. Why am *I* the one being asked to explain myself?

His shoulders sag, and he sighs. "I'm sorry, it's my fault. I really shouldn't leave you like that. You're obviously lonely."

Me? *Okay, Miguel. Whatever you need to tell yourself.*

Except . . . he's not wrong. This is precisely what happens when you spend so much time with a single person: You begin to mimic them. Resemble them, even, which might explain why the fur over my eyes is losing its color at the same rate as his curls. If I'm not careful, I'm going to morph into Miguel before I'm able to help him.

The truth is, I may need someone other than him, too. But even thinking that makes me feel guilty. It's not just that Amelia didn't make that my mission; it's that I don't *want* to want anyone other than her.

He sits on the edge of the bed, then sinks back into the mattress.

"What a waste. An hour in the car to have a three-minute conversation with the most closed-minded people I've ever had the misfortune of knowing. And you know what, Harold?"

I lie next to his feet and wait for him to go on.

"I asked them why, if they think romance is so immoral, they've been accepting Amelia's royalty checks," he says. "And they said that if she'd wanted that money to go to me, she would've married me."

No, they did not!

But of course they did. They're not kind people, which is exactly why Amelia didn't want to get married. Miguel asked her all the time, but she told him she simply couldn't do anything that upped her odds of turning into her parents.

"I told them they knew full well that we were life partners. For fifteen years, five months, and twenty-eight days, we shared everything. And I said that cashing in on their dead daughter's novels instead of supporting her legacy by helping her store was the ultimate hypocrisy. Then I left."

He doesn't say anything else for a while, just lies there breathing shallowly. Finally, he hoists himself onto his feet.

"I'm going to take a shower. You can be on the bed if you want. It doesn't matter."

While I'd love to accept his long-overdue invitation, he's going to shower only because he needs to cry. Which is my fault, because I get upset when he's upset and that makes him feel even worse.

He's in there for a long time, oblivious to the fact that the crack under the bathroom door allows me to listen to his labored sobbing. When he finally emerges, I try to huddle close to him, but he pats me and wanders downstairs to the kitchen. He serves me my food, but instead of making a bowl of cereal for himself, he stands beside the counter and watches me.

"Harold, I'm okay," he says when I don't immediately stick my face in my bowl. "Really, go ahead and eat. I just . . ." He squeezes his lids shut for a second, and his shuddering sigh sounds more horse than human. "I still don't have any ideas, but one thing's for sure."

I lift my head, waiting for him to reveal this so-called certainty.

"It's going to involve as few people as possible. No people, no pain." He nods decisively, then adds, "Thank goodness you're a dog. You'd probably have me committed if you could understand half of what I'm saying."

Oh, Miguel, I think, inching closer to him. *Sometimes you have the sense of an inbred turkey.* People are the opposite of pain; Amelia taught me that. And if Miguel interacts with them even less than he already does, then the man will truly be marooned on misery island.

And I—

I will have failed.

Seven

I don't have to wake Miguel the following morning. "Team meeting today, dog," he says, pulling on the same shirt and shorts he wore yesterday. "But are you sure you're up for walking to the store? It's cooler than it has been, but it's still a little swampy out here."

I stare up at him. Does a cat piss in a pan full of gravel? I may be old, but I am *not* about to miss the opportunity to sniff dog puddles and munch on rabbit droppings.

Wait, forget about snacks—this is a chance to find Miguel a mate! We're out and about so infrequently that I must remind myself of what I've been charged with. I tug on the leash to tell him I'm raring to go.

Raina's pulling into her driveway as we're leaving. Miguel's never been big on small talk, but he used to be the one neighbors turned to if, say, they needed help hauling an oversized Christmas tree into the house. Now Raina pretends not to see Miguel, who either pretends not to notice or simply doesn't care, and I can't decide which is worse.

As we make our way down Main Street, he grumbles about this rickin' frickin' sidewalk and that family that hasn't mowed their lawn since May. I ignore him and busy myself by searching for suitable partners. A cheerful woman on a bike whizzes past us, and while I'm guessing she'd like her smile returned, perhaps she prefers the brooding type. Unfortunately, Miguel doesn't even seem to register her. Nor does he notice the woman in a pantsuit who's clearly checking him out as we stroll past the little café with the big metal spoon over the door. I personally can't tell what makes humans hot for each other, but Amelia often told Miguel how handsome he was; I don't think the shadows under his eyes or the rug on his face or even the cloud of grief hanging over his head have negated that.

No, the trouble is that Miguel lost a fundamental part of himself when Amelia passed. Because once upon a time—well, he loved love, too. He'd hum salsa songs and spin Amelia around the kitchen as she laughed and laughed because even with his help, she had the rhythm of one of those capybaras I saw on Animal Planet, which Miguel leaves on for me when he goes out for groceries. Sometimes he'd tuck a tiny note under the guava cakes he baked for her and deliver them with an espresso while she was wrestling with a tough chapter. And though they'd been together for years, his face lit up when she walked into the room. Every time!

Just like most of the characters Amelia wrote about, they were a pair of opposites who couldn't help but attract. While Miguel would have lived in a book if he could have, people loved to talk to Amelia—and she loved to listen. "That's half a novelist's job," she told Miguel over dinner one evening after he'd been teasing her about collecting "randos." "How am I supposed to write convincingly about the lives of others if I don't know how they live?"

"Read about them like I do and call it a day," said Miguel with mock seriousness, and she threw her napkin at him and laughed.

Oh, but they were perfect together.

Now the oven's cold and the house is quiet, and I can't remember the last time I saw Miguel pick up a book outside of work. No wonder Amelia said she was asking the impossible of me; I'll learn to meow before I find someone like her for him to love. She was the most wonderful human I've known. She was irreplaceable.

I'll just have to find Miguel a person who understands this. Someone who won't mind that he can't be the way he once was. Except . . . who would accept being loved a little when you could be loved all the way?

I'd better not think about it too much, lest I get discouraged.

We turn the corner, and he ties me up outside the bakery that sells the good donuts. Excellent—he's getting food for everyone. He hasn't done that since Before. "Have to get the team revved up. We need all hands on deck now," he says, patting me before he heads inside. "I'll be as fast as I can, Harold."

He returns a few minutes later holding a box full of something doughy and delicious. It's that time of year when the sky's bright until the fireflies take over, but it isn't intolerably warm. Still, my hips feel like they're on fire as I rise from the pavement. I can't let the pain bother me, though. Not when Miguel's actually trying. It's unfortunate that it took a series of calamities to get him to care, but at this point, I'll take what I can get.

When we reach Lakeside, Riley unlocks the front door for us.

"Sorry I'm late," says Miguel. Under his breath, he adds, "I didn't want to come."

She laughs. "I heard that. I also noticed you brought provisions, so all is forgiven."

"Don't thank me yet—we've got a lot to discuss," he says as we make our way to the reading nook. He sets the box in the center of the wood coffee table that Amelia bought at a garage sale back when I was still young. Someone, probably Dane, has set out a pot of coffee and brought over my water bowl from the stockroom. I slurp down its contents, splashing Natalie's toes in the process. She's a college student who's worked here the past few summers, and she's on the couch beside Brenna. Riley and Brenna used to sit together, but that was before they broke up. Now they act like a couple of people who can't stand the smell of each other. Dane's seated in a folding chair across from them. Riley takes the folding chair next to him, and Miguel takes the last one in the row.

No one sits in the yellow armchair. That's where Amelia used to sit.

"Good to have you here, chief," says Dane, reaching for a donut.

"Yeah, I'm sorry I've missed the last couple. It's been a busy summer," he says, as though we don't all know that his idea of busy is having to leave the house for groceries. "But I'm here now, and unfortunately, I've got some not-great news." His eyes roam the store for a second. "For anyone who hasn't already heard, our rent's raising in September."

"How much?" asks Brenna. She's not a big talker, but Amelia used to say that if you needed to figure something out, you could give it to Brenna and she'd have three solutions for you in an hour.

"A lot." He swallows hard, then says, "A thousand a month."

Dane whistles.

"It's not ideal," Miguel acknowledges. "I understand why Kathy has to do it, but we're all aware that Lakeside's barely scraping by these days. Brenna, how are July sales?"

She tugs on her tie, and I find myself wondering, not for the first time, why some humans willingly collar themselves. "Not awful, but down almost ten percent compared to this time last year."

He grimaces. "That seems to be the trend. A couple years ago, I wouldn't worry so much, but prices are up on everything, not just our rent. Kathy mentioned the war, but I wonder if this is the reality of running a bookstore in the new millennium. Maybe people just want to buy everything online now."

Riley drops a piece of donut in front of me, then asks, "And JMB?"

Miguel looks down. "His assistant doesn't know where he is."

"Someone asked for a refund for the event yesterday," says Natalie, nearly whispering.

"Did you give it to them?"

She grimaces, then nods.

"It's okay," he assures her. "We can't say no. But it's only a matter of time before more people ask, and I can't promise a rain date when I have no idea where he is or how to reach him."

Dane raises his hand like a kid at Story Hour. "If we're tight on cash, I could work for free. I've got savings."

"That's generous, but I'm not going to *not* pay you," Miguel tells him. "No one's working for free except me—and no one's losing their job, either. Amelia was adamant that you all are the heart of this business, and since she's been gone, I've learned just how right she was about that." He swallows hard. "I know I haven't been around enough the past year, but that changes now."

"Boss, we're fine holding down the fort. You've got to take care of yourself," says Riley.

"I appreciate that, but it's time," he says, meeting her gaze. "It's been time. I need to step up again and right the ship, and I can't do that without being here more often. Of course, I'll have to be careful with Harold," he says in my direction. "He can't be home by himself for long stretches, but sometimes he overdoes it when he's here. If you all see him wearing himself out, please let me know."

I turn and give him a withering look. I do not *overdo* anything. In fact, I feel my best at Lakeside. He's not the only one who needs this place.

"We'll be careful with him," Dane says, scratching my head. "He's our mascot, after all."

I sit up on my hind legs to indicate that I accept the honor.

"Boss, Dane and I were talking, and we do have one idea . . ." Riley begins.

Miguel groans. "Not online books again. We already know that there's no competing with tech giants. Our ethernet barely works half the time."

"We're not suggesting we compete." She glances at Dane, who nods. "Just join the game. We could put a selection of romance books up—I know some of Amelia's colleagues are selling well online."

He shifts in his seat. "We're running a skeleton crew here, and I'm not sure we're equipped to deal with delivery, never mind the whole online aspect. Besides, our romance sales are down right now."

"Only three percent," Brenna volunteers.

Riley steals a quick glance at Brenna before looking at Miguel. I still don't know how they went from love to loathe so quickly, but I wish they'd make up already. "I think that's because we're not marketing them effectively. Sales go up when we display them on the front tables. I have to wonder if we should move Romance up to where Nonfiction is. Aside from a couple bestsellers, that category's definitely not selling as well as it should."

Miguel frowns. "I really feel we should be going harder on literary fiction, since that's what the people who signed up for JMB's event are into."

"I'm sure a good number of JMB's readers read lots of genres, just like us," she says, gesturing to the rest of the staff.

Maybe they do, but Amelia used to joke that Miguel only read serious books by authors named Jonathan and David. "There's barely enough time to read what I already know I like," he told her once when she pressed one of her friend's novels into his hands and said he had to give it a shot. "That's why I'm not going to make you suffer through *Infinite Jest*—you have your own favorites. Our taste is what makes Lakeside so great. There's a little bit of something for everyone," he said, and kissed her neck in the way that always made her shiver with delight.

"Maybe, but I don't know that anyone spending fifty dollars

to see Jonathan Middleton-Biggs is into romance or thrillers," Miguel tells Riley now. "We need to get the right books in front of them when they come back in here. We want them to leave with a book in hand and the impression that this is the best place to buy literature, since a lot of the people who own vacation homes around here end up coming back for a week or two in the fall and winter. If we can do that, we could boost revenue long-term. But I'll tell you what, Riley—as soon as I find JMB, we can have a conversation about romance."

When he leans forward and puts his hands on his knees, there's a glimmer of the man he used to be—just a glimmer, but it's enough to give me hope.

He turns to Dane. "While I'm going to skip the whole kidnapping thing, you're right on one count. I need to go to Chicago and track down JMB. Is there any way you can watch Harold for me?"

Eight

I'll admit, I'm not excited to rise and greet the following day.

In fact, when I nose Miguel and he groans and says, "Five more minutes, Harold," I go back to my bed and give him a whole hour. Who cares if he lets me out now or later? It's going to be the same yard with the same smells. Then I'll eat the same kibble while Miguel's off gallivanting in Chicago.

Without me.

Now, it's not like my life with Amelia was filled with adventure. After our early walk, she and I spent most of the morning in her office, where she'd clack-clack-clack on her keyboard and drink coffee and clack some more. Sometimes she wouldn't even pause to eat lunch at the normal time—she probably would have skipped it altogether if it weren't for my pestering. Still, I loved to watch her write. She put a big floor pillow beside her desk for me and would read me lines from her drafts.

"'His smile was more a gift than a facial expression' . . . Ooh, that's pretty good, don't you think, Harold?"

Very good, I thought, lifting my head in affirmation. *How lucky your readers are.*

Most afternoons, we'd head to the bookstore, and that's when the fun began. Who would drop in? Would they have their dogs with them, their other children, contraband snacks? There was even a student who came by with his cat. Technically, cats aren't allowed in the bookstore—not because Amelia and Miguel disliked them, but it's dicey with the place teeming with my kind. This fellow, however, wore a backpack with a plastic enclosure at the top, so his cat could see out. She always seemed incredibly bored, but the rest of us weren't when she was around.

I take it back: Life with Amelia was very much an adventure. And now it's not.

But as I watch Miguel throw clothing into his suitcase, it occurs to me that this isn't over yet. He's still here, which means I have time to prove to him that I am not too old to travel, nor would I be better off with a sitter. I must convince him that I am a dog with the ability to go to the big city and assist in the finding of one Jonathan Middleton-Biggs.

He's just closed the suitcase when I begin to whimper and nudge his leg with my nose. It takes a minute, but he finally gets the hint. "You must really need to use the bathroom," he grouses as we descend the stairs and head to the kitchen.

I do not, but once I'm out the door, I muster up enough urgency to lift my leg and wet a bush so that it doesn't look like I've roused him for no reason. Then I begin the new, improved routine I've just devised. Around and around the yard I go—one lap, two, another and another. My knees now ache as much as my hips, but there's no slowing down. Not yet.

"You're not a mustang, Harold," calls Miguel from the back door. Then he mutters to himself, "What has even gotten *into* him?"

You have, I think as I zip past him. *Do I look like an animal past his prime? I think not.*

He shakes his head and wanders back inside the house. I do a few more laps, then collapse on the weathered wood deck, panting far more than I'd like. It's already warm, and I'm going to need a bucket of water as soon as I catch my breath and find the energy to get back on my paws.

My torso's still heaving when I sense something—almost like a bug on my back, but heavier. I turn my head and realize it's Miguel's gaze; he's cupping a mug in his hands and staring at me from the windows that overlook the deck. He appears . . . concerned.

Doggone it. Of course he does. The way I'm breathing probably makes me seem like I need to be hauled to the emergency vet, who's twice as expensive and three times as scary as the normal one. Though my tongue's still dangling out of the side of my mouth, I attempt to smile to assure Miguel that I'm happy as a hairy clam. He frowns and doesn't move from the window—almost like he's waiting for proof that I'm all right.

And I *am*. That's why I was able to cover so much ground just now. But Miguel isn't of the canis genus, and he doesn't know that my recuperation is well within the realm of normal.

What else must I do to convince him?

Then I spot a squirrel in the garden box, rooting around where she has absolutely no business being. Now, I come from a long line of hunters—but personally, I've only ever been a companion. As such, I've never attacked anything more than a murder of crows, who then attempted to murder *me* for an entire season, because it turns out their memories rival an elephant's.

Still, Amelia loved everyone, but not everything. The squirrels continually raided her beloved bird feeder, which now sits empty. She even bought pricey, spicy birdseed to try to deter them—apparently birds are immune to heat—but the rodents managed to build up a tolerance to the stuff. She'd grab the broom and wave it at them, yelling her head off as Miguel stood by and laughed. She never did hit a squirrel, and eventually she'd end up laughing, too.

But she did loathe those grubby little creatures. And I must believe she'd approve of what I'm about to do.

I start slowly, crouching as I advance toward my target. The squirrel doesn't see me, and even if she did, she probably wouldn't care. They're pretty far down the intelligence chain. They do, however, learn to assess threats quickly. And because I have not once chased their lot around these parts, she's not expecting me to do so now.

I'm nearly at the garden box, and the squirrel's still squatting in the dirt with her back to me. She's eating something that landed in the soil—a mulberry, perhaps?—and I remind myself to stop thinking about what she's doing and focus on the task before me.

I take a deep breath, lunge, and—

The noise hits me first, and oh my dog, it's *terrible,* like someone has punctured a balloon but also poked a human baby and combined them into the most awful, high-pitched distress call I've ever had the misfortune of hearing. Reality sinks in at the same rate my teeth sink into her coarse fur: *I've caught the squirrel.* She is clawing at my face like—well, like something trying to survive, twisting and attempting to bite me and, *ouch,* I think she just did. And yet I am jerking my head this way and that, just how I used to annihilate the squeaky toys Amelia gave me. This, however, is markedly less fun. Worse, I can't seem to stop.

"Harold!"

Miguel's running across the yard, holding the same broom Amelia used to wield at the squirrels raiding her bird feeder. I can only hope that Raina and the Bergers, who live on the other side of us, aren't around to get the wrong impression. Because Miguel's waving the broom at . . . *me.*

It works. I immediately drop the squirrel, who tries to dash away but can't, and ends up sort of limping sideways to the fence. She slips through an opening and disappears behind the garage. I want to feel relieved for her, but I know—I just know—that she will not survive the hour.

What was I thinking? Amelia would've been horrified. *I* am horrified.

I look up at Miguel, who's no longer waving the broom, and I feel so, so sad.

"Oh, Harold." He's kneeling now, and he has one hand on my back and another gently on my jaw. "*Pobrecito,*" he murmurs, examining my face. "That's not like you."

Well, it wasn't—but now it is. And although Miguel's being more tender with me than he has since the end of everything, that's not comforting. At *all.*

"Were you trying to show me something?"

Yes, I was! I was trying to prove to you that I'm fine, Miguel! Fine fine fine fine fine! Take me to Chicago!

"I'm going to have to call the vet," he says, standing. "I think it might be time for doggy Prozac."

I don't know what Prozac is, but he believes something's

wrong with me, which is the opposite of what I was going for. I hobble behind Miguel, barely in better shape than the squirrel I just mauled.

Maybe he's right.

He's definitely right. I'm *not* fine.

How will I ever fulfill my duty in this sorry state?

I've just hid myself under the love seat in the living room when the front doorknob starts to rattle. "Miguel, it's me! Open up!" yells Dane.

"*Dios mío,*" mutters Miguel, shaking his head. He yanks open the door and squints at Dane. "You do know we have a bell? Or you could even, you know, knock instead of scaring the stuffing out of the neighbors."

"Sorry, chief," says Dane, running a hand through his hair. "I was just excited."

"To . . . dog-sit?"

"No, dude. I mean, no offense, Harold," Dane says to me quickly.

None taken; as much as I enjoy Dane, I don't want to be cooped up with him any more than he does with me.

"It's just that I brought you a little gift." Dane pulls his backpack off his shoulder and reaches into it. Then he hands Miguel a stack of papers and a tiny piece of plastic with a metal end. "Thumb drive *and* the dead tree version, since I know you're not big on computers."

"I'm fine with computers. Not as skilled as you, but that's only because I have better things to do than play Dungeons and Dragons all day. What is this, exactly?" Miguel asks, holding the papers right in front of his nose.

"It's a report." Dane bounces on his toes, waiting for Miguel to respond.

"What *kind* of a report? I can't really make this out without my reading glasses."

"Why didn't you say so, chief?" He plucks the papers out of Miguel's hand. "I've put together a rundown on the comings and goings of one newly infamous Chicago author. See, here's his favorite bookstore, and then this is where he apparently likes to grab a beer, and this is his home address," says Dane, pointing at some scribbles on the page. "I also printed a bunch of comments from some of his, ahem, ardent fans, which might contain other clues I didn't catch yet."

"Where did you even find all that?"

"Chat rooms, mostly. Also, on a forum for Chicago librarians, and a few other sources I probably shouldn't reveal. But my dude, there's more where this came from."

"Where?" says Miguel, peering around the papers. "And . . . just, why?"

Dane pats his backpack. "Got my trusty laptop with me—and a change of clothes. And because what I've found might just be the start of our mission, you'll need me."

"Wait one second. This is a solo endeavor."

"Nah. You of all readers should know no hero's journey is complete without a guide."

Miguel looks him up and down. "So, you're . . . Gollum in this scenario?"

Dane wrinkles his nose. "I was thinking Yoda to your Luke Skywalker. 'Cause Yoda put Luke up in his swamp crib, and as it happens, I actually do have a place we can crash."

"I wasn't planning to stay overnight."

"While I'm stoked that you're thinking ahead, chief, what if you don't find JMB right away? Or if you do and you need to,

I don't know—*convince* him? That could take time. And I'm not on the schedule until tomorrow afternoon, though honestly, Brenna and Riley should be fine without me if we get back late. Sure, Riley'll be mad that I'm not there to be her buffer—but she and Brenna are gonna have to work it out at some point."

Miguel is clutching his forehead the way he sometimes does when he hasn't had enough coffee, and also after he's had too much. "You have a bachelor pad in Chicago you haven't told me about?"

"Nope, but I have a good buddy there, and his place is always open to me. He's in Thailand right now. Or maybe it's Santa Monica. Doesn't matter for our purposes."

"I can stay in a motel if I need to. Or just sleep in my car," says Miguel.

"Danger, Will Robinson," says Dane in a robotic voice. "Carjacking in three, two—"

"Okay, okay—I won't sleep in the car. But why on earth would I take you with me?"

"Because you need me," Dane says, like this is the dumbest question he's ever heard. "And I need to get out of this town for a hot second before I lose my mind."

"What about the dog?" asks Miguel, turning his attention to me. "He's been kind of weird for a while, and he nearly killed a squirrel today. I'm not sure traveling's a good idea."

Nearly! As ashamed as I am, he could at least give credit where it's due.

"That's because he's bored, too." Dane leans toward me and scratches my head. "Look at the old boy—he needs another romp or three before he calls it a day. My buddy loves dogs and won't care if he stays with us. What do you think, Harold? Wanna head to the Windy City?"

I grin up at Dane, because while Miguel may not love him, I sure do right now.

Let's go, let's go, let's go!

Nine

Some years ago, when I was neither young nor old, Miguel, Amelia, and I drove all the way to Michigan's Upper Peninsula. I held it together as long as I could but ended up throwing up in a rest stop parking lot. Amelia was so worried that she sat beside me in the back for the next couple of hours, petting my head until I finally passed out. When I woke again, we'd just pulled up in front of a lake. Like the one we live near, this lake was great, too, and stretched the length of the horizon. Even so, the beach was especially light, and there were rocks upon rocks just beneath the water's surface. "I warned you!" Amelia laughed when Miguel stuck his foot into a wave and immediately squealed like a piglet. "Superior's an ice bath!"

Then he laughed and picked her up and pretended like he was going to toss her into the water while I ran circles around them.

Barfing aside, that was a great trip.

This time, I don't get carsick. That's probably because I was so excited that I could barely eat my lunch before we left. Miguel's excited, too. I can tell because he's humming again, and he's wearing a shirt with buttons and pants that don't smell like weeks of living. Dane sits beside him up front; as usual, I'm in the back. I start off in the place where feet go, but it's hard for me to contain myself and I immediately hop up onto the seat. Miguel must really be in a decent mood because he doesn't bark at me to get down like he normally would. "If he starts sliding around or looks like he's going to vomit, make him get back on the floor," he tells Dane, who salutes him in agreement.

Dane does most of the talking. He tells Miguel about how he was supposed to be a lawyer like his dad and grandfather and most of the other men in their family, but how he left law school after the first semester and traveled the world, eventually landing in West Haven and working for Lakeside.

"Good for you for doing what you wanted to," Miguel tells him.

Dane's face lights up. "Thanks, chief. Life's too short to live for other people. Now I just gotta find someone to spend mine with."

"Do you? It's better being alone," Miguel mutters.

"I heard that, and I disagree. After all, you'd be having a way worse time if I wasn't here."

"If this is the upgraded experience, I think I'd prefer economy," Miguel says, but Dane just laughs and puts his feet on the dashboard.

The drive's not too long, and before I know it, I see a bunch of buildings touching the sky. My ears lift. This must be the place!

Miguel scowls. "I hate driving in cities."

"Chicago's easy," Dane assures him. "I lived here for a while after college. Everything's a grid and the people are chill—or they are when they're not behind the wheel."

That may be, but we have to do an awful lot of stopping and starting to get to Dane's friend's house. My gut's just begun churning when Dane announces that we're almost there.

"This was a terrible idea," says Miguel as we inch down the block.

"Was not. Pull in here," says Dane, pointing at an alleyway. It's next to a big house made of pale stone. It has a pointy tower jutting from the top, and it's not attached to the other buildings, the way a lot of the houses in this area are.

"Whose place is this again?" Miguel asks as he parks in front of the garage in an adjacent alley behind the house.

"It belongs to Tony, an old buddy of mine," Dane says. "We went to prep school together."

"Prep school, huh?"

"Yeah, out east. Hated that my parents shipped me off, but I met some super cool people, including Tony. He's a consultant, and he's always jetting around. He bought this place right out of college as an investment, and the neighborhood's just gotten wild since then. *Expensive* wild," he clarifies, catching Miguel's alarmed expression. "I've stayed over a bunch of times. It's totally safe—if you can forget that safety's only the illusion of control."

"That's reassuring," drones Miguel. "Meanwhile, I had no idea you were hanging out in Chicago."

"Everyone's got secrets, chief. Mine's that I get restless if I'm home for too long, which is why I like working retail instead of being stuck behind a desk five days a week. And yours is that you like me."

Miguel snorts, and the three of us scramble out of the car. They pull their suitcases from the trunk, then Dane directs us through an iron gate, down a stone path, and to the front of the house, where the porch's floor and ceiling have been painted the color of the sky in early spring. Dane retrieves a key from under a planter, opens the huge wooden door, and waves us inside.

Ooh—fresh smells! I'm getting Thai takeout with hints of indoor plants and the slightest whiff of bright blue cleaning spray. And . . . a dog? If my instincts are right, the last one in this place was tiny.

"You're sure it's okay to have Harold here?" says Miguel. The house is as fancy as it is large. There's a statue of a dancer at the end of the wide hallway, and we pass a tall stand with a fern perched on it. This is one of those rare occasions I'm grateful to have just a bit of tail left; otherwise, I'd be covered in soil right now.

"Totally," says Dane. "Tony's got two of those little punters."

"Punters?"

"Football-sized dogs. They stay with his sister when he's not here."

Two! I'm seriously off my game. What else have I missed? Actually, I'm not sure I want to know.

"This is an awfully nice place for one guy and two dogs."

"Yeah, Tony's from money, though if you met him, you'd never know it. Let me show you where you can crash," he says, then leads us up a long, curved staircase. "This is you and Harold," he says, opening a door for us. "Make yourselves at home. I'm going to set up in the room at the end of the hall. There's a bathroom right next to your room, and another on the first floor. Meet in the living room after you get settled?"

"Sure," says Miguel, peering around. "I . . . I really appreciate you arranging this for us."

If Dane realizes what a big deal it is for Miguel to thank him, he doesn't let on. "I got you, my dude. See you downstairs."

I'm itching to go sniff around some more, but for a man on a mission, Miguel's in no hurry. Instead, he takes out each item of clothing in his suitcase, carefully folds it, and places it inside the drawers of the dark wood dresser that's opposite the bed. This, after plucking his daily attire from the laundry basket—and, let's be honest, the hamper—for more than a year! Then he lines up his shoes and hangs a bag with his bathroom things from a hook on the wall.

When he begins to rearrange the pillows on the bed, I realize we could be here for months if I don't do something. So, I make my saddest face and whimper at the door.

"Fine, Harold," he says with a sigh. He glances at his reflection in the mirror on the wall, which strikes me as a positive sign. "I'm just a little nervous. What if we can't find JMB? Then what am I going to do?"

I really hope I won't need to come up with an answer for this.

We amble downstairs. The living room's especially big, with high ceilings and a fancy glass light fixture overhead. "This used to be a ballroom!" says Dane when he sees us. "Nice, right?"

"It's certainly grand," says Miguel, circling the perimeter. He stops in front of a painting of colors smeared in every direction and a big bright ball rising in the center, like the sun in the early morning.

"If you're into art, we could hit the Art Institute while we're here." When Miguel shakes his head, Dane says, "I get it—you're more in the mood for an adventure."

"No to that, too. I've already had my fair share of adventures," Miguel tells him.

"Oh yeah? I'm all ears."

Miguel frowns, and I almost expect him to change the subject. But then he clears his throat and says, "Me and my sister, Miriam, would pack a little sack full of food and spend the night at the beach, or the local park, and practice being orphans."

Did they? This is the first I'm hearing of this.

"That's rad," Dane tells him.

"Not really, since we practically *were* orphans," says Miguel, but he doesn't sound upset. "We were worried my Aunt Ceci could die suddenly, too, just like my mother did."

"Oh," says Dane softly. "What happened?"

"Heart attack, even though we have no family history of heart problems. It was right after she found out my dad had started another family a couple miles away from where we lived. She'd loved him since they were kids and thought they'd be together forever. Finding out he didn't feel the same way was too much for her."

"I'm sorry. That must have been rough on you. And then Amelia having heart problems, too . . ."

"It is what it is," says Miguel, shrugging. "But Miriam and I decided we should figure out what to do, just in case."

Dane walks over to him and puts a hand on his shoulder. "That's a heavy load for a kid, chief. Good thing you have Miriam—she's the bomb. I always wanted a sibling, but no dice."

"Miriam's the best," Miguel murmurs in agreement.

"She's smoking hot, too."

"Dane."

"Just sayin'."

"Maybe don't." Miguel shakes his head. "All right, enough chitchat. The only adventure I'm interested in now is one that results in me not having to refund eight thousand dollars to angry customers."

"Done and done," says Dane, clapping his hands together. "Let's go find our absconding author."

Ten

"You sure this isn't creepy?" Dane whispers.

If you must ask that question, the answer's almost certainly yes—*that* is what I'm sure of. Nonetheless, we're in front of Jonathan's townhouse, so I gently nudge him with my nose to indicate that there's no turning back now.

"We're just being pedestrians," says Miguel, squinting at the boxy modern building. The walls are mostly glass, though the inside's hidden by thick curtains. The lawn, which is behind a tall metal gate, is covered with pebbles instead of grass. In its center, there's a sign with a picture of a dog squatting with a circle around him and a line through both.

So JMB's not a dog lover. Yeah, well, now I'm not such a fan of his, either.

"Uh, I feel like we're gawking more than we're walking," says Dane.

Miguel ignores this comment. "You're sure you got the right address? This doesn't seem like him. I was imagining, like, something classy with red brick and window seats. You know—bookish."

"I'm as surprised as you, but of course I'm sure. Found his address in last year's tax records, and there's been no sale on this property since then."

"Tax records? Now who's creepy?"

Dane frowns. "Thought you wanted to find JMB."

"I do," Miguel says quickly. "In fact, I'm almost impressed. I just didn't realize you had the *cojones* to pull that off."

"I told you, I'm good at tech stuff. If you're ever ready to set up an online store . . ."

Miguel holds up a hand. "Focus, Dane."

"I'm focused, chief! Should we go knock?"

"Not just yet." Miguel looks down at me. "Harold, I wonder if maybe I should have left you behind. Might be weird bringing you to the front door, especially given that no-dogs sign." He rubs his head and thinks for a moment. "Let's walk the block first, observe the area as casually as we can—just in case anything's amiss or he's out and about."

"I wonder if we should come back when it's dark?" Dane seems unusually nervous for someone whose first idea was to stash Jonathan in the trunk. "The guy's probably way too used to people getting all up in his business."

"No one's in anyone's business—we're just out for a walk. So, let's walk."

A lot of people must live in JMB's neighborhood, because as we make our way back down the block toward the car, we weave through strollers and gaggles of teenagers and loads of dogs and their humans. I can tell the crowd's making Miguel twitchy, but the truth is, we'd never be this invisible if we were in West Haven.

"I'm just going to talk to him, man to man," says Miguel, but now he's talking to himself. "If he can see my face, realize that I'm a real person and that his decision has impacted me personally, then surely he can be reasoned with."

"You nervous?" Dane asks.

Miguel shoots him a withering look. "It's not like the future of my business, which happens to employ you, is on the line or anything."

"Fair, but you'll be fine. Just be . . ." He trails off. If I had to guess, he was about to tell Miguel to be himself. But that self isn't around these days.

We've reached the end of the street, so we cross to the side opposite Jonathan's house. Miguel's mouth forms a tight line as we begin walking toward it. "Be on the lookout for signs of life," he instructs Dane.

I personally see plenty of those—and they're all squirrels whose beady eyes are boring holes through my fur. I don't have to speak rodent to know their sharp squawking proclaims a killer's in their midst. We're almost directly across from the house when Dane stops abruptly. "Chill."

"What?" says Miguel, glancing around.

"Chief, that is *not* chill. Slow your roll and check out eleven o'clock—balcony. Tell me what you see."

"Uh . . . oh! Someone's up there," whispers Miguel.

I follow his gaze to the flat surface on the second floor. It's only sort of visible from where we're at. But a person's definitely there, sitting in some sort of lounge chair.

"I think it's a woman, but that's strange—I'm almost positive JMB doesn't have a partner," Miguel says in a low voice.

"Maybe it's a house sitter or something. I can go ring the bell if you want."

"Then you *do* know how to use a doorbell?"

Dane grins. "Don't tell my boss. Why don't you hang back and let me and Harold handle this?"

I get to help? I'm so excited I pee on the pavement, just a little.

"I don't think that's a good idea," says Miguel, but Dane's already marching across the street and tugging me behind him. When he reaches the gate, he presses a button on a box near the top of it.

"Go away!" calls a voice from above. The voice is . . . young, it seems, but deep and serious sounding.

Dane looks up with surprise. "Hiya! We just want to ask you a question!"

The person is at the edge of the balcony now, leaning over a metal railing. I still can't really make her out, but she seems small.

"You never heard of stranger danger?" yells the person. "Shoo!"

Dane glances over his shoulder at Miguel, who's already making his way across the street.

"Um, that's a *child,*" Miguel says, just loud enough for Dane to hear him. "Does Jonathan have a daughter?"

"According to the internet, no," says Dane, shrugging. "But I'm gonna press the doorbell again. Maybe he'll answer this time."

"I said go!" hollers the girl. "If you don't, I'll call the cops and tell them you're stalkers."

"No one's stalking anyone!" Miguel calls up to her. "We're looking for Jonathan!"

"No duh!"

We're clustered together at the gate now, and admittedly, I

can see why two men and one dog loitering in front of a famous novelist's house might seem a bit suspicious.

The girl eyes us, then says angrily, "I'll count to five and then I'm going to go dial nine-one-one. One . . . two . . . three . . ."

The vein in Miguel's neck is throbbing like it's trying to find a way out. "We're just worried about Jonathan," he tells her. "I know him. Well, sort of—he was supposed to come to my bookstore last week, but his assistant said he went missing. Lakeside Books in Southwest Michigan? Maybe he mentioned it?"

The girl opens her mouth to say something, then pauses.

"Seriously, we're not stalkers, and we're not strangers. I spoke to Jonathan's assistant myself. I just need to know why he didn't show up at the event. Can you go get your parent?"

"No, I cannot go get my parent," she says in a mocking tone. "Now get lost!"

But someone has appeared beside her, someone much taller, with long hair that's blowing in the breeze. Unless Jonathan has made some big changes since he took his super serious author photo, it's not him. Before I can further examine the figure, they both step away from the balcony and disappear.

"Bummer," says Dane.

"No," says Miguel firmly. "*Not* a bummer. Though that obviously wasn't Jonathan, we have confirmation that he lives here. And whoever that was knows where he is—I can tell. Now we just need to convince her to get that adult to come out and speak with us."

"We could throw rocks at the glass," Dane volunteers. "That's gonna get annoying real fast."

"The number of suggestions you make that could result in jail time is astonishing."

"Dude, I'm not the one trying to talk some kid into giving me info about her dad."

"I was not trying to talk her into anything. Besides, I think we'd know if he had a child."

"Not if it was a *secret love child,*" says Dane, his eyes wide.

They're so busy bickering that they haven't noticed the woman walking down the path that cuts through the pebbled lawn. I start circling Miguel to try to get him to look up.

"One second, Harold," he tells me.

If he's proof of evolution, I'm not sure the experiment worked.

"Hi there," says the woman through the gate, and Miguel startles.

He whips around to face her. Then he stares . . . and stares. I'd say the cat's got his tongue, but for the life of me, I don't know what a cat would be doing in a human's mouth. "Uh, hello," he finally manages.

"Hello. May I ask who you are?" The woman's voice sounds like a babbling brook. She's—well, to be honest, she looks like a lot of the women who come into the bookstore, if taller than average. Loads of hair, mostly dark with lighter threads that catch the light. She's wearing a long dress that's the color of daffodils. Her glasses make her eyes big, like a lemur's.

And I know, the way a dog just does, that she is a good person.

Miguel clears his throat. "I'm Miguel Rivera, the co-owner—er, the owner—of Lakeside Books, where JMB—I mean Jonathan—was supposed to do an event for us earlier this week."

The woman sighs. "Oh, dear. I'm sorry."

"Sorry he didn't show?" asks Dane from behind Miguel. "Because so are our customers. And we're here to demand a do-over. Oh, I work with Miguel. Obviously."

"Do you know where he is?" Miguel asks her. "Like my colleague Dane just said, I only want to speak with him and explain what his absence has cost us, with the hopes that he'll make things right. I haven't been able to get ahold of him, which is why we're here." He cringes as he hears himself say this. "I swear, we're really not stalkers."

"Believe it or not, I didn't get the impression you were," says the woman pleasantly.

"Well, good," he says, and this is the longest he's made eye contact with someone other than me in eons. "I know it was Jonathan's idea to come to the store in the first place, and I almost thought it was a prank, but he *said* he would be there, and it was supposed to be the biggest event in Lakeside's history. We were really counting on it for the income and to help people learn about our store and decide to buy their books there instead of online. And—" Miguel catches himself and looks at the woman. "I'm so sorry, I'm rambling. I didn't even ask you your name."

The woman, who has been calmly listening to him, flashes him a smile that Amelia would've described as dazzling. "I'm Fiona Foster," she informs him, sticking her hand through the gate. He's still staring, but he takes it and shakes it wordlessly as she adds, "Jonathan Middleton-Biggs's sister."

Eleven

Miguel drops her hand like it's just burned his palm. "You're—Jonathan's sister?" he sputters.

The woman I now know to be Fiona is grinning like she swallowed something delicious. "You don't recognize my voice?"

He shakes his head, bewildered.

"We spoke several times. I called you to set up the event, and then you called me the other day to see if I knew where he was."

"Right. But I thought you were his . . . assistant?"

"I am, sort of. I help Jon with his calendar and events and whatnot. He's a tad reclusive."

Miguel's eyes immediately narrow. "Too reclusive, if the other night's any indication."

"I know. I really am so sorry about that. As I mentioned, I've been trying to get ahold of him for days." Her eyes lower and land on me. "Oh," she says, and though the gate is still closed, she takes a big step backward.

I know that "oh," and it's not good.

"Sorry," says Miguel. "Are you allergic?"

Fiona shakes her head. "No, it's not that. I'm . . . not a dog person."

What? But I just liked *her*!

"Harold's not a dog," says Miguel, and although this is patently untrue, I'm pleased by his defending me. Seeing her confusion, he says, "I mean, technically he is. But he's . . . Harold."

She's still regarding me fearfully. "I'm sure he's lovely. I had a bad experience, though, so . . ."

"Bummer. Just takes one," says Dane. "But this li'l puppers might be the dog to help you change your mind. I mean, look at his mug," he says, pinching my jowls the way people do with human babies. "This guy wouldn't harm a soul! Unless it belonged to some creeper who was bothering you. Then he'd defend you to the death."

"Mm," says Fiona, who's clearly not convinced.

"You're sure Jonathan's not here?" Miguel asks, looking past her.

"I wish he were. I'm just down the street, so I stopped by to water his plants and bring in his mail. Since you're here, too, would you like something to drink?"

Personally, I'd love to be watered. But she must have just remembered I'm here because she glances nervously at me.

"I can take him to the car if you need," Dane quickly tells Miguel.

"It's too hot to just leave him outside, and he doesn't really like to be alone," Miguel explains to Fiona.

She pivots to look over her shoulder, which is when I remember the girl on the roof. Where is she, anyway? I don't see her looking over the edge anymore. "I guess it's okay," she says, turning back to us. "He seems tired, and it *is* hot out."

"He's just old. Around fourteen, we think," says Miguel. "He's never bit anyone in the entire time I've had him."

Except that poor squirrel, but I'm happy to keep that between us.

"I'm glad. Just . . . hold on to him?"

"Of course," Miguel reassures her. "Thank you for the invitation—I'd really love the chance to speak with you about this situation."

"That makes two of us. While this is a bit of a surprise, I'm glad you're here." She opens the door and waves us inside.

The house is new; the smell of plaster and paint competes with the perfumed air wafting from the candles in the hallway and living room. I'd love to sniff everything, but Miguel's got me on a tight leash, and I don't want to mess things up for him, or worse, be sent to the car.

The kitchen's big, with a stove twice as large as ours. The spotless surfaces tell me no one's cooked here, or even served a bowl of cereal, in a long time. "Wow," says Miguel, glancing around. I can see the wheels turning behind his eyes; he's thinking about how this is what JMB sees every day before he sits down to write.

"Please, make yourselves comfortable," says Fiona, gesturing to the long counter in the middle of the room. There's a bowl of glass fruit on one end of the counter, which is probably for the best; I once scarfed down an entire chicken after Miguel and Amelia made the mistake of mating before eating the bird he'd just pulled from the oven. Amelia said she couldn't help herself when he cooked for her—and apparently, neither could I.

Dane seems nervous, which is really him looking like most people normally do instead of half-asleep. I wonder if it has anything to do with Miguel's *not* being so wound up for a change. If I didn't know better, I'd think he was happy to be hanging out with a stranger.

"Tea?" asks Fiona.

"I'm good, thanks," says Dane.

"I'll take tea if it's not too much trouble," Miguel tells her.

Wait, did he just accept the beverage he usually refers to as swamp water? His eyes follow Fiona as she retrieves a kettle from one of the tall cupboards and fills it, and I decide this is a stellar sign. He's intrigued enough to stay and sip his least favorite beverage.

Then it hits me: I have identified a contender!

My elation is immediately replaced with guilt. I want to make Amelia proud. I do. I only wish she'd asked me to help him—well, with almost anything else.

Fiona sets the kettle on the stove and lights the burner, then turns to Miguel. "Again, I'm so sorry Jon didn't show up to your event."

Miguel leans toward her. "I appreciate that, as we're in a bit of a pickle here. How soon do you think JMB—er, your brother—could do a makeup event? Our customers are incredibly unhappy, and we need to reschedule right away to reduce the number of refunds we'll have to issue. I don't want to get into it too much, but the short version is that we can't afford to pay them back."

She frowns. "I'm not actually sure when he'd be able to reschedule."

"What do you mean, you're 'not actually sure'?"

"I mean that in the literal sense of the words I used," she

says, lifting her chin like she's testing him. But instead of this irritating Miguel, his lips twitch upward.

Yes, that's the way! I mean, sure, Chicago is an hour and a half from West Haven, so that's a bit of an issue. Also, this Fiona Foster doesn't like dogs. Still—she could be the person Amelia told me to find for him; I just know it.

"Is life imitating art?" he asks.

"Is that a *Missing Person* reference?" Of course, because Miguel has yapped so much about this novel, I know that the main character is haunted by his parents' death, and after he gets dumped by his girlfriend, he heads to Europe to grieve with nothing but a backpack and a book without telling anyone where he's disappeared to.

"Perhaps."

She laughs, which makes his face brighten. "Well done." The kettle begins to whistle. "Let me grab that," she says.

I watch her as she busies herself filling two mugs with boiling water and tea bags. Fiona may be good, but there's something she is not saying. Dane's unusually stiff spine tells me he's picked up on that, too.

"Here you are," she says, passing Miguel a mug and one of those plastic bears.

"Thank you." When he's done emptying way too much of the bear goo into his mug, he clears his throat and sputters, "Michigan. Our bookstore. What happened?"

Fiona wraps her hands around her mug. "I wish I knew. He said he was going to go to your event, and then . . . he went somewhere else."

"If you don't know where he's disappeared to, is there at least a way I could speak directly with him to help him understand the impact this is having on us?"

She glances toward the hallway. "I'm afraid not."

"Is he *alive*?" presses Dane.

"Alive? My brother's not dead. And he *did* intend to go to your store. We discussed it back in April." Fiona's teeth land on her bottom lip. After a moment, she adds, "I thought it was perfect for him."

"You did?" says Miguel.

She nods. "I coordinate most of his events, and I'd heard about Lakeside from another author. And while I've never run a shop myself, I know enough about the business to understand it's hard to keep a bookstore open these days. Jon and I, we try to support literary underdogs—not just writers, but also stores where their work is sold."

"With all due respect, this underdog is running out of time," Miguel says quietly. "If I have to refund that money, I won't be able to pay my employees next month."

Dane stands and shakes out his legs. "Fiona, you seem chill, but let's cut to the chase."

"Dane—"

"Chief, I got you." He turns back to Fiona. "We know you and your bro had a lousy childhood. That's why my dude here likes his book so much—he and his sister had one, too. But judging from this crystal palace, seems like JMB's success has made him lose touch with reality. Otherwise, he would understand how bad this is for us."

Miguel clears his throat.

"No, it's okay," Fiona says. She pushes her glasses up on her nose. "Kitchen aside, I don't like this place, either. I chose this neighborhood because of the schools, and this was the house Jon decided to buy so he could be close to us. And you're right. It was crappy of him not to show."

Miguel immediately softens. "I'm sorry. I don't mean to insult you or him. I've just had a rough couple of years, and this feels like the rotten cherry on top of the *mierda* pie life has served me."

Fiona chuckles lightly, and though he probably doesn't realize he's doing it, Miguel cracks a faint smile.

"Really, I appreciate you having us in your home when you don't know me from Alejandro," he tells her. "I just want to get Jonathan to come to our store like he said he would, preferably as soon as possible. I have more than a hundred people waiting for a rain date."

"Psstt."

Before I even cock my head, I catch a whiff of an apple-ish fragrance, maybe from shampoo. It's her, the girl who was on the roof! She's crouched down in the doorway, waving at me. Fortunately, Miguel's let my leash go slack, so I slowly scoot across the tile and around the corner.

"Finally!" the girl whispers. She bends down and reaches for my collar. She smiles as her eyes move across the letters on my heart-shaped tag. "Harold!" she says, peering into my eyes. "That's a funny name for a dog."

I'm so dumbstruck that I just sit there drooling all over the floor.

"I'm *so* happy to meet you, but you'd better get back in there," she tells me. "My mom gets weird about dogs. Between you and me, she gets weird about everything—driving on highways, cellphone towers, even cheese puffs, which she calls fluffy food coloring disguised as sustenance. But dogs *really* freak her out."

She's petting me so softly that I don't want to return to the kitchen, but I really do need to check on Miguel.

"I understand your frustration and promise I'd help if I could," Fiona's telling him as I round the corner. "But as I said, Jon doesn't want to be found."

"If that's the case, then we should jet," says Dane, frowning at Fiona. "When you finally find him, tell your brother he's gonna be the nail in Lakeside's coffin."

The girl jumps over me so fast I don't even have a chance to be startled. "Don't say that about my uncle!" she yells, putting her fists on her hips and glowering at Dane.

Before Miguel or Dane can respond, Fiona rushes over to the girl and wraps her arms around her. "Amelia Mae!"

Instinct is my first language, so I immediately do what a dog does upon hearing his owner's name exclaimed loudly: I start barking my mother-loving head off and zipping around the kitchen to locate her. I've just circled the counter a second time, leash dragging behind me, when I run smack-dab into reality.

A name is not a person. Is not *my* person. That wasn't Miguel speaking, either, and he's the only one who regularly called Amelia by her first and last names.

I don't know what just happened, but I don't like it. Did my judgment fail me? It must've. A good person wouldn't say a bad thing like that.

I'm not the only one who's upset.

"Is this some kind of joke?" says Miguel, shoving off his stool. He's not just mad; he's a whole swarm of yellow jackets. Which is . . . kind of terrifying. I've seen him like this one other time, and in that case, Amelia's parents had it coming.

He glares at Fiona and the girl, then turns to me and Dane. "We're leaving. *Now*."

Twelve

Oh my, oh my, oh *my*. I still don't understand what's happening, but I know enough to put myself between Miguel and Fiona. While I'm not pleased with her, either, Miguel isn't himself these days, and I don't want him to do anything stupid. We need him, even if he forgets that.

Fiona blinks. "I beg your pardon?" She pulls the girl back a bit farther. "Is he going to attack us? Dogs sense anger, and you're clearly very angry, though I have no idea why."

"He's harmless, Mom," the girl tells her, but Fiona's staring at me fearfully.

Miguel grabs my leash from the ground without answering her. "The World Wide Web was a mistake. Sickos put everything on there." Dane's frozen in place, so Miguel turns back to him as he tugs me toward him. "*En serio*. Let's get out of here."

"I'm very sorry I've offended you, but I truly don't understand what I did," warbles Fiona. She glances around, and the girl takes the opportunity to slip out of her mother's arms. "Amelia Mae!" she exclaims. "Get away from the dog!"

"That," growls Miguel. "*That* is what you did wrong. *You said Amelia May.*"

"Yeah, because that's my name," the girl growls back. Her voice gets surprisingly deep for such a young human. Now that I'm examining her, she looks sort of like a smaller version of the woman, except her skin's darker, like Riley's, and her flashing eyes say she does *not* care about being nice. "I'm Amelia Mae. A-M-E-L-I-A M-A-E. And you," she says, jabbing a finger at Miguel, "are being mean to my mom."

Miguel's face has gone pale. And Dane, who's beside him now, is as still as a stalk of bamboo on a breezeless day. He opens his mouth to say something, but Miguel beats him to it.

"I—that's my partner's name. Amelia May." He swallows. "By which I mean, it *was* her name. She's . . ."

I hang my head. Six seasons later, she's still gone for good. No—gone for *bad*. Because it's forever.

"Oh, I'm so sorry," says Fiona in a choked voice, and she sounds like she means that with every fiber of her human being. "How stupid of me. She owned the store with you and . . . you didn't know she and my daughter share the same name. Though Mae," she says, lifting her chin at the girl, "is Amelia's middle name, not her surname."

"No, I didn't know," says Miguel bluntly. "How could I?"

A tear's trying to escape the corner of Fiona's eye. If my Amelia were here now, she would've given her a big hug and told her it was going to be okay. But Miguel just stands there with his arms hanging at his sides.

"I'm sorry," she says again. "I didn't mean to upset you, or overreact about the dog, either."

"This isn't just some dog, Mom. It's Harold," says the other

Amelia, kneeling beside me. She puts her arms around my neck again.

"Love bug, please be careful," says Fiona, who's batting her lids like she's caught in a sandstorm.

"Can't you tell he's nothing like the kind of dog you're afraid of? Are you?" The other Amelia's peering into my eyes again. Strangely, I don't want to look away. "Can they stay a while so I can hang out with him?"

"No, sweetheart." She turns to Miguel. "I'm afraid I've already made a bad situation even worse."

He glances down. "It's not your fault. I should take a cue from your brother and steer clear of people for a while. Or more like indefinitely. Regardless, I apologize for overreacting. It's still kind of . . . fresh."

No one says anything now, and for once, I don't feel like filling the silence by making someone pay attention to me.

"We'll be going, then," Miguel finally tells her, then he motions for Dane to follow him to the front door.

"I really do feel terrible about all of it. How long are you in town?" asks Fiona as she trails after us.

The lines between his eyebrows deepen as he turns and regards her. "We're supposed to leave tomorrow, but I'm not sure there's any point in staying overnight now that we know Jonathan's not here."

She glances away quickly.

"Why do you ask?" says Dane, examining her.

"It's just . . . I feel like I should be able to figure out something for you all—some way to help the store," she says, raising her eyes again. "Are you free for dinner tonight, by any chance? Everyone's invited."

"Even Harold?" says the other Amelia, who still has her arm around my neck.

Fiona smiles tightly. "Even Harold."

"Yay!"

I couldn't have said it better myself! But those lines between Miguel's eyebrows appear to be stuck, and he's shaking his head. "I appreciate the invitation, but now's not a good time," he tells her.

What is this animated meat sack talking about? Now's the best time! After all, it's the only time we really have, and I'm certainly not getting any younger over here.

"Drinks, then? We don't have to do a meal," Fiona says. "I'd really like to hear about Lakeside."

Miguel at least has the decency to look sheepish. "I'm sorry, but I don't want to leave Harold by himself in the home we're borrowing from Dane's friend. He might take the opportunity to leave a pile in the corner."

Must he shame me? I only did that once or thrice when he overslept.

"I mean it—he can come, too," she says, but she sounds uncertain. She reaches into the canvas bag on the counter and retrieves a small card, which she passes to him. "If you change your mind, here's my number. I don't know how, but I'd like to make this up to you."

Miguel examines the card. "No," he says softly.

"That's it?" Fiona pulls her head back, incredulous. "Just, *no?*"

"If you won't put me in touch with your brother, then there's nothing you can do to make this up to us."

Us. Maybe he just means me and Dane, but I somehow doubt it, and now I feel sad again because he's back to thinking he's failed Amelia. And his "no" means I'm almost certainly going to fail her, too.

Fiona smooths an imaginary wrinkle on her dress, then meets his gaze. "Isn't that what you came here for? To get help?"

"I came here for answers."

"And I don't have the ones you want."

"I guess not. But again, thanks for inviting us in." He begins shuffling toward the front door, with me and Dane following behind him like ducklings.

I, for one, would very much like to return for dinner, even if I'm mildly insulted that Fiona fears I will hurt her daughter.

The other Amelia must be disappointed, too, because she gives me a mournful look.

Now, I am highly aware that this is *not* about me. It is about fulfilling my duty by doing what's best for Miguel. And everything from Fiona Foster's bright eyes to her brilliant smile tell me that she would make a great mate for Miguel.

Or at least she will once I turn her into a dog person.

It just so happens that Fiona's a package deal. So, you can't blame me for wagging my nub when her child, who just happens to go by the best name in the world, grabs me before I leave her uncle's glass house and whispers in my ear, "Don't you worry, Harold. This isn't the last we'll see of each other."

Thirteen

I don't care what Miguel says about cities; I love Chicago. So many things to see and smell, so many people and pets! Even an old dog can have a good time in a place like this. Sure, I'm here to help Miguel find JMB—and, of course, love. And yes, I do wish the girl were here with me right now. Still, who am I to protest when Dane convinces Miguel that we should shake off our disappointment by exploring his friend's neighborhood?

Dane's yapping like a coyote at dusk as he guides us from this block to the next. "The area's way different from when I lived here. I was over on North Wolcott, just off Division," he tells Miguel, pointing down the street. "Used to be able to score drugs on all four corners of that intersection. Not that I did—but, you know, the vibe was way different."

"And that's how you ended up in West Haven?" Miguel asks. "I know I should know this, but it occurs to me I've never asked."

"Nah, but it's okay. I showed up for a buddy's wedding and liked that I could see the water from almost everywhere I looked. Two months later, I packed up my truck and made my way to the other side of Lake Michigan."

We've stopped at another intersection. "Chief, this is your show," Dane says to Miguel. "What are you in the mood for?"

Miguel squints. "You have that list you showed me at home?"

"Sure do." Dane rifles around in his backpack for a moment, then pulls it out.

Miguel takes it from him, then steps under an awning to get out of the sun. I stand next to him, but it's not much help. My paws are sweating like crazy, and no amount of panting seems to cool me down. Miguel must realize this, because he looks at me and says, "Harold, should we take you back?"

I close my eyes and pretend I didn't hear him.

"Okay," he says, though it's not clear if he's speaking to me or Dane. "I say we try the sports bar, since it's within walking distance."

"Solid plan," says Dane. "But, uh, what are we going to do when we get there?"

"I don't know, but we'll figure it out."

When we reach the bar, I half expect that I'll have to continue to barbecue myself on the sidewalk, but Dane ducks inside, then quickly returns to say I can come with them. The space is narrow and deep, with a long counter in the center and some small tables with metal chairs hugging the walls. It doesn't look like a great spot to get writing done, but maybe JMB comes here to meet his writer friends.

Miguel and Dane sidle up to the bar and order a couple of beers. The man helping them is about Dane's age, with dark hair and thick lines drawn over his lashes that make his eyes look like they have stingers.

"Thanks," Miguel says when the man sets a couple of tall

glasses in front of them. He's using his bookshop voice, the one that's calm and confident and in charge. That used to be how he spoke all the time. "I didn't catch your name."

"Enrique," says the man. "You?"

"Miguel. My friend Dane and I are in from West Haven, just around the bottom of the lake in Michigan. You ever been there?"

Enrique's lips twist to one side. "That near New Buffalo?"

"Yeah, about twenty minutes north. We run a bookstore over there—Lakeside Books. You should check it out if you're in the area."

"I'm more of a city mouse, but if that changes, I'll definitely swing by," says Enrique.

"We'll remember you if you do." Enrique's about to leave when Miguel adds, "Hey, I'm wondering if you happen to know someone named Jonathan Middleton-Biggs—he's said to be a regular here? Mid-thirties, white guy, probably six foot or so, sandy hair that kind of falls into his eyes? He's an author, so I'm guessing he typically has a notebook with him."

Dane leans on the bar. "Or, you know, his computer."

"Right." Miguel lifts his pint glass and mutters, "To technology, the downfall of civilization."

Enrique's smile has just upended, but I don't think it's because of Miguel's commentary. "Why do you ask?"

"Then you *do* know JMB?" says Dane.

"I know most of our regulars," says Enrique, looking them both up and down. "And I know they like their privacy."

Dane takes a long swig of his beer. "We totally get that."

Beside him, Miguel's shaking his head. "We're not asking for his Social Security number or anything. But are you aware that Jonathan may be missing?"

Enrique's eyes go buggy. "Missing? I thought he was on vacation or something."

"He didn't show up for an event at our store a couple days ago," says Dane. "And nobody seems to know where he is."

Miguel gives Dane a look, which probably means he's revealed too much. "Does he ever talk about his writing with you?" he asks Enrique.

"Um, I'm not sure how much I should say."

"I promise, we're here to help," Miguel tells him.

Enrique sighs, then says, "Jon never said anything about his books, and none of our regulars ever bugged him about that stuff. He liked that. Mostly we talk about the White Sox, sometimes the Bulls during the offseason. But usually baseball."

Dane and Miguel immediately turn to each other. "I thought Jonathan didn't like sports," says Miguel.

"Trust me, he's into the game—big-time. The guy knows more stats than anyone I've ever met. You can be like, 'Hey, how many strikeouts did Loaiza have last season?,' and he'll just rattle the numbers right off." Enrique looks over his shoulder. "Let me grab her a drink," he says, nodding toward a woman on the other side of the bar. "I'll be back."

"What do you think?" Dane whispers to Miguel.

"What I think is that that's super strange. Sports? Baseball stats? I've never once heard him mention that in an interview."

"Well, like that Fiona chick said, he's pretty private."

"Chicks are prepubescent fowl, Dane. Fiona's a woman," Miguel says.

"Yeah, she is," says Dane, wiggling his eyebrows. Miguel's just opened his mouth to respond when Enrique reappears.

"You good on beer?" he asks.

"Great, thanks," says Miguel.

"But while we have you . . ." Dane pulls a book out of his backpack and passes it to Enrique. "You sure this is the same dude you're talking about?" he says, pointing to the photo on the back cover.

"Where'd you get that?" Miguel asks him.

"Uh, there's this super cool little shop in a town called West Haven that sells books? You heard of it?"

Miguel shakes his head, but Enrique's peering at the paperback. He looks up. "Unless he's got a diabolical twin who also goes by Jon, that's him. I know people recognize him sometimes—but in here, he's just a guy who likes to watch the game and have a beer, and that's really all I know. I guess you could ask Vik, but I haven't seen him in a while, either."

"Who's Vik?" Dane and Miguel say in unison.

"Jon's friend. They come in here together a lot, or at least they did. Hey, sorry, but I've got to help these people," he says, referring to the group that just streamed in from outside. "Nice to meet you both."

"Of course. Thanks for your time," says Miguel.

Dane's just scribbled something on a napkin, which he hands to Enrique. "Do us a solid and call us if you hear anything about JMB—uh, Jonathan."

Enrique shoves it into his back pocket. "If I do and he's okay with my calling you, sure. But Jon's a great guy. If he didn't show up to your store, he had a good reason."

"I hope you're right," says Miguel, standing from his barstool. Just under his breath, he adds, "But I'd like to be the judge of that."

Fourteen

"You sure you don't want to call her?"

"Call who?"

We're back at Dane's friend's house, and Dane and Miguel are sprawled out across from each other on the identical sofas while I rest next to the vent, where the cool air streams at my face.

"You know I'm not talking about Riley. Though we could call her, too." Dane grins as he looks up from his laptop, which is connected to a couple of cables that lead to the wall. "I'm talking about JMB's sis, chief. Remember, she gave you her digits? She can tell us who this Vik dude is, because so far, I can't find anything online. Though I guess not everyone has a Friendster profile. And without a last name to go on, I can't scour my usual databases."

"Given how tight-lipped she was earlier, I don't think Fiona's going to suddenly give us a list of her brother's trusted contacts," Miguel says.

"Eh, maybe she would. She likes you."

"She was being nice, Dane."

"How come she wasn't that nice to me, then?"

Miguel rolls his eyes. "Because you're a doofus."

"You say that like it's an insult," says Dane. "Still, if you're going to call names, I'd rather be known as Lakeside's idiot savant."

Miguel's trying so hard not to laugh that it escapes like a cough. "Consider it done," he says, hitting his chest with his fist. "But only because you've gotten us this far."

"Yeah, I have." Dane pulls his laptop closed. "Wanna check out the bookstore everyone says Mr. Future Pulitzer likes before we find some grub? Maybe someone there will know who Vik is."

"I guess that wouldn't be the worst thing."

Dare I trust my ears? Miguel always wanted to visit the local bookstores first when we traveled. And even though he didn't have to, he often left with a big bag of books. This is an excellent development.

"Sweet. We'll have to drive over there, since my guy Harold can't take the L with us, and he probably doesn't need to keep baking in this heat."

"I'm up for driving, but we should leave Harold behind. Most bookstores don't allow dogs inside."

"You said you were worried about him dropping a pile on the floor here."

"I was just saying that to get out of dinner."

"Sharing the trade secrets! I feel special," says Dane, mussing up his hair.

"Don't." Miguel sighs loudly. "Well, Harold, this is more action than you'll probably get again in this lifetime—but it sounds like you're coming with us."

I do wish he wouldn't talk like that. Of course I'm not excited about heading to the big doghouse in the sky. But I'm far more worried about time—and geography. If Miguel won't even *call* Fiona while we're here, how will I ever get them together?

We pile into the car and drive across town. After enough circling the block to make me worry my kibble's going to come back up, Miguel finds a parking spot down the street from the bookstore.

The bookstore's smaller than ours by a lot and has a blue awning and a narrow glass door. I don't go inside—as Miguel suspected, this shop isn't dog-friendly—but Dane waits with me. It hasn't cooled much since earlier, so we shelter under the awning, and he lets me drink straight from his water bottle to keep from overheating. When Miguel emerges fifteen minutes later, he's carrying a plastic bag with a distinctly rectangular bulge. Is it? Could it be?

But yes: The man has purchased at least one book, and maybe even several! Oh, I'm so happy I could chase my own backside. If the only thing he leaves with is a reignited interest in reading, this trip won't have been a complete waste.

"Whoa," says Dane. "You trying to put yourself out of business?" Seeing Miguel's face fall, he quickly adds, "I'm just kidding, chief. You know there's no such thing as too many books."

"There *is* such a thing as too little money, though," says Miguel, frowning. Then he reaches into his pocket and pulls out a piece of paper. It's long and thin, like the paper that our cash register spits out. He waves it at Dane. "I do have some good news."

"They gave you Vik's number!"

"No, but almost as good. I have his full name."

Dane lifts his hand to high-five Miguel, who hesitates but then slaps his palm against Dane's. "How do you feel about sushi, chief?"

"Uh . . . what does that have to do with this?"

"It doesn't, but there's a killer takeout place right around the corner, and my stomach is about to eat itself. Let's go get some food—my treat—then we'll head home so I can find this Vik fella."

An hour later, I have learned the hard way not to eat the spicy paste that's served with sushi, but I can't bring myself to care too much about the stuff that's still stuck at the top of my mouth. Not when we're back in the car and off to yet another adventure.

"You're positive it's the same Vikram Choudhary?" says Miguel, hands wrapped tight around the steering wheel.

"Positive? No, sir. But he's the right age, and I'd rather start in Lincoln Park than drive all the way to Naperville."

"I hope this isn't a dead end," says Miguel.

"It's only dead if we stop trying. Let's go."

Traffic's far worse than when we arrived, and it takes a good half hour to go just a couple miles. Miguel can't find parking, so Dane offers to circle the block to look for something while he goes up to the apartment. To my surprise, he takes me out of the car with him. "You've been my lucky charm so far, Harold."

Have I? Come to think of it, I *am* rather fortunate.

"Maybe we can finally make real progress this time," he adds as we climb the steep cement stairs to the large stone building where Vik supposedly lives.

When we reach the door, Miguel hits one of the many buttons on the panel. There's a loud buzzing noise, but no one lets us in. He hits the button again. "He must be out right now," he murmurs. "Wonder if he went with JMB to . . . well, wherever he is now."

"Excuse me."

There's a guy behind us dressed in an all-blue outfit, the same kind Raina wears to her job at the hospital. I can't be certain, but the man's long, straight nose and bulgy arms make me think people would describe him as handsome. In fact, I can imagine him in one of Amelia's stories.

"Sorry," Miguel tells him, stepping out of the way.

"No worries," says the man, sticking his key in the lock. He's nearly inside the lobby when Miguel shoves his foot in the door to keep it open.

"Hey," says the man, spinning around. Miguel's tall, but this man is taller. "I can't let you inside—building policy. You'll have to wait for whoever you're trying to visit to buzz you in."

"I'm looking for Vik. Are you him? You fit the description I was given."

The man frowns.

Miguel tries again. "Vik Choudhary?"

"I'm not sure what this is about, but I'm not interested," says the man, pulling the door closed.

Miguel moves his foot, so it doesn't get slammed in the doorframe. Instead of leaving, though, he taps on the glass. The man spins and looks at him. He shakes his head. After a moment, he opens the door again and steps onto the stoop. "What do you want?" he says wearily.

Miguel seems surprised. "Um, to ask you a few questions about your friend Jonathan Middleton-Biggs."

Vik's eyes immediately drop to Miguel's waist, like he's expecting him to pull something out of his pocket. Miguel must notice this, too, because he raises both of his hands. "I'm not sure what you're thinking, but I'm just a bookseller—I own Lakeside Books in West Haven, Michigan. My name's Miguel Rivera."

"Okay . . ." Vik's frowning, but he doesn't smell so nervous anymore. "Why are you here to see me, then? I'm not an author, and I don't have enough time to read all that much."

"Because we're trying to find Jonathan."

Vik laughs bitterly. "He's definitely not here."

Miguel examines Vik. "I got your name from Enrique. Well, your first name, and then we went to Roundabout Books, and a woman named Keisha knew who you were."

"Ah, that explains a lot. She and my sister went to school together." Vik glances away. "I'm still surprised you got this far. Jon doesn't like anyone prying into his personal life. Everyone who knows him knows that. Including Keisha."

"I gathered, and believe me, I had no intention of poking into his affairs until he didn't show up for his event earlier this week. I'm now on the hook for thousands of dollars, and it might put my bookstore out of business. I'm just trying to find Jonathan so I can convince him to come in and do the reading and signing like he said he would."

"I'm sorry to hear that, but I have no idea how I could possibly help you when I haven't seen Jon in a month."

Dane's making his way around the block again, and he rolls down the window and sticks his head out. "Everything good, chief?"

Miguel flashes him a thumbs-up. Dane must not believe him because he frowns, but the car behind him is honking now, so he rolls the window back up and drives away.

"Did something happen, that you stopped talking?" Miguel asks Vik.

"Something happened, all right—but I'm not so pissed that I'm going to run my mouth about it, even if you do seem innocuous. Or at least more so than most of his stalkers." Vik adjusts the strap of the bag on his shoulder, then looks down his perfectly straight nose at Miguel. "I wish I could help you. I really do. But if you want more information, you'll have to ask Fiona."

Fifteen

When we get home, Miguel finds the little card Fiona gave him and calls her. I can't hear what they're talking about—he leaves me in the living room with Dane and shuts himself up in the bedroom during the conversation—but when he emerges, he tells Dane to change.

"Nah, I'm good," says Dane from his spot on the sofa.

Miguel looks from Dane's face to his shirt and back again. "You're wearing half the sushi you ordered earlier."

"You suddenly the sartorial police? 'Cause you and I are practically twinsies these days. Though I must say, you're sharp as a shiv tonight."

Miguel glances down and seems surprised to find himself dressed in a short-sleeved linen shirt. It's the pale yellow one Amelia bought him, and even *I* can tell he looks nice in it. "Thanks, I think."

"You're welcome, I think. Anyway, I'm not going with you."

"Why not?"

"How'd we go from 'this is a solo endeavor' to 'Dane, you play Luke'?"

"I am *not* asking you to play Luke. I just . . . expected you to join me."

"Miguel, as much as I'm geeked you finally want to hang, you're *good*. Fiona likes you. If she didn't, she wouldn't have invited you over a second time." Dane rises from the sofa and ambles over to the fireplace, which Miguel's standing in front of. He claps him on the shoulder. "You leaving our dog friend with me? Seems like Fiona's not as big of a fan of his."

"I got that impression, too, but she told me to bring him."

Did she?

"She said the girl wants to see him," Miguel adds.

Oh, I can barely contain my excitement.

"Then there you have it. It's a double date!"

"It is not a date of any sort, Dane. I'm just going to have a drink with her and see if she'll put us in touch with Jonathan."

"Okay. But chief, your face."

He reaches up and touches his beard, which he trimmed before we left town. "What? Do I have something on me?"

"Nope. You just look . . . happier than usual."

Miguel immediately scowls. "I won't be happy until JMB's at the podium at our bookstore. And if I play my cards right tonight, that might finally happen."

"There you are!" Her voice is higher pitched than when she growled at Miguel. But it's her, the other Amelia, who has spotted me and thrown open the front door of her house. "I knew you'd come," she says, guiding me into the townhouse. With its deep brick façade and wavy windowpanes, her home looks far more like Miguel thought Jonathan's would. "But it took you long enough—it's ten minutes past eight! We're going to have to have a talk about your owner's punctuality, Harry."

Harry! I've always wondered what it would be like to have a nickname. Now I know: It's a warm hug made of sound.

She ignores Miguel, who's standing mutely behind me, and points at the small bowl of water she's placed on the floor. "That's for you. Not sure what you eat, but it's hot out, so I got you something to drink."

I glance up in appreciation, then slurp greedily, even though I suspect I'm splattering all over the tile.

"Bet you feel better now," she says when I'm done.

I do, and I rub against her leg to thank her.

"You're sweet, but we have work to do. You," she says, finally addressing Miguel. "You'd better be nice to Fiona tonight."

"Fiona?"

"My *mom*. Duh."

"Yes, I'm aware," he says with amusement. "I'm just surprised to hear you call your mother by her first name."

"She doesn't like it, either, but the Stone Age is over." She points down the hall. "Go on, she's in the kitchen. I'll take care of Harry."

"Harry, huh?" says Miguel.

"Yeah. No offense, but who calls a dog Harold?"

"I'm not offended. That's the name he came with. Are you sure—"

"Of *course* I'm sure," she interjects. "I turn twelve in two months, which is legally old enough to babysit siblings in plenty of states. Not that I have a sibling, but if I did, I'm sure

Harry would be way better behaved. Besides, Fiona will be less anxious if she doesn't have to see him too much. Now go, and please *be good.*"

She doesn't check to see if I'm trotting behind her as she makes her way up the stairs; we both know I am. "Sorry," says the other Amelia when we reach the second level. "I know you've had quite the day. I have, too. But I'm glad you're here again."

How can I not be charmed, when she's talking to me just like my Amelia used to? Of course, Miguel rambles at me plenty, but this is different. She's doing it because she wants to, not because it's compulsive and there's no one else to listen.

"Well, here's my room," she says, directing me inside.

I know right away that this is the best spot in the house. The walls are mostly built-in bookshelves, and there are a bunch of beanbags and blankets strewn about in front of them. The floor's littered with books and notebooks and markers, too.

My Amelia would have loved it here, and for some reason, that makes me a little sad for feeling this excited about having a new friend who shares her name.

"Make yourself at home," she tells me, plopping down in front of a blue armchair in a corner. She shoots me a skeptical look when I sit tentatively beside her. "*Home,* Harry."

Home. The word nearly sounds right coming out of her mouth.

"Come on, feel this carpet," she tells me, bending to rub her hand on the floor. "It's so soft. You can lie down on it and listen to me read."

Yes, I think I'd enjoy that. I stretch out as she grabs a paperback from beside the chair. She flips through it for a moment, then says, "I'm sure Fiona would prefer I was reading *Anne of Green Gables* or *The Secret Garden* or even *The Baby-Sitters Club*—but between us, I'd rather peruse the junk mail. Anyways, I have a feeling Stephen King's the only one who can help us right now."

Help us? Does he bail out bookstores?

"This is called *Misery*. It's about a writer who gets kidnapped by a crazy fan. I'm wondering if it'll give me some ideas about what's going on with Uncle Jon. My mom's trying to act like everything's fine, but she's being way too weird, and something's up. I can tell. I just don't want her to be upset—she's already been through so much with my grandparents getting killed in a car accident and then my dad taking off on her."

Hmm, that is a lot. I wonder if she realizes it's a lot for her, too. And if Amelia Mae doesn't know where her uncle is, that means her mother probably doesn't, either—which isn't ideal. But she's beginning to read, so I close my lids. Even though I don't fall asleep, by the time she's done, I feel every bit as rested as if I had.

"I'm glad you liked that," she says, patting my belly. "I wasn't sure how the whole leg-breaking thing would go over with you. Just remember, it's only a book. You can always turn the page if you aren't feeling it."

"Love bug," calls Fiona. "Come say hello! And please bring the dog with you—carefully!"

Amelia Mae frowns. "Drat, we're being summoned. Come on, Harry. Let's go make an appearance for the fogies. We've gotta show her we're fine together."

Fiona and Miguel are in the kitchen, which is smaller than

Jonathan's and smells like food. There are loads of photos on the fridge. Like with her room, you can tell someone actually lives here.

"There you are! I wanted you to say hello to Miguel," says Fiona, who's seated across from Miguel at the counter.

"We spoke," Amelia Mae assures her mother. "Before I took Harry upstairs. And since you're going to ask, he's on his very best behavior today."

Fiona's eyes dart to me, and I flash her my teeth. She turns to Miguel. "Am I losing it or is he smiling at me?"

"Dogs do smile," he says. He knows this because my Amelia read him something about it after he told her that wasn't a thing. "Harold must like you," he adds.

"Really?" she says with surprise.

I smile even wider to reassure her that I'm willing to let bygones be bygones if she will, too. Miguel nods, then takes a sip of the pale liquid in the glass he's holding.

"You know, I didn't even ask you if you would have preferred red," she twitters. She suddenly seems nervous, and for once, I don't think I'm the cause. "I have a cabernet. Or sparkling water if you don't drink—oh goodness, I didn't even ask you that, either."

"This is good," he grunts, sounding way too much like his prehistoric ancestors.

"Did Fiona show you the balcony yet?" Amelia Mae asks Miguel.

"The balcony?"

"It's like the one I yelled at you from, but nicer. We have plants and stuff up there."

"Oh." He seems uncertain. Probably because he hasn't spent much time around younger humans since he was one himself—even when he wasn't always running from customers, he left the kids up to my Amelia and Beth, who used to run Story Hour before she left to have her own baby. "No, your mother hasn't mentioned it."

"Amelia Mae's right. It's lovely," says Fiona, who seems unable to hide how uncomfortable she feels saying her own daughter's name in front of him.

Miguel must pick up on this because he gives her a reassuring smile. It probably pains him to hear it, but maybe it's getting easier already.

"Would you like to see the view?" she asks. "Maybe we can keep talking shop up there."

"Sure," he agrees.

Amelia Mae stands and claps her hands. "You kids have fun—I need to pee. Harry, think you can deal with the stairs again? If you go with them, I can meet you up there."

I'm *not* sure; it's a lot of up and down, and I'm more worn out than I care to admit. But she's already disappeared, and I really should keep an eye on Miguel, just in case he says something stupid to Fiona again. So, I follow them to the second floor and down a long hallway to a small study that opens onto the balcony.

In the study, Miguel stops to examine a tall bookshelf that's much like the ones in the other Amelia's bedroom.

"This is my office," says Fiona from behind him.

Miguel turns to her. "I don't mean to pry—I just can't help but check out your selection."

"Never trust a person without bookshelves filled to the brim," she says, and he laughs lightly.

"Agreed. Ah," he exclaims, spotting a thick book on her

shelf. "*Brief Interviews with Hideous Men*—that's one of my recent favorites."

" 'One never knew, after all,' " she says.

" 'Now did one now did one now did one,' " he recites.

As they smile at each other, I'm reminded that there's a special language shared between two people who have read and loved the same book.

"Admittedly, it doesn't hold a candle to *I, Edward,*" he adds.

"Different style from my brother's—but thank you. Not that I can take credit, of course."

"Your brother is a genius. Safe to assume it runs in the family."

"Genius is overrated, and you're kind." She turns and slides open the glass door, and they step onto the balcony. I'm about to join them when Miguel pulls the screen door in front of my face. "It's way too hot out here, Harold," he says. "Stay in the air-conditioning and go find your friend."

"We can keep the glass door cracked to keep an ear on them," says Fiona.

I know she most wants to keep an ear on *me*. I'm willing to overlook that, though. Because for all his nerves, Miguel may not be completely happy right now—but he's content. And that's owing to my stellar taste in potential mates; I just know it.

"So . . . why did Vik tell me to ask you about your brother?" he asks after they've sat down in the deck chairs. The patio overlooks the city, which is starting to blink like a yard full of fireflies now that the sun's slipping in the sky.

Her eyes sweep Miguel. "You have a sibling, right?" she asks after a moment.

"A sister," he says cautiously. "Miriam. She still lives in Puerto Rico."

"Are you close?"

Now he doesn't hesitate. "Very."

"Then I assume you know and care more about your sister than almost anyone else," she says, then lifts her glass to her lips and takes a sip.

"Well, yes," he admits.

"Same with me and Jon. As you know, we lost our parents when he was young, and I helped raise him. I still feel the need to protect him all these years later."

Miguel nods. "We did, too. Miriam and I, we lost our mother when I was twelve and she was nine, and our dad had already been in the wind for a while at that point. We felt . . ." He glances away for a moment before looking at her again. "Well, like we weren't enough for him to stay. But after our mother passed, then it was like we were truly alone in the world and had only each other to rely on. I think that's why your brother's work has always resonated so much with me. Orphan as origin is a story I know a little too well, and the way he described your relationship—it's a lot like how I feel about Miriam."

"I'm glad it resonated, but I'm also so sorry for your loss," she says quietly.

"Thank you. I'm sorry for yours, too."

Neither of them says anything more for a while. It's a comfortable silence, though. So comfortable that I startle when I feel a hand on my back.

It's Amelia Mae, who has snuck over to the study and is beside me on the floor. She holds a finger to her lips to indicate I'm not to announce her presence. We both lean silently toward the screen door.

"I promise I'd share more if I could, but I honestly don't know what's happening with Jon," Fiona says quietly.

"You could at least tell me how to reach him. You must have his number."

"Of course I do, but if he won't pick up for me, he's definitely not going to answer for you."

"Are you sure he's all right?"

"Sure? No. He and Vik got in a fight a month ago, and he hasn't been the same since. But I'm not worried he's going to hurt himself, if that's what you're asking."

"So, he and Vik are together?"

"They were."

"I had no idea."

"It's not because he's trying to conceal their relationship. He just doesn't want people to know *anything* about him, including who he dates. And I have to respect that."

"Right," Miguel agrees. "All the same, I would like the chance to speak with him."

I jump up suddenly, like a flea bit me, but it's not bugs that have me bothered. Amelia Mae isn't here anymore. Where'd she go?

"Harold," says Miguel, spinning around. "What's wrong?"

Fiona's eyes flash with fear. "Amelia Mae?" she yells. "Where are you?"

Sixteen

She isn't in her bedroom or Fiona's. She's not in the kitchen, either. I dart from one place to the next as fast as I can—which is admittedly not very—because if I slow down, Miguel might catch me. Unfortunately, Fiona seems to be under the impression I'm the reason Amelia Mae's missing and is scrambling behind us. Did she have to run past a pack of hyenas to get to school when she was a child? Granted, I've been threatened by some naughty dogs in my day. But it was really their owners who were the issue, and she can clearly see that Miguel—well, he may not be dog dad of the year, but he cares entirely too much about me and would never let me hurt anyone. Especially her daughter.

"Harold!" he calls as I slip around another corner and out of his sight. To Fiona, I hear him add, "Don't worry, he has a great sense of smell. He's just trying to find her like we are."

This is true, but as much as I'd love to relish his compliment, I have more pressing matters to attend to. As it happens, I've just discovered a fresh trail of apple shampoo, and it's leading me straight to the front closet.

"*Shhh!* Get down, Harry!" exclaims Amelia Mae when I stick my snout inside. She pulls me into the small room and closes the door behind me. "I don't want Fiona to realize I took her phone." She flips the shiny plastic device open and hits a bunch of buttons. I hear faint ringing, then some sort of robotic voice. She presses another button, then repeats the process a few more times. Finally, a real man's voice comes on.

"Fiona? Is everything okay?"

"Uncle Jon, it's me! Amelia Mae!" she whisper-hisses. "You're not kidnapped! Wait—you probably can't tell me if you are. Say 'pepperoni' if you're not safe, okay?"

I can't hear him anymore, but her smile tells me that he's all right. "Phew! I was worried you were tied to a bed and some lunatic was making you write another book." She nods. "Yeah, I know it sounds like *Misery*. That's where I got the idea! Oh, Uncle Jon, you worry too much. It's just a book! But seriously, where did you go, and why didn't you tell us you were leaving? And what happened with Vik? Are you two fighting?"

The doorknob rattles, and suddenly Fiona's standing over us. Before I can warn Amelia Mae, Fiona grabs the phone out of her hand.

"Mo-*om*!" she protests, but Fiona's already lifted the phone to her head.

"Hello?" she says. Her eyes narrow. "Yes, I told her you were fine. Repeatedly. But given that I was clearly upset and couldn't say where you were, she was bound to pick up on the fact that something was wrong. Yes, I know. I *know*." Fiona sighs and gestures for Amelia Mae to vacate the closet. She hangs her head and complies, as do I.

Fiona's still holding the phone to her ear when we join her

in the hallway, but she's looking at Miguel now. "Since I finally have you on the phone, do you want to tell me where you are and why you didn't show up to the reading at Lakeside Books?" she says to Jonathan. "I'm actually with the bookseller now, trying to smooth this over. You standing him up has put them in a bad financial situation. Yes . . ." She flashes a closed-lip smile at Miguel. "I understand, but this is not the end of our conversation, Jon. You can't just—" She stops abruptly and listens to whatever he's saying. Then she hands the phone to Miguel. "It's for you. It's on speaker."

Miguel's standing at attention now. Truly, I haven't seen him this alert since he nearly got us both flattened by a car walking across an intersection a few weeks ago. "Jonathan? This is Miguel Rivera. I was really hoping we could reschedule your event at my bookstore. Maybe we could put something on the books while I have you?"

"I'm sorry I didn't make it," says Jonathan. But he doesn't sound sorry; he sounds grumpy. "You'll have to excuse me, but I'm done doing events."

"I understand your desire to avoid the public—believe me, I do—but you don't strike me as someone who would promise something as big as a ticketed signing and then suddenly back out. And Fiona, as you can hear, has been far more generous about this than I would have been if I were in her shoes," he says, staring at her. "Now, this event would make a huge difference to Lakeside. In fact, if I have to refund the tickets, I won't be able to pay my employees next month and may end up closing the store. So, can we schedule a rain check for the end of August, maybe September at latest? I'll take any day you're able to come in."

"No."

Miguel yanks his head away from the phone like Jonathan has just reached through it and slapped him. "What? You're kidding, right? You *said* you would. You offered to do this. Fiona told me that supporting small bookstores is important to you."

"It is. Fiona, please write him a check."

"I offered that already, Jon," she says into the receiver.

Did she? They must have discussed that while Amelia Mae was reading to me.

"This is about more than just the money," says Miguel. "I've squandered our goodwill with our customers—people are angry that there's no rain date. They *expected* to meet you. And we were hoping that your coming into the store would help boost our sales by putting Lakeside on the map."

"I'm truly sorry that your plans aren't working out, but I'm sure this isn't the first nor the last time life will disappoint you or your customers." In a softer tone, he adds, "Amelia, love, are you there?"

She's leaning against the wall and rubbing a strand of hair between her fingers, suddenly looking less like a shrunken adult and more like the child that she is. "I'm here, Uncle Jon," she says quietly.

"I'm really sorry I worried you. No one kidnapped me, and I'm already looking forward to seeing you again soon. I'm just going to travel awhile longer before I come home. Think you can hold down the fort?"

"Sure," says Amelia Mae in the quietest voice I've ever heard her use. "I was just worried because . . . I guess it doesn't matter. I'm glad you're okay. But Uncle Jon?"

"Yes, kiddo?"

"Where *are* you?"

I can hear him sigh through the phone. "I'm in Copenhagen. That's in Europe."

Miguel's eyes bulge, probably because that's the city where a lot of *Missing Person* takes place, too.

"Will you do me a favor and take care of your mom until I get back?"

She nods solemnly. "Okay."

"Thanks, love. I love you. Now, everyone, please excuse me. It's the middle of the night here and I'm going back to bed."

And with that, the phone goes silent.

Fiona's face has just shifted through nearly every feeling I can identify in a matter of seconds, but Miguel's expression is unreadable. "I'm so sorry," she tells him. "Let me at least write you that check. You can just take it with you in case you change your mind."

"I won't," he says, and for whatever reason, this makes her crack a tiny smile. "I can't accept money from you when this isn't your fault. But even if your brother himself was handing me a stack of cash, I can't take funds for an event that never happened. I shouldn't have counted on it in the first place, and that's on me. Anyway, Harold and I should be going. Thanks for the wine."

She places her hand on his shoulder. "Of course. I really am sorry, but I'm glad we were able to connect. Maybe we can come see Lakeside Books for ourselves sometime."

He doesn't blink as he looks at her. "If it's still there when you're in the area, we'd love to have you."

That's it—we're leaving, with no promises to see them again? My heart feels heavy. But then Amelia Mae sticks her face in my fur and whispers, "This story isn't over yet, Harry," and everything lightens and brightens.

She's right, of course; I'm not thinking this all the way through. Because Jonathan Middleton-Biggs going on a walkabout that led me and Miguel straight to her and Fiona?

That could not be a coincidence.

Seventeen

When we drive home the following morning, the tall buildings disappearing in the car's rear window make me lonely. Which is strange, since Miguel and Dane are right there.

But maybe that's just how you feel when you can't be with the person you want to be with.

I wonder if Miguel's feeling that way, too, because he barely says a word to me and Dane on the drive—and for once, Dane mostly lets him sit in silence. In fact, Miguel's not even muttering to himself. What's going on inside that giant skull of his? And why didn't he properly invite Fiona and Amelia Mae to come visit us while the store was definitely still open? I'd like to show it to them. Really, this week would be ideal, and later today would be even better.

When we reach West Haven, we drop Dane off at the coffee shop so he can caffeinate himself before he starts his afternoon shift at Lakeside. Then Miguel and I head to the house, where he hauls in his suitcase and my things while I tend to my needs in the yard. I'm on my way back inside when I hear Miguel's voice, faint and floating from the second floor. I rush upstairs to find him and end up scraping my undercarriage on the stairs in the process. The bedroom door's closed, but even from the other side, I can tell he's speaking Spanish.

And for a split second, I forget she's gone.

Amelia's Spanish was dreadful, but she tried anyway because she loved Miguel and making him laugh—and oh, how he laughed when she confused verbs or unintentionally lapsed into French, which she'd studied in school. "*Ay, amor,*" he'd say, mock-chiding. "*Eres tan mona cuando intentas hablar español.*"

Yes, she was quite cute. But I've just remembered that it's not her talking now, that I'll never hear her voice again, and wish my memory hadn't failed me.

So, he must be on the phone with—well, let's be honest, it's got to be Miriam; he doesn't really speak with anyone else, regardless of the language, but they rarely speak English or even Spanglish when it's serious. He's telling her about Amelia's parents and our trip and how JMB's in Copenhagen. She must be interjecting soothing noises and comments because his agitation quickly gives way to melancholy as he explains that he's done all he can and is really and truly out of options.

"*Tendré que cerrar la tienda en septiembre,*" he adds woefully.

Close the bookstore in September?! What happened to that being like "losing Amelia all over again"?

Oblivious to my panic and his own shortsightedness, Miguel begins to babble justifications: I should have done it a while ago. I don't even read anymore, so I'm obviously in the wrong business. It's not the same without Amelia here.

Of course it's not. Nothing is. That doesn't mean he can just . . . *quit.*

I'm sure Miriam's responding in all the ways I wish I could:

telling Miguel to hang in there, not to give up so soon, to leave space for things to work themselves out and maybe even a miracle or two.

She must have just told him to take the money Fiona offered, because he says sharply in Spanish, "I don't *want* her money. I'm not so desperate that I'm going to let her spend all that cash to clean up his mess. Even if he pays her back, it isn't right. No, Miriam, I'm not being self-righteous . . . it's called having principles. Besides, just getting through August and even September won't save us when the business is clearly broken, and Amelia's parents are heartless. I don't see the point."

She talks for a while—I know because he's silent until he tells her he'll be okay, just like he always does, and that he'll call again soon. Then he hangs up, flings open the bedroom door, and spots me hovering in the hallway. "Eavesdropping, Harold?"

Me? Never.

"Don't give me those sad eyes," he tells me. "I know you miss the girl, and I'm sorry about that. I never should have dragged us to Chicago in the first place. What an absolute waste of time and energy."

Yes, he should have! And yes, I do miss her—probably far more than I should. I'd like her to read more stories to me, even if they aren't ones she plans to write when she's ready. I'd like to hear about the things she puts in the notebooks she has strewn all over; I'm willing to bet Fiona and Miguel made it onto her pages last night.

I squeeze my lids closed and remind myself that this is about Miguel. Of *course* I know that; it's the last and most important thing my Amelia asked of me.

But a small, selfish part of me can't help but wish he would think about what I want, too.

My eyes spring open again, and though the sun streaming through the small window in the hallway burns them, it's all right. Because in imagining what Miriam said to Miguel, I have conjured a memory that doesn't hurt quite so much and might—just might—help a little.

I never believed her then, but my Amelia always swore thinking about someone could make them appear. "You were *just* on my mind," she'd say with delight when she answered her phone or ran into a friend around town. "I must've conjured you!"

I suspect she spent a lot of time thinking about a lot of people she cared about, which I suppose is its own form of magic, if not the sort she thought it was. Yet . . . it worked. All the time. And though I don't know if it'll work for me and Miguel, I'm willing to try anything, and I do mean anything, to get Fiona and Amelia Mae here.

So, I squeeze my lids shut, imagine a tall, sunny woman and her perfectly cloudy child, and tell them to find their way to Michigan—fast.

Eighteen

We're back at the bookstore the next morning, but it's just me and Riley; Miguel drops me off so she can keep me company while he runs an errand—to do what, he doesn't say.

I'm still feeling blue, but I'd rather be blue here, especially now that I know the store's future is even more tenuous than it already was. I follow Riley around as she puts this book back and rearranges that shelf and pulls a well-read copy of a picture book from the children's section. Dog-eared, she calls the books that the kids love most, and while that doesn't make sense to me, I certainly don't hate the comparison.

It's an overcast, sleepy sort of day, and the only person who's stopped in so far is a college-aged student. She approaches the register with a book, but she looks like she's about to buy a block of manure. When Riley asks her what she prefers to the novel she's purchasing for school, she confesses she'd rather watch TV. Minutes later, the student's clutching a second paperback and has promised Riley she'll report back as soon as she's finished *Circle of Friends*.

Miguel's walking in as the student walks out. Riley spots him and waves from the register. "I want to hear about your trip to Chicago! How was it?"

He takes a sip of the coffee he must've picked up while he was running errands, then says, "You first. How did closing go yesterday?"

"Kind of you to ask, but it was business as usual. So? Chicago?"

He glances down. "I'm surprised Dane didn't already tell you—it was a total bust."

It was *not*. How can he say that?

But he's not looking at Riley anymore. Instead, his eyes are roaming the room, and they just landed on the Romance section. I don't know what he's thinking, but I do *not* like the way he's regarding those shelves.

"What happened?" asks Riley. "Dane said you met JMB's sister and the two of you really got along. She should be able to talk him into coming in, right?"

"I thought so, too, but that's not happening." He shakes his head. "JMB's in Copenhagen and is done doing events."

"*Copenhagen.*" Riley practically spits the word out. "Like in his novel?"

"I thought it was an odd coincidence, too, but maybe he's trying to relive his past. Whatever he's up to, it sounds like he's done being an author. Which means we're in serious trouble."

"Crap. Well, maybe we can get someone to take his place? I've been looking into possible replacements."

"Thank you," he says with surprise. "I appreciate that."

"Don't thank me yet. Amis charges for events," she says,

rubbing her finger and thumb together. "So, he's out. Coetzee's and Lethem's teams didn't call back, and Atwood said she can't commit to anything right now."

"Probably for the best—people would fuss about it not being Jonathan, so I'm going to end up refunding the tickets one way or another. Which, as we all know, we can't afford."

Riley squares her shoulders. "I was actually hoping to talk to you about that."

He sets his cardboard coffee cup on the counter. "I'm listening."

"So . . . we're struggling."

"We have been for a while, and I know that's my fault."

She shakes her head. "You don't run this place on your own. It's on all of us. Dane said Brenna's trying to reduce our returns, and I'm helping Natalie get better at hand-selling—but respectfully, those moves are only going to get us so far."

"*Por favor,* not e-books again," Miguel says, wincing. "I can practically see Walt Whitman rolling over in his grave."

"Miguel, if Whitman were alive, he would have been at the forefront of Project Gutenberg and figuring out how to get his books on your phone. Well, not *your* phone—that thing's a brick with buttons," she says, and he pretends to be offended. "But yeah, I think we should have a real conversation about e-books. They're gold, and we don't have to miss the rush." She holds up a hand before Miguel can protest. "I am well aware of your feelings on the matter, so that's not the main thing I'm proposing. Instead of leaning so heavily on literary fiction, we could get more romance readers into Lakeside. Romance authors, too. After all, we know so many of them—and didn't Amelia always say that romance readers were the most voracious? Nearly every bookstore from here to Timbuktu sticks romance in the back or in some far corner like it's shameful. We don't have to do that. We *shouldn't* do that. We have an opportunity to serve those readers. And yes—make money doing it."

The lines between Miguel's brows deepen. "Amelia and I were always clear that this is a store for *all* readers. Not just one type."

"It still will be, but romance could be our differentiator. Like Brenna said in our last meeting, our romance sales are slipping right now, which doesn't reflect industry trends. Even if that weren't the case, they could easily be twice what they are now. We could do a big romance event here. An entire conference, even, where we have authors come and sign books and do readings and—I don't know, there are probably a bunch of things I'm not even thinking of. We have the space," she says, gesturing to the center of the store. I can see what she's saying. Most of the tables could be moved so that readers could mingle.

Riley continues. "The romance book club that meets here every month said they'd be all over it, and said they'd tell other readers who aren't in the immediate area. They'd help publicize it for us."

"You already asked them?"

"Hypothetically, and strictly for research purposes," she says breezily. "We could capitalize on the fact that we're in the Midwest instead of on the East or West Coasts—not everyone wants to fly to New York or LA to see their favorite novelist, and most of the big-name writers don't even live there. Off the top of my head, there are a bunch of local authors who might be willing to come. We could ask Amelia's network for help—I'm sure they'd be willing to show up. This could really put us on the map."

"That's what JMB's event was supposed to do. And frankly, I don't want to do a romance conference or festival or whatever." He reaches over the counter, grabs a pile of unread mail from a shelf, and begins rifling through the envelopes, ignoring Riley's incredulous stare.

"Why?" she demands. "It's a good idea. A great one. Brenna thinks so, too."

"So you two are back on speaking terms?"

Riley sighs deeply. "Not exactly, but I'm making an effort because I know it's awkward." Miguel keeps looking at her, so she adds, "And yeah, because I do feel bad and my first apology didn't really seem to do the trick. Point is, given that she used to do the accounts at Borders, Brenna of all people understands what works and what doesn't. You think the JMB reading was supposed to be big? Well, this would blow it out of the water. We need to think bigger if we're going to survive. With a little testing, who knows—maybe we could stop worrying about rent and buy the building."

"That's not going to work," he says simply.

What's wrong with him? Romance's the antidote to the dumpster fire that is the world: That's what Amelia liked to say when someone asked her why she didn't write something "serious." She was joking . . . but also, she meant it. And Miguel's being ridiculous and irrational.

"At least let me move the Romance section to the front of the store so everyone sees it when they walk in," says Riley.

He shakes his head. "Not now. We're teetering on the edge of closing. This isn't the time for experiments."

"This is the *exact* time for an experiment." She tosses her braids over one shoulder and crosses her arms. "Miguel, I know you don't have the money to pay me like a manager, but I'm already functioning as ours. I have been since Amelia got sick and you couldn't come in as much."

"Riley," he begins, but she doesn't give him a chance to continue.

"I'm not trying to make you feel bad. I've loved doing that work, which hopefully I've made clear. But you and I both know I deserve a spot at the table when it comes to decisions, and I'm asking you to let me make one of those decisions while there's still a chance. More important, I might be the only person around here who knows what you're going through. I'll never get over losing Jamal in the terrorist attacks. When I close my eyes at night, I still think about how I couldn't call him and I couldn't get downtown, and how I felt like my whole life had ended as I watched the smoke from the towers from our apartment on the other side of the river. Then came weeks of waiting—even though I knew, I *knew,* he was gone. I miss him every single second I'm conscious, Miguel, and most of the ones when I'm not. I'm not sure that I'll ever recover, which is probably why Brenna and I never stood a chance," she says, her eyes glistening with tears. "So, I'm not going to be the one to tell you to get over it; you probably won't. But also, I'm not going to pretend like you're okay anymore. I've known for a while that you're not, and I'm sorry that I didn't bring it up sooner. I didn't want to offend you or make it worse. I should have known that that was a mistake."

Now he gives her his full attention. "I'm not offended by you taking credit for what you do. You're a great employee, Riley, and I am a hundred percent aware that the store couldn't have survived this long without you. If I haven't said that before, I'm truly sorry."

"Thank you, but that's not what I mean. Can you watch the register for a second?" She jogs back to the break room without waiting for him to respond. A minute later, she returns with a piece of paper, which she presses into his hand. "Here."

"What's this?" asks Miguel, glancing down at it.

"The name of my therapist," Riley tells him. "She's phenomenal, and she specializes in grief. Call her."

He's holding the paper like it's coated in bird droppings. "My sister already tried this. I *don't* need a therapist."

She gives him a knowing look. "That's what I said. Now I wish I'd gone sooner. You know I was still hardly functioning when I showed up here. I don't blame myself, but I realize now that I needed someone else to nudge me. Did you know Amelia was the one to encourage me to go get help? I'm not sure if she ever told you that. She was already starting to feel unwell, yet she was worried about *me*." Riley's getting choked up. "And she would have wanted you to get help, too, Miguel."

"I appreciate your concern." Except now he doesn't sound appreciative at all. "But therapy isn't going to fix my grief."

"There's no fix—well, aside from time and being around people you love. But it would help you deal with the pain. And maybe you could talk to the therapist about whether your aversion to romance is because it reminds you of Amelia."

He rubs his forehead, and I can tell that his measured breathing is deliberate. "Even if it does, Riley—and maybe you're not wrong about that—it's a moot point. You should be the first to know that it's extremely likely we'll have to close at the end of August. If you started looking for a new position, I wouldn't blame you. In the meantime, you're right: You should be allowed to make big decisions. Rearrange the store however you want. You can even move the Romance section to the front if that's what you'd like to do."

Instead of responding, Riley looks around Lakeside. Almost like she's attempting to imagine what the space would be if it weren't a bookstore.

Or maybe that's just me. And try as I might, I can't picture anything between these four walls besides books and the people who love them.

But what if this *isn't* the place where Miguel can heal? Just like Riley needed to leave New York to get better, what if he needs to leave Lakeside and West Haven to find love?

I close my eyes, rest my head between my paws on the tile, and make a wish . . .

That moving on doesn't have to mean letting go.

Nineteen

We don't go to the store the following day, or the next. Instead, Miguel takes up residence in front of his computer. As far as I can tell, he's poring over the same bills and accounts he's seen a million times (though what do I know? In what strikes me as a true injustice, I cannot read). Regardless, I am almost certain that he's avoiding Lakeside, probably because he doesn't want to see what Riley has done with the place or be reminded of his own perceived failings.

Silly human.

Usually when it's just the two of us, Miguel's so worried about me that he anticipates my every need before I do. Which, to be honest, can be incredibly annoying sometimes, even if he means well. Now, however, it's like I barely exist. This is nothing if not further evidence that he needs other people—because I'm sure not keeping him going. But not just *any* people. Why doesn't he call Fiona, tell her he's sad and lonely and that the only time in recent history that he really felt good was when she was around?

Unfortunately, I can't dwell on it too much this morning, as I have an urgent need to empty my bladder. So, I whine at Miguel until he rises.

"Should've gotten a dog door," he says when he lets me out.

Should've? I may be old, but I'm still here, Miguel! Stop acting like it's too late to make a change!

When I return, I look expectantly at his car keys, which are hanging on a hook on the wall. Surely, we can't stay here all day *again.*

"No," he says firmly. "I'm going to do some research about liquidating book stock and maybe call Miriam back. So, don't get your hopes up."

Don't get my hopes up! He might as well command a fish to swim through the trees. Hope got me through a year in a crate. It kept me going in the animal shelter until Amelia arrived.

And at once, I realize that I need that hope again—for both of us. Fortunately, I know exactly where to find it . . . and it's sure as sugar not in this house.

It takes me a while to think of a strategy that doesn't involve begging. By the time lunch rolls around, however, I have devised a plan.

Act normal: This is my first order of business. I clang my bowl, as per usual, then suck up my kibble like a tornado in a cornfield. Immediately after, I rush to the door and cast deliberate glances at my leash. Miguel still has no intention of walking me, but my ruse works, and he opens the door so I can run around the backyard.

If I had the time, I'd work the latch on the gate. However, my second order of business is to escape while he's still looking but before he can catch me. I jump up on the garden box and, after a few shameful seconds of hesitation, leap over the wooden fence and tear off down the driveway.

People are always amazed that dogs can find their way home from long distances. They shouldn't be. All creatures have a natural homing instinct; it's just that dogs take care to develop ours, as we know there's likely to be at least one occasion in which it's required for survival.

Except in this case, it's Miguel I'm trying to save.

The sun's high and the heat's as heavy as a wet towel as I sprint down the side street leading to the big road. On and on I run, darting by the mail carrier, past a woman with a stroller who startles when she sees me, and around cars blocking the intersections.

It's probably a mile from the house to the bookstore—hardly the stuff of *The Incredible Journey,* which is a Story Hour favorite, but no jog in the dog park, either. Just when I fear I can't go on, I spot the telltale stretch of street signs and lampposts. I've made it downtown! As tempting as it is to scavenge for sidewalk scraps or stick my head inside the antique store with all the odors, I continue until I reach Lakeside.

Then I collapse in front of the door, too parched and winded to bark to be let inside.

The thud-thud-thud coming from under my ribs isn't quite right. Maybe it's my heart murmur. Amelia had one, too. Doctors said it was no big deal, but it turned out to be a little part of a very big deal. At any rate, I still remember how astonished she was when the vet told her about me.

"Oh, Harold," she said, hugging me. "Of course you do. Of course, because I do, too! You and I really were meant to be together, weren't we?" Then she looked at the vet. "Will this hurt him?"

"Probably not in the short term," he told her. "As he ages, though, his heart may get weaker."

My heart *does* feel weaker, though that might just be from missing Amelia. Either way, we're well past the short term now. But a dog's duty is a vow—a sacred promise that can't be broken.

Miguel better get here soon.

Twenty

"Harold, you lunatic! What were you thinking? It's nearly ninety out."

I'm so happy to see Miguel that I'm not even concerned that his hands are balled into fists and he's walking a lot faster than normal. Besides, while he may holler on rare occasions, he's as scary as a garden snake.

He kneels over me on the pavement. "You're the weirdest dog, you really are. I thought your runaway days were behind you. Are you trying to pull a JMB on me? Are you all right?"

Better than I was a few minutes ago, though that's not saying much; perhaps sprinting wasn't my most evolved idea. Miguel opens the door, and I force myself onto my paws. My legs are trembling as I make my way into the bookstore. Dane, who's at the register, sees me and grabs his water bottle from the counter. "Here you go, bud," he says to me, holding the bottle over my mouth. "Sorry I didn't see you out there sooner."

"I can grab his bowl from the back," Miguel tells him.

"Dude, he's wilting! Time is of the essence!" Dane says as I greedily gulp. Is there anything better than a cool stream of water on a hot day to remind you of how good it is to be alive? I think not.

"Thanks, but that's disgusting," says Miguel, because I did just lick the bottle.

Dane shrugs. "Their tongues are super clean. I read it online."

I bathe my bottom with my mouth, so I'm not too sure about his sources. But I rub against his leg in gratitude.

"Welcome, Harold," he tells me.

"Dog, are you okay?" says Miguel, kneeling beside me. "You look like you need to rest."

That's an understatement, but I just stick my tongue out farther and wait for him to appreciate the ambience.

"Since I'm downtown, I do need to run over to the accountant really quick," he tells Dane. "Do you mind watching Harold? Just call me if he seems like he's struggling."

He's leaving so soon? But he just got here! And yet again, my plans have failed.

"On it, chief," says Dane.

"Thanks. By the way, I fed him before we left, so don't let him trick you into giving him more food."

Food? I'm still so winded that eating sounds as fun as licking sand. So, I go find my usual spot in the sun on the braided rug. I'm about to doze off when I hear someone whispering.

"Shhh! Harry, over here!"

Dare I trust my ears? Actually, I don't have to—because my nose has just picked up on a now-familiar shampoo scent.

It *worked*!

My conjuring worked, and Amelia Mae is here, in Michigan, in our bookstore! I leap to my feet, ignoring the fact that my hips are on fire, and rush to the reading nook.

She's slouched in the yellow chair, holding a book in front of her face. She lowers the book when she sees me. "Harry, I've been waiting for you! Not too long, though, so thanks for that."

But *how*?

"I hopped on the train right after Fiona dropped me off for camp," she explains. "Union Station's not far from the drama center, and turns out they'll sell a ticket to anyone with a note written in careful cursive. Anyways, it was a fast ride, and I sat next to a nice old woman who gave me part of her cookie. Course, we're not going to tell that to Fiona, who'll worry I got poisoned. But I could tell that the woman was just lonely and wanted to make her feel a little better. She said I should read Shirley Jackson sometime."

I'm so excited that I've begun pacing back and forth in front of her without even realizing it.

"You're sweet, Harry. You know why I'm here, right?"

I cock my head and wait for her to explain.

"Obviously, I'm lonely and I missed you. That's reason enough—but also, Fiona's been *miserable*. She's stopped journaling in her zillion notebooks, and she got in another huge argument with Uncle Jon. They're always on the same page, so this is bad news. I told her we needed to come to Michigan, and she said no, not right now. Between us, I think this is about more than Uncle Jon—though she does hate the highway. I'm positive she's lonely and Miguel made her realize that, deep down. Now we just gotta bring it to the surface."

Fiona's lonely, too? I don't want to be pleased about that, but I can't help it. Not when she might just need Miguel as much as he needs her.

She continues, "I had to take matters into my own hands.

The minute Fiona learns I'm here, she'll come running. Er, driving. Which is good for her, since she needs to work on her hang-up about highways. And then we'll let these two imbeciles take it from there." She pats the ground in front of me, and I sit at her feet. "Perfect," she says. "Let me read to you for a while until they figure out what we're up to."

She begins, but she hasn't made it through the chapter when I hear Riley call me, and I leap back onto my paws. Oh, good—Riley's a rule follower, and certain to rat on us.

"Hello there," says Amelia Mae, glancing up from her book. "You must be Riley; Miguel told my mom about you. Great bookstore you have here. At least as good as the couple near me in Chicago. Maybe even better."

"Thank you . . ." Riley says cautiously as she examines her. "Is your mom here with you now?"

"Nope. But according to the states of Michigan and Illinois, it's perfectly acceptable for a person of my age to be alone for reasonable amounts of time. And in case you're wondering, I'm almost twelve, and they don't define 'reasonable.'"

Riley's eyebrows shoot up. "That may be, but does your mom know you're reading *The Dark Half*?"

Amelia Mae lifts her chin to challenge her. "She doesn't need to. We Fosters don't believe in literary limitations. What you make of a book is about *you*—not whether it's 'good' or 'bad,'" she says, making air quotes.

"You're precocious!"

"No," she says sternly. "I'm not precocious, and I'm not gifted, either. I just read a lot."

Riley laughs. "Your point."

"Thank you!" Her smile fades. "Sometimes I annoy the kids at school. But Harry actually likes to listen to me. That's why I just took a train around the lake to get to this place. I'm Amelia Mae, by the way."

Riley has grown very still.

"I know that's weird that I have the same name as the woman who owned this bookstore, but let's call it a coincidence. Just like Uncle Jon being gone when Miguel and his friend Dane showed up at our house, which led to him hitting it off with my mom."

"Wait, you're—"

"Fiona Foster's daughter," she offers. "Who's the sister of Miguel's favorite author, Jonathan Middleton-Biggs. Aka my Uncle Jon, aka the no-show."

"I see." Riley pauses, then says cautiously, "Is your mother in town here with you?"

"Nope." Her hair flies back and forth as she shakes her head. "That's the whole reason I'm here. She hates anything she thinks is even sort of unsafe for me, and somehow traveling to Michigan made the list. So, I decided to help her rip off the Band-Aid and get over it."

"Oh, my word," says Riley, agog. "You do know I'm going to have to call Miguel so he can call your mother, right?"

"That's the plan."

"I guess I'm somewhat relieved to know this is intentional. Can I trust you to stay put?"

"Obviously," says Amelia Mae with a hint of amusement. "I'm here until Fiona is. And hopefully after that, too."

"Well, good. Harold, please keep your new friend company while I go sort this out."

Yes, she is my new friend. And having a new friend never gets old, even if the same cannot be said of me.

"Ruh-roh, Harry," she whispers as she watches Riley walk

to the counter. "I have a feeling it's about to get real around here."

"Yep," I hear Riley say as she cradles the phone between her shoulder and ear. "For about ten, fifteen minutes, maybe? I don't know, but it couldn't have been that long." Her eyes dart to us as she listens to whatever Miguel is telling her. "Uh-huh. Uh-huh. Yep, that's her. Okay . . . thanks, boss."

She hangs up the phone, then calls to us, "You two, don't go anywhere until Miguel arrives. He's going to call your mom."

"*Miguel,*" says Amelia Mae, rolling her eyes at me. "Dum-dum needed me to disappear just to pick up the phone and call her. Sorry, Harry—I don't mean to say mean things about your owner. The good news is, once they get here, I'm going to insist we stay awhile. I packed extra clothes." She points to the backpack next to the chair, then winks and adds, "I'll even cry if I have to."

My Amelia was clever like that. When she told people how she became a writer, she'd talk about only being allowed to read religious material growing up. "I'm exaggerating, mostly," she'd say with a grin. "But don't you know, the Song of Solomon was my gateway drug to Johanna Lindsey and Judith Krantz. The rest is herstory."

Oh, how I miss her.

But the other Amelia has decided that I'm too far away and has put her legs right next to my body and begun reading aloud to me again. And even though it doesn't make me miss my Amelia any less, I still somehow feel better.

I just hope Fiona's arrival will make Miguel feel that way, too.

Twenty-One

A few hours later, the sound of sandals slapping on the floor startles me awake.

"Amelia Mae!" Fiona's striding toward the reading nook, where her daughter's set up shop. Not that she had a choice—Miguel brought her a sandwich and a candy bar and has been watching her like a hawk from the register. Except he's not there now. Where did he disappear to?

"Over here," says Amelia Mae, waving her fingers in the air at her mother. "In Michigan, where I told you we should come visit? And whaddaya know, I already love it!"

Fiona throws her arms around her daughter. When she's finally done squeezing the stuffing out of her, her expression says she can't decide whether she's proud or angry. "It's a good thing I could get on the train right away."

"You didn't drive?"

Fiona shakes her head.

"Drat. I was hoping you'd work on your highway paranoia."

"I do *not* have a paranoia—I just happen to have firsthand experience with the dangers of driving at high speeds. Regardless, I was on the verge of panicking, thinking of you making that trip all by yourself. Please don't scare me like that, love. You know you're all I have."

I side-eye Fiona; she sounds exactly like Miguel right now.

"Technically, I had company," Amelia Mae tells her. "I counted fifteen other people in my train car."

Fiona looks like she might pass out.

"Don't worry, I sat next to a very nice old woman, and we talked about books. So . . . you're not mad?"

"I'm not *happy,* but no—I'm not mad. Which doesn't mean you should ever pull something like that again. And drama camp is not cheap. You should've told me you didn't want to do it."

"I did! Seven times! You didn't listen." Amelia Mae widens her dark eyes. "So, did you talk to Miguel yet?"

"Fortunately, I had the good sense to answer his call even though I was in the middle of canceling everything on Uncle Jon's calendar. Though honestly, I did have a hunch that there was a disturbance in the Force. How did you even find this place?"

"I asked someone at the train station where it was, then walked. Less than a mile, door-to-door. At least that's what the guy told me. How'd *you* get here?"

Fiona reaches for the bookshelf to steady herself. "A taxi. Sweetheart, someone could have snatched you!"

"I know I said I was worried about Uncle Jon getting kidnapped—but I did some research, and it turns out that random kidnappings are a statistical anomaly. Not that you need another worst-case scenario to haunt your dreams, but I'm more likely to choke to death on a fish bone than be abducted. Besides, I was walking through town, not down some eerie dirt road—though I bet we could find one around here."

Amelia Mae crosses her arms over her chest. "The main thing is that I promised Harry that I'd see him again, and whether you like it or not, I'm a girl of my word."

I give Fiona my biggest puppy dog eyes, and she *does* seem to soften. "The dog. Of course. You are sort of compelling, aren't you?" she says to me.

Am I? Do I still have it? She didn't even say anything about my eyebrows!

"Still," says Fiona, "this dog—"

"Harry," Amelia Mae interjects. "Best friend to Miguel, *your* new friend, who you've been miserable without. Like I told Harry, you haven't touched your notebooks since he left."

Fiona adjusts her glasses. "Darling, I appreciate your thinking about me, and I find it sweet that you somehow believe your old mom's obsessiveness is a good thing. But the notebooks aren't important, and I've had my hands full with—well, your uncle's decision."

"You're not old."

"Thank you, love, though I noticed you didn't refute my obsessiveness. Now, why wouldn't you tell me you were going to come here?"

She sighs heavily. "I *did*. And again, you didn't listen. 'Too far.' 'Not right now.' 'Maybe later,'" she recites, making puppets out of her hands.

"Well, I *am* your mother. Last I checked, that makes me the de facto decision-maker in these scenarios."

"Um. Hi," says Miguel, who's just loped over from the bathroom. "Thanks for—well, I guess you had to come."

"Hello there," says Fiona in her singsong voice. Though her sweat smells nervous, too, she's a cool breeze compared to him. "And yes, yes, I did. But now that I'm here, I'm glad. I like your bookstore quite a bit. Jon really blew it not coming to his event."

Amelia Mae steps in front of Miguel and addresses Fiona. "I told you this place would be *amazing*. Wait until you see Stabby Peeps!"

Miguel raises an eyebrow at Riley across the room, who holds her hands up and tries to suppress her smile.

"I could live there. Though you'll probably like the back of the store better," she says, referring to the Romance section, which Riley hasn't moved yet.

"Are you going to run off again?" Fiona asks her.

"How many times do I have to remind everyone that it's perfectly legal for me to be on my own?"

Fiona looks over the top of her glasses at her daughter. "The legality of your great escape is debatable, dear heart, and I suspect Child Protective Services might have something to say about you checking out of camp without my permission, to say nothing of your train voyage. How did you pull that off, exactly?"

"I may or may not have forged a letter from you saying I had therapy. Aren't you always saying reading is therapeutic?"

"Good-*ness,* Amelia Mae," says Fiona, making that angry-proud face again. "What am I going to do with you?"

"Buy me this?" she says, holding up her novel.

Miguel sighs. "The book's on me."

I wonder why the man would give away a book when the bookstore needs every dollar it can get.

Then it finally sinks in: He really likes them. Or at least he really likes Fiona, and since she and Amelia Mae are a bonded pair, that's enough for me.

"That's generous of you, but I'm happy to pay for it," says Fiona.

"Mom, never turn down a genuine offer. Especially if it's a free book. And this one's very important—so thank *you,* Miguel."

"Don't mention it. But out of curiosity, why's it so important?" he asks.

"Well, I'm worried about Uncle Jon, and I have a strong suspicion that *The Dark Half* is going to help me figure out how to help him."

"Didn't you just tell me kidnappings are a statistical anomaly?" Fiona says, cocking her head at her daughter.

"I haven't been worried about him being kidnapped since I talked to him in the closet," she says slowly, like she's explaining this to a child. "But I heard the two of you arguing the other night, and I know he's being weird. What if there's a voice in his head, telling him not to write anymore? What if it's his secret *twin,* buried in his brain?" she says, covering her face with her hands as she pretends to be horrified.

"Love, that's a whole lot of storytelling right there."

Miguel clears his throat. "Um. Fiona? Is there a chance that your brother's actually struggling? After all, he doesn't believe in writer's block. He's said that repeatedly in interviews—that you can solve for it with desire and discipline."

Fiona frowns, searching for the right words. After a moment, she says, "No, it's nothing like that. Jon's just doing the living he didn't get a chance to when he suddenly skyrocketed to success. He claims he's had enough of being in the public eye. And I quote: 'The frickin' internet ruined everything.' "

"Okay, Flintstone," says Amelia Mae. She drops her hand

from her face and frowns at her mother. "So . . . you like the bookstore?"

"Of course," she says, glancing around. "It's practically perfect in every way."

"Thank you," murmurs Miguel.

"I knew you would," says Amelia Mae. "I had a feeling even before I came here. But now that we know for sure how great it is, we have to do *something* to help them out."

"You're sure you won't take the check?" Fiona asks Miguel.

He shakes his head firmly. "I really can't accept something for nothing, nor your money. I appreciate that you like the store—it means a lot to me. But you didn't get us into this problem, and it's not on you to get us out of it."

"I know that, but I like you, and my daughter likes your dog."

He thanks her with a shy smile.

She smiles back. "Actually . . ." She puts a finger under her daughter's chin. "You've raised an interesting point. We *should* help Uncle Jon make things right—and I might have a few ideas. I want to strike while my mental iron's hot, and there's no way I can work on the train." She turns to Miguel. "Would it be a terrible bother if we stuck around a little while longer?"

"It's no bother at all," says Miguel, whose flushed cheeks tell me he means it.

"Terrific. Then let's see if there's a hotel around here where we could spend a night or two."

Amelia Mae turns to me. "Hang on to your harness, Harry! I have a feeling we're in for some fun."

I'm enjoying a late afternoon snooze when I hear Miguel scrambling around downstairs. I swear he's speaking to someone, and he's making a terrible racket. Then I remember that Amelia Mae and Fiona are here, in our town. Maybe they've stopped by our house for a visit!

But when I make it to the kitchen, Miguel's alone, scooping food into my bowl.

"Eat up, and then we're going out," he tells me.

I eye him with equal parts suspicion and incredulity. Does "out" mean back to the bookstore? He *is* dressed in clean clothes, even if his freakishly long toes are poking out of his sandals—that's one feature about humans I'll never warm to. I bet we're heading around the block, since he'd tell me if we were seeing our new friends. Well, I suppose anything's better than sitting here.

I tend to my bowl but don't finish my kibble; it's too much effort for too little pleasure. Then I walk to the door, where Miguel clips the leash to my harness. But rather than heading down the driveway, he directs me to the car. "You've got to be on your best behavior," he commands as he points at the space behind the front seat.

"Best behavior" means we're not going to the bookstore, since I don't need to be told how to act there. Where to, then? It'd better not be the vet.

Darn it, it's probably the vet.

And after my squirrel mauling and great escape, who could blame him? Dread seeps from my head to my heart to my gut. I try to pace in the place where feet go but there's not enough room. So, I do what I'm not supposed to and hop up on the seat and press my face against the glass.

I'm still waiting for Miguel to yell for me to stop licking the window when he pulls into Lakeside's parking lot. *Not* the vet—we're back at the store! Have Fiona and Amelia Mae returned? Oh, I hope so. This must be why Miguel's been extra quiet. He's excited, too, and it's been so long since he's felt that way that he doesn't know what to do about it.

But once we park, Miguel grabs my leash and leads me away from the store, toward . . . the café? Listen, I like Spoon. After all, they allow dogs inside, which is more than I can say for most of the shops around here. I've never misbehaved there, though, so it's weird that he felt the need to instruct me.

Then it suddenly clicks, and I bound through the door so fast that Miguel nearly trips on his way in.

"Easy, dog! Easy!" he says, but being old does have its advantages, because he's not yanking on my leash hard enough to deter me. Dragging him behind me, I hightail it to the corner where Amelia Mae has already stooped down to hug me.

"Harry!" she cries.

Amelia Mae! I think, sticking my nose into her soft, scented hair. It's not the same as being embraced by my Amelia. But in this moment, in her warm arms, it's enough.

Fiona, who's still seated at the table, clears her throat.

"Sheesh, Mom!" Amelia Mae chides without letting go of me. "Pretend he's a cat or something!"

"I didn't say a word, dear heart," she says. To Miguel, she adds warmly, "Well, hello there. I'm happy to see you."

"Hello," he says stiffly.

Miguel, it seems like you're the one who needs to be reminded to be on his best behavior. But I can't be too mad at him—not when he's making an effort to be with the person I've selected for him.

"I didn't realize you were bringing the dog," she says, casting a glance at me.

"I'm sorry," he says, frowning. "I just thought . . ."

Fiona's gaze shifts from me to Amelia Mae, who's still kneeling. "Okay, I'm being silly. I know you said he doesn't like to be alone."

"I was thinking of your girl," he says gruffly. "She seems to like him."

"Harry doesn't say I talk too much," Amelia Mae says in a quiet voice. "And I can tell he likes me, too."

He looks at her with surprise. "Harold *loves* when people talk to him. And he definitely likes you." To Fiona, he adds, "I promise, he's harmless—he's too old to hurt a fly."

I'll have you know that I ate a fly just yesterday, I think, narrowing my eyes.

"How old is he, exactly?" asks Fiona. Her expression looks calm—serene, some might even say. But I can smell lingering anxiety on her skin. It may take some work to persuade her that I'm nothing like the mangy mutt that charged me and Amelia when we were out walking one winter night. I don't know what triggered him—dogs and humans aren't that different, in that our emotions sometimes come rushing out for no apparent reason—but I'll never forget his enormous, frothing jaw snapping mere inches from my neck, and how Amelia managed to get us both behind a fence before he could hurt us.

"Almost fourteen, we think," Miguel tells her.

He doesn't realize that he's speaking like our Amelia's still here. I close my eyes for a minute, just to see if I can pretend like she is.

It doesn't work. But at least the other Amelia still has her arm around me.

"He does seem harmless," says Fiona, widening her smile to try to prove she's not afraid. Which tells me she absolutely is. "If you ask my daughter, I'm prone to overreacting. Please, sit," she says, gesturing to the chair across from her.

Miguel slides into the chair. "You said you had a bad experience as a child. Did you get bit?" he asks, resting his elbows on the table.

"Don't expect to get anything out of her," Amelia Mae tells him as she finally leaves my side to sit down. "I know she seems chatty, but Fiona's actually a vault with no combination."

"Now, sweetheart, that's not true at all," Fiona chides cheerfully. "Your uncle is very private, and I simply try to respect that."

Amelia Mae raises her eyebrows at me. "My uncle," she says in an exaggerated whisper. "Riiight."

Fiona sighs without breaking her smile. "I did get bit, in

fact. Neighbor's dog, the one everyone said was so gentle. I still have a scar," she says, instinctively touching a spot on her forehead where the skin rises slightly.

"Oh, I'm sorry," says Miguel. "I promise, Harold won't do that to you."

"I'm sure he won't," she says, but there's a hint of a question in her voice.

"Do you know what you'd like to eat? I can go order," he asks her.

Good boy! I take back everything I thought about his behavior.

"A caprese salad, if you don't mind," she says.

"White wine?"

"If you're having some, sure."

"Oh, I definitely am," he says, nodding his head, and she laughs. "And you?" he says to the other Amelia.

"Grilled cheese, please!" she says.

"On it. I'll be right back."

"Isn't this great, Harry?" Amelia Mae says to me, watching Miguel at the counter. "I didn't think he'd call today, but he came through. I want us to spend as much time as possible together while we're here."

"Love, I can hear you. And as a reminder, we're only here to deal with your uncle's mistake," Fiona tells her. "You need to get back to camp, remember?"

"Drama camp," she says, rolling her eyes. "Now *that's* an oxymoron. It's as dramatic as watching paint dry."

"All the same, you are going when we return. I paid for it."

She sticks her bottom lip out. "You offered to write an eight-thousand-dollar check to make up for Uncle Jon's

Houdini routine-y. Something tells me we can afford for me to miss camp."

"Goodness, Amelia Mae," says Fiona in a low voice. She glances around the café. It's nearly full, but save for a stinky French bulldog a few tables away, no one's paying attention to us. "For the record, your uncle would be covering that—not us. But can we please not discuss this in public?"

"All good?" Miguel's just reappeared and is somehow holding two glasses of wine and a cup of water—oh, to have opposable digits. "These are pretty full, so be careful. I'll be right back with our plates."

"Thank you. That was kind of you," says Fiona when he returns. She smooths out her skirt before she lifts the glass he's set in front of her. "Though shouldn't I be the one treating you?"

"No," he says simply, and I wonder if he notices that she's smiling into her wine.

"So," says Miguel.

"So," she says, looking back up at him. "I read that profile you wrote about my brother for the *Michigan Quarterly Review*."

His eyes widen. "You did? That was what, four years ago? I thought no one saw that."

"It was very good," says Fiona, nodding, "though I would have taken the opportunity to dig deeper about why Jon feels so confident writing female characters the way he does."

"Touché," replies Miguel, but he's clearly pleased. "I'm no expert."

"From what I read, you know more about my brother's work than a closet full of English professors."

"I'm not sure how many English professors you can fit in a closet, exactly."

"Believe me, plenty. Their egos, on the other hand—those require an additional storage unit."

The corner of Miguel's mouth ticks up. I'm pleased, too; I can't remember the last time he was this engaged in something other than bills and staffing schedules. "I can't disagree. But how'd you find that article, anyway?"

"I spend a fair amount of time online and know where to search. I was a journalist in another life."

"Another life? Do tell."

She waves at the air, but their eyes are locked. "It's really not interesting."

"Maybe not to you," he says, leaning forward. "How'd you get into journalism?"

"Curiosity, I suppose." Amelia Mae's seated beside her, finishing off the last of her sandwich, and Fiona reaches across to touch her head. "I wanted to learn about lots of things, and journalism offered an opportunity to get paid to find out about them."

"That's smart. What kinds of things?"

"Mostly environmental stuff," she murmurs.

"Mom could have been famous," says Amelia Mae, nodding.

Miguel arches an eyebrow.

"Oh, she's just talking about the story I'm best known for. Back when I was at the *Post,* someone tipped me off about a major pharmaceutical manufacturer dumping toxic chemicals into Illinois's waterways. It didn't take a whole lot of digging to figure out that officials knew and were looking the other way. Jon helped me sort through their corporate records and evaluate the water samples. We caught them red-handed. But that was a lifetime ago, or so it feels."

"Wait." Miguel leans back and eyes her. "You're *that* woman? Like the Erin Brockovich of the Great Lakes water system?" I have no idea who he's talking about, but it must be someone important because the man looks like he finally met JMB himself. "I had no idea."

"I don't usually talk about it," says Fiona, smiling.

He shakes his head. "You should—I'm seriously impressed."

She beams. "Thank you. Most people don't seem to think it's a big deal, so I rarely mention it."

"Idiots," he says, and her grin widens. "But how did you go from uncovering a public health crisis to working for your brother?"

Good questions are how you make friends; good listening is how you keep them. That's what Amelia said. She'd be proud of him right now.

"Well, Jon's career took flight right around the time I had Amelia Mae, and . . ."

"My dad's a bum who flew the coop when I was a baby," Amelia Mae supplies.

Fiona's smile tightens. "Sadly, that's accurate. What's more, I got laid off the minute my pregnancy became obvious. Jon and I were already used to being a team, as you know, so he stepped in to help me raise Amelia Mae, and I helped him navigate his career. I guess nothing much has changed, since we live right down the block from each other. Though given his surprise European vacation . . ." She trails off.

"I don't mean to pry," says Miguel.

"As a former journalist, I can say with certainty that it's only prying if the other person doesn't want to disclose. It's obvious that I'm happy to yap your ear off," she says, and they smile at each other before finally turning their attention to their food.

Amelia Mae rolls her eyes at me, but I can tell she's happy, too.

Between bites, Fiona and Miguel talk about nothing at all, which is a rare human skill I'm not envious of. They're nearly finished when Amelia Mae, who's back on the ground beside me, looks up at Miguel. "Hey, you have a car, right?"

He nods.

"Can you give us a tour of the town before it gets too dark? We've never been to West Haven before. Mom and I want to see everything. Or at least I do."

He frowns. "Aside from the lake, there's not a whole lot to check out."

Even if that's true—which it isn't—why wouldn't he take the opportunity to spend more time with Fiona? But then he surprises me and says, "I suppose I do live here on purpose. I'd be glad to drive you both around and let you form your own opinion."

"Thanks! Harry's coming, right?" she says, and Fiona laughs nervously.

Miguel looks down at me, then back at Fiona. "He'll grow on you," he assures her.

"I don't know about that, but he does seem sweet," she says, regarding me.

I am! And it's extra easy to be that way on a day like today, when I get to ride around in the back seat beside Amelia Mae and listen to Miguel chitchat with Fiona, still talking about little of importance yet sounding more like himself than he has since Before.

If only life could be like this all the time, I think, sticking my head out the window as Miguel drives us down Main Street, then loops over to the road that leads to Lake Michigan and shows them all the big houses along the lakeshore.

"Aren't these weird old homes the *best*?" says Amelia Mae, who's stuck her head out the other window. "Some of them are practically haunted! It's like the entire town is set up like a horror movie—you know, the part when the kids are still riding their bikes under tree-lined streets and the guy with the knife hasn't shown up to murder everyone yet."

"Well . . ." says Miguel, glancing at her in the rearview mirror.

"It's a compliment," she assures him. "Mom, this is way better than Chicago, and it's probably safer, too—I was totally kidding about the serial killer. I bet the kids are nicer than they are at my school."

Unfortunately, it's not that hard for me to imagine some students being unkind to her. My Amelia said that growing up, all her best friends were books, because childhood is hardest for those who don't seem like everyone else.

"And imagine all the writing I could do if we lived in a house with a turret!" she adds.

Fiona twists around to face her daughter. "I don't think we're moving anytime soon, but I do like the idea of you writing. You take after your uncle that way." To Miguel, she adds, "How'd you end up here?"

"Amelia," he says quietly.

Fiona doesn't ask him to elaborate, but maybe one day he'll

tell her that this is where my Amelia was born and raised. When she was young, she dreamed that eventually her little town would have a bookstore where people like her would be able to find the books they loved—even the ones that others stuck their noses up at or tossed in the trash, like her parents did when they found her stash of romance novels under her bed. They met in Ann Arbor, where Miguel had moved to attend college and never left; she'd arrived there to work as a copyeditor at a local paper. A few years later, after her parents had moved farther north, she and Miguel packed up and headed across the state to West Haven.

"We found the perfect place for our happy ending," my Amelia would sometimes say when she told others about the store's origins.

That was one of the only things she was wrong about. Endings can't be happy, because they're the opposite of forever—and no one wants to spend the rest of time without the one they love.

"Well, here we are," says Miguel, pulling up in front of the bed-and-breakfast. It's a big house, not unlike the spooky ones Amelia Mae pointed to on our drive, with dark paint that's peeling in places and vines creeping up the sides.

"Already? That was too fast," Amelia Mae pouts.

"I wasn't kidding when I said there wasn't much to see."

"Love, you've had a very long day. It's time to wind down and get some sleep," Fiona tells her. She turns to him. "That was lovely—thank you. But we never did talk shop."

"That's okay," he says. "This was nice, too."

"Well, I'd still like to if you're game. We're free tomorrow if you want to get together to discuss it," she says, climbing out of the car.

He opens his mouth, but no words come out.

We'd like to get together! I think, slobbering on Amelia Mae to make sure she gets the message. She giggles and wipes her cheek before stepping onto the sidewalk.

The passenger door's still ajar, and Fiona leans in to address Miguel. "Just give me a call if you feel up to it, okay?"

"Will do," he says, and if that's not a lingering gaze he's giving her, then I'm an overgrown ferret.

"Bye, Harry!" Amelia Mae calls, walking backward as she waves. "I had the best time with you today!"

I did, too.

She and Fiona disappear into the bed-and-breakfast, but Miguel doesn't drive away. Instead, he grips the steering wheel and stares at the lake in the distance.

Finally, he glances back at me and mutters, "Harold, if only feeling good for a change didn't make me feel so bad."

I know, Miguel, I think. *I know.*

Twenty-Three

I have not fulfilled my duty, but I am closer than I have been at any other point. Despite his guilt, Miguel was humming last night as he did the dishes that had been piling up in the sink. He even washed his sheets—and what is spontaneous laundry-doing if not a sign of a man who has found a reason to care again?

He does not love Fiona yet, but I believe he could.

He *could*.

Yet to my dismay, he does not call her the morning after our around-town excursion. And when he tells me he's going out to run errands, I'm certain he's not attempting to bump into Fiona and Amelia Mae at the farmer's market, or wherever it is he's going; otherwise, he'd say so, and probably bring me along for the journey. When he returns, I demonstrate my displeasure by refusing to look at him. Except he doesn't even seem to notice! He just commands me to go outside because he was watching me like a hawk when I went into the yard this morning and he knows I didn't finish my business. "Don't run off again," he warns when he opens the back door for me.

I couldn't if I tried—my whole dog's barking today—but I suppose I do want to see if that dreadful possum's been sniffing around the raised garden box again. I mosey over to it, checking for the decaying meat odor that lingers long after the beasts are done playing dead. But no tomatoes have been planted this year, no basil or kale—and so there's no reason for the possum to do anything but pass through. I make a pile in a corner of the yard, then circle the yellowing grass for good measure before letting myself back inside, as Miguel has left the door cracked for me.

There's a smell that's at once familiar and foreign wafting from the kitchen. I trot over to Miguel, who's at the counter. That's when I see he's wearing an apron.

He's making food? Dare I trust my (admittedly hazy) eyes?

I lift my head, trying to figure out precisely what he's working on up there; the only scents I can detect are flour, butter, and powdered sugar. I've still got my snout in the air when the phone rings. As he bounds across the kitchen to see who's calling, I take the opportunity to put my front paws on the edge of the counter.

"Eh, I'll call Miriam back later," he says when he reaches the phone. I've just spied a bowl, a spatula, and a plastic tub of some unidentified substance when he spots me. "Harold! Get down right now! I can't have you getting fur in the guava cakes."

But . . . I don't smell guava. And he only baked those for Amelia.

I'm not sure if I like that he's making them now. In fact, I feel oddly protective, like the time Amelia's friend brought over her Maine coon—that cat was a real show-off, chasing after a tennis ball like it was some kind of puppy. Couldn't he bake something else for Fiona?

This means your plan is working, Harold, I remind myself. *You don't get to pick* how *he's being romantic. Just enjoy your victory for a hot second.*

"Can't believe I have to substitute quince," he says, frowning at the tub.

Quince? Phew.

He continues. "Maybe after the bookstore's closed, I'll open a *tiendita*—someone needs to stock guava paste and plantains around here." He sticks the end of a spoon into the container, then puts it into his mouth, oblivious to my incredulous stare. He may be half joking, but I don't like him talking so casually about closing the store. "Hmm. Acceptable." He tosses the spoon into the sink, where it lands with a clang, then says, "Sorry, dog, these are for our picnic. But be patient, because I'm sure your little friend will slip you one when I'm not looking."

For once, I don't care about free human food. We're going on a picnic? With Amelia Mae? Two get-togethers two days in a row is well beyond Miguel's limit. He's doing even better than I've given him credit for. And maybe I should give myself credit here, too, because didn't I help summon Amelia Mae and Fiona to town?

I spend the next hour pacing in nervous anticipation instead of napping like I should. Miguel finishes baking the cakes, then packs them up and directs me to the car. I expect him to keep humming, but he's quiet on the short drive to the bed-and-breakfast. I myself am having trouble focusing, but that's mostly from feeling tired and wired. But I forget all about my exhaustion when I see Amelia Mae skipping down the front walk toward the car.

"Hiya, Harry," she says, sliding next to me in the back seat. "I'd give you a squeeze, but—" She gestures to the large picnic basket she just placed between us. "The inn had a basket we could borrow, and Fiona took it as a personal challenge to fill it to the brim."

"I might have," says Fiona, who's just gotten into the passenger seat. She's changed into a short blue dress today and has a big straw hat on her head, while Amelia Mae's dressed in dark colors and is wearing a pair of very big sunglasses. "I appreciate you picking us up," she says, leaning across the armrest to give Miguel a hug. He accepts, but I can't help but notice he looks like a person who's never had a pair of arms around his shoulders before.

"No worries. You look nice," he says.

A compliment? I take it back. Heck, I'd give him a bone if I could. He's being such a good boy!

"Thank you. I found a place to pick up some clothing, since"—Fiona raises an eyebrow at her daughter—"this was an impromptu trip."

"Since you haven't gone on vacation in a million years, you're welcome," says Amelia Mae.

"Thanks, I suppose," Fiona says, but she's smiling at Miguel now. "At any rate, I'm so glad there's a breeze. It's perfect weather for a picnic."

"Isn't it?" he says. "I think you'll like the park I've picked out."

The park's really just a stretch of grass that runs along the beach. My Amelia liked to come here sometimes because tourists didn't know about it; even in the middle of the summer, it was often just the three of us. There are only a few other people in sight this evening, too.

"Don't go in the water," Fiona warns Amelia Mae as she spreads out the blanket that Miguel has retrieved out of the trunk. She pulls sandwiches and fruit out of the basket. She's packed plates and little glasses, too, and a bottle of some sort of beverage, and—ooh, is that a bone?

"The bone is from me, Harry," Amelia Mae tells me. "But you'll have to wait until dinner to have it. In the meantime, let's go check out the lake."

A gift to gnaw on? Could this day get any better?

"I'm serious about the water, love. There could be a rip current," Fiona warns her.

She glances down at her shirt and shorts. "Do you really think I'm going swimming in this getup? I'm just going to go to the edge and stick a toe in. Then I'll find a nice stranger to accept unwrapped candy from."

Fiona balks, but Amelia Mae's already turned to me. "Harry, you don't have to if it's too much."

It probably *is* too much, but that's never stopped me before. I stick my tongue out and wait for her to pick up my leash.

It's hard to walk in hot, dry sand, but soon we reach the firmer sand at the shore's edge. And maybe because I'm so poky, she decides it's best if we sit. Her eyes rove along the water, which sparkles in the low sunlight. "I like it here," she says after a while. "At home, everyone thinks I'm the know-it-all with the famous uncle. I can't change their minds, but I could make new friends somewhere else. I bet this could be a good place for a fresh start."

It was once that exact thing for me. I still remember the first time Amelia brought me to the lake. She thought I would swim, since I'm a bird dog who's supposed to know how to find ducks or whatever it is my ancestors were bred to fetch, but the water was so cold that I decided to drink it instead, and she laughed and laughed.

That was long ago. Now I just hope this will be a good place for a slow finish.

"Fiona's being weird," Amelia Mae tells me. She's running her finger along the sand and writing something—of course, I don't know what it says, and even as I'm wishing I did, a wave comes and washes it away. "I asked her why Uncle Jon left, and she said she doesn't have the faintest idea, but I don't believe her. My mom isn't perfect, Harry, but she never lies to me. Why would she do that now?"

I sigh and rest my head between my paws.

"I don't get why Uncle Jon would take off like that—it's not like him. He *owes* my mom. I'm not supposed to think that, but she took care of him after my grandparents died even though she should have been off at college doing whatever college kids do." She lowers her head for a second. "It's probably my fault. He must have gotten tired of trying to fill in for my dad. Uncle Jon's always telling my mom to get out more, to go live a little instead of doing everything for me. But he never really did that, either. Maybe that's what he's off doing now. Living."

She puts her hand on my back. I wish I could tell her that these are big worries for such a small human, that none of this could possibly be her fault.

"They like each other," she says, glancing over her shoulder. "Can you tell?"

I turn to see what she's looking at. Fiona and Miguel are each propped on an elbow, so they're facing. Even from here, I can tell that Amelia Mae is right—they *do* like each other. Oh, this is all coming together so perfectly!

"The question is, which one of them will mess it up first? Probably both now that I'm thinking about it." I must give her a funny look because she laughs and jumps to her feet. "Don't poop on the messenger, Harry! That's just what adults do—make simple things complicated. Hopefully they'll listen to us if it comes to that."

Miguel and Fiona are still sprawled out on the blanket when we return to the grassy area. They're so deep in conversation that neither even glances at Amelia Mae as she grabs a sandwich and passes me my bone.

"You really haven't read *Stoner*?" Miguel asks Fiona.

"Nope. I've heard of it, but so many books . . ."

"So little time," he finishes. "You should—it's one of my favorites. But one caveat: Williams doesn't get his female characters right. At least, that's my take."

"And I should read it because . . ." she says teasingly.

He laughs. "I know, I know. I'll argue it's still worth it. Maybe if he'd written it a little later, he'd have known better. I mean, don't you think some of the nuance your brother brings to his work is because he was born in this era instead of another?"

Above us, the sky is clear and sparkling, but a shadow crosses her face.

"And from your input," Miguel quickly adds.

She manages to smile again. "You don't have to say that."

"I mean it, though."

"Thank you. That means a lot to me from you."

His fingers linger on hers as he passes her one of the little cakes he made. She takes a bite, then closes her eyes for a second. "Oh, my word. This is divine."

His smile's tinged with embarrassment. "I'm a little rusty, and the ingredients aren't quite right."

"If that's true, I'm afraid to see what you can do when you're well oiled."

They're staring at each other now, and neither one is smiling anymore. When dogs look at each other like that, it's a challenge. This is, too—but a different kind.

"May I ask how you got into such a tight spot at the bookstore?" Fiona asks after a moment. "Like I said, I understand that it's hard to be a bookseller, but I really didn't know Jon's event could be a make-or-break for you."

"It's kind of a long story."

"I've got time if you want to tell it."

A muscle in his jaw twitches. "The thing about my Amelia was . . . she was generous. She used her royalties to pay off the mortgage on our house, then subsidized the store with anything she had left over."

"I apologize if I'm being too forward, but wouldn't her royalties keep coming to you?"

"No, they go to her parents now." His brief laugh's more weary than bitter. "We were together almost sixteen years, but we never got married. I would've married her in a heartbeat—I used to propose to her all the time—but she didn't want . . . well, she didn't want to become her mom and dad. Unfortunately, she didn't have a will, because who expects to die at thirty-nine? And common-law marriage doesn't exist in Michigan."

"Why would they take that money from you instead of sending it to the bookstore?" Fiona says, aghast.

"They're not nice people. Never have been—they were terrible to Amelia when she was a child and weren't much better once she was older. They didn't like me, and they hated that she wrote romance. They thought her books were trashy."

"For heaven's sake. They're love stories," says Fiona, shaking her head. Then she reaches out and touches his arm. "I can tell how important the store is to you. Tell me again why you won't accept my check?"

"Honestly? As much as I'm glad you decided to come, this isn't your mistake to fix."

"I want to, though," she insists. "Jon will reimburse me."

He looks down at the blanket before meeting her gaze again. "I'm going to be honest with you, Fiona—I don't know if your brother showing up would've saved us. He probably would have bought us more time, though. I'm not much of a people person, and lately, I can't even say whether I really want to run a bookstore anymore. But I do care about my staff, and Amelia's legacy."

"I understand that, which is why I'm still working out how to make this right," she tells him.

Before Miguel can respond, Amelia Mae interjects. "Does that mean you're going to go on another date before we leave?" she asks, her eyes wide with excitement. "Because that would be getting it right."

"It's not a date," say Fiona and Miguel at the same time. They look at each other and laugh nervously.

"Besides, love, we're leaving tomorrow morning," Fiona reminds her.

Already? Date or no date, they haven't spent enough time together to realize that they simply *must* make a habit of each other's company.

But Amelia Mae grins mischievously at me, and that's when I realize: *I* may not know how to accomplish my mission, but something tells me she can figure it out.

Twenty-Four

Humans do all sorts of things that will never make sense to me. For example, why are they so preoccupied with whether anything's coming out of their noses? Why do they make important life decisions based on pieces of paper with dead people on them? And don't get me started on how eager they are to see one another's hairless bodies, yet they insist on wearing clothing all day.

But the way they can't stop saying the name of the person they're smitten with: *That* I understand, as nothing made me happier than when my Amelia said my name. And, of course, Miguel was so enamored with her that he used both of hers.

So, when his face brightens the next morning when he tells Dane about his picnic with Fiona, I know—I just *know*—that she is taking up space in his mind in the exact way I've been hoping she would. Still, I'm not prepared when Fiona appears at the bookstore a little while later with Amelia Mae, and he leans in and kisses her cheek. It's not a mouth kiss, but I'll confess: There's a tiny part of me that feels sad. Because if I could have anything I wanted, Fiona would be my Amelia, who would be alive, and my mission would be to love her—not replace her.

But a duty is not up for debate, and who am I to judge when he finally seems, well, nearly normal again?

Behind the register, Dane's making googly eyes at Riley, who's pretending to straighten up the magazine racks as she tries not to laugh. Then they're in on this, too. Excellent.

"We get the official tour before we leave?" says Fiona, directing her dazzling smile at Miguel.

"Absolutely—I apologize for not doing that when you were in the other day."

"No apology needed," she tells him.

"Well, *I've* already seen the whole store," says Amelia Mae. "I'm going to go sit in the reading nook, then maybe peruse Stabby Peeps again while I still can. You kids go on without me."

Fiona laughs, but she smells a little anxious, too—and finally, it's not on account of me. I decide to trail after them to keep watch.

"Ooh, you moved Romance to the front of the store?" she says to Miguel as they pause in front of the shelves Riley and Dane just finished setting up. "That's a rare and welcome sight."

"It was Riley's idea," he tells her. He keeps walking until he realizes Fiona's paused and is browsing the titles. He frowns. "I didn't take you for a romance reader."

She plucks a paperback from the shelves. "I read all kinds of stories," she says, her eyes running over the words on the cover. She returns the book to its spot, then looks at him and smiles. "And who doesn't like love?"

I almost expect him to balk, given how he responded to

Riley after she suggested the change. But he just touches Fiona's back lightly and smiles, and then her expression morphs from sunny to a full solar flare. She likes him, too—a whole lot, especially the way he responds to her, the way he sees her. I couldn't be more pleased if he'd just given me a whole roast chicken with a donut on top.

"Remind me, how many people were you expecting for Jon's event?"

"More than a hundred." She whistles, which makes him laugh. "People came in from all over the area. About twenty-five of those were VIP tickets—they paid extra to meet with Jon after his talk."

"You have capacity for that many?" she asks, glancing around.

He nods. "Amelia always thought big. We rent the building from Riley's Aunt Kathy, and she gave us a steal on the lease. Unfortunately, our rent is going up significantly in September. Even beyond the event and the issue with Amelia's parents, that's another part of the problem."

" 'You mustn't confuse a single failure with a final defeat,' " says Fiona.

He cocks his head. "It's a great quote, but Fitzgerald died with a pickled liver thinking the world had forgotten about *Gatsby*. Not sure we should be taking life advice from that guy."

"You know he was sober and in love?" she volleys back. "He fell for Sheilah Graham, a gossip columnist who lived in his building. She helped him give up booze and find some happiness in his last act."

"You're like a literary encyclopedia."

"Wait until you meet my brother." She cringes as she realizes what she said.

"I suspect that won't be happening this century," he responds, but for once, he's not upset, or even melancholy. In fact, I daresay there's a spring in his step as he shows her Stabby Peeps and the children's section and then shuffles her over to Historical Fiction. They've just finished up in Sci-Fi when she gestures for Miguel to walk with her toward the window. I follow them, pretending like I'm trying to find the right place to lie down on the rug.

"The bookstore is wonderful," she says. "As I thought it would be—but still."

"Thank you."

"I do have an idea about how to help. With the store, I mean."

"As much as I appreciate your offer, I'm never going to cash a check from you," he says, shoving his hands in his pockets.

"I know. But I'm not talking about a freebie, since you've made your feelings on that clear. I could give you a loan, or even buy a minor stake in Lakeside."

He shifts uncomfortably. "I don't mean to be presumptuous, but because your brother has written extensively about your childhood, I'm guessing you're not sitting on a trust fund."

"You're right, but I'm in a good financial position. Jon pays me for the work I do for him, and I've been a careful investor, especially these last few years. This would be another investment."

"But . . . you're in Chicago."

"I'm not suggesting we move, but I like it here—as Amelia Mae's pointed out, the town's extremely charming. I guess I'm thinking of her in all this, too; she's taken a shine to Lakeside Books, to say nothing of your dog."

I'm already grinning when he glances at me. *This is a brilliant idea! The best yet! Say yes, Miguel!*

Fiona continues. "I wouldn't want to tell you how to run your shop, and your team seems incredibly competent," she says, nodding to where Riley and Dane are standing, heads together, near the register. "And you're obviously working hard to come up with new plans. I guess what I'm saying is that I have faith that you'll figure it out, and maybe this could help in the interim. It wouldn't be a burden for me and Amelia Mae to take the train to Michigan from time to time without being under your feet too much."

"You wouldn't be under anyone's feet," he says, his voice even lower than usual.

"No?"

Miguel hesitates, then says, "I'd like to see more of you."

She swallows hard. "I'd like that, too."

I'm ready to start barking with excitement when he adds, "But . . ."

"Go ahead," she tells him. "I hope by now you've gathered that you can be honest with me."

He wrinkles his nose. "It's just that I'm not sure I want investors."

"You're right," she says quickly. "Jon's always saying I'm overly optimistic about my ability to fix things."

"I don't think that's a bad trait," he says, reaching for her arm.

"So you won't mind too much if I keep trying to come up with some way to help?"

"While you really don't have to, I'm honored that you'd want to try."

"It's not so much a matter of wanting as being unable to turn my brain off," she says.

He smiles. "That's one of the best things about you."

"That opinion puts you in a very small pool of people, so thank you." Fiona looks past him at the big clock on the wall behind the register. "I hate to say it, but our train leaves in just over an hour. I should probably round up Amelia Mae and head back to the bed-and-breakfast."

"Do you need a ride to the train station?"

She shakes her head. "The owner offers a shuttle." She hesitates, then leans in and hugs him. "It's been wonderful spending this time with you."

"I'm glad you came," he says gruffly. In a lighter tone, he adds, "I hope the next visit doesn't involve your daughter getting on public transportation alone."

"Does that mean we can come back sometime soon?" says Amelia Mae, who's just popped up between them.

"I'd like to." Fiona looks at Miguel. "If you're okay with it, that is."

"Absolutely," he says.

He sounds like he means it—and I'm sure part of him does. But having spent nearly my entire existence with the man, I don't need to speak human to know what he's not saying: He's afraid of betraying the one person he will always love more than life itself.

The question is, is that enough to keep him from loving Fiona, too?

Twenty-Five

For reasons I cannot explain, I slink off to the stockroom before Amelia Mae and Fiona leave the bookstore. Of course, Amelia Mae has already hugged me a whole bunch of times and vowed to return before I even realize she's gone. I still can't help but feel . . . well, a bit abandoned. Sure, there's a lake between us, and that's a reason to not be together.

But it doesn't seem like reason enough.

Eventually I venture back out to the main floor. Riley's making adjustments to the new Romance section, Dane's behind the register, and Miguel's at the end of the counter. His bent neck and tight expression tell me there's nothing good about the goodbye he just said to Fiona. I expect him to go take my place in the stockroom or announce that it's time to go home. Instead, he lifts his head and regards Dane, who's just finished ringing up a customer. "So, where are you drifting to next?" he asks.

"Whaddaya mean?"

"You said you don't like to stay put for too long," says Miguel. "So, where's the next adventure?"

Dane, who seems genuinely surprised by his question, considers it for a moment. "Well, at some point I want to hit up Morocco, and Guatemala's for sure on my list. But you know Michigan's the best place to be in the summer. If you're in the Northern Hemisphere, at least—otherwise it's New Zealand. I'm thinking I'll explore more of the east side of the state sometime soon, since I still haven't been to Lake Erie. Wait a minute—is this your sneaky way of letting me know you're getting rid of me?"

"No, Dane. Well, I might have to get rid of everyone if we can't keep the store open. But in this case, I was just thinking about what you said about being restless."

I expect Dane to crack a joke, but he leans forward and says quietly, "I'm good for now. How are *you* feeling, chief? Guessing having them in town felt like a lot, even if you liked it?"

"Who says I liked it?"

"Your face."

"Okay, okay. It was . . . nice."

"Yeah. I know we got off to a rocky start there in Chicago, but Fiona seems cool. The kid's not half-bad, either."

Miguel nods.

"You think you'll see her again?" Dane asks. "Like, in a romantic way?"

He looks across the room for a moment before turning his attention back to Dane. "I don't know. It feels early. It feels weird."

Dane twists up his lips on one side of his mouth. Then he sighs loudly through his nose, like I sometimes do. "Yeah, I get that. Reminds me of after my parents split."

"You didn't mention your parents were divorced."

"Happened right after they shipped me off to school."

"Guessing that sucked."

"It did," Dane says matter-of-factly. "And less than a year later, my mom introduces me to this guy named Silas, who she's really, really into. I'm like, ugh—no thanks, I already have a dad, and this dude's obviously a rebound, right?"

". . . Right," says Miguel. I don't know where Dane's taking this, either, but we both keep listening.

"Well, Silas ended up sticking around. They dated for a couple years, and I basically couldn't stand him, even though my dad, not Silas, was the reason my parents broke up. Now, I'm not on the best terms with my dad, since he's always made it clear I wasn't the kind of son he was hoping for. But I still thought liking anything about Silas was betraying him."

"I'm sorry," says Miguel. "About your father, I mean."

"Yeah, me, too," says Dane, and there's a skosh of sadness in his voice this time. "When I was almost done with college, my mom and Silas finally tied the knot. I came home one summer. I didn't usually do that, I always tried to be somewhere else—but this time, I spent a couple weeks with them because my mom was really nagging me about giving Silas a chance."

"I'm not angling to be a stepfather, Dane."

"Dude, I hope you know that's not my point."

"I continue to await said point."

Dane waves at an older couple who has just entered the store, then returns his attention to Miguel. "Turns out Silas is the bomb. Like, he knows how to get bees to make honey in his backyard and speaks all these languages, and you can ask him about, I don't know, some obscure detail in the Constitution or the origins of punk rock and he'll have the answer. The funny thing is, he's a lawyer, too, and in a weird way, he helped me understand my dad better. But he's actually the one who told me I didn't have to become one. He said I should go live and be happy."

"And . . . are you?"

"Mostly, yeah. I'd like to fall in love again. It's the best feeling in the world, and I'm thinking there's some possibility that with the right person, that feeling could last a long time, just like you had with Amelia," he says, nodding at Miguel. "Which is I guess the point I didn't know I was trying to make. I know you miss Amelia more than anything, and that's a sign of how solid you two were. But it's okay to trust your feelings. The new ones, I mean."

Miguel's making the same twisted-lip expression Dane was earlier. "And if those feelings are in conflict with the old ones?"

"Welcome to being a human, my dude."

His smile's only a little sad. "Dane?"

"Yeah, chief?"

"You're not half-bad yourself."

Dane claps Miguel on the shoulder. "I knew you'd start to come around. I'm here if you need me."

The phone on the wall rings loudly, startling Miguel.

Dane spins around to answer it. "Lakeside Books. Oh, hey—you don't say! Yeah, he's still here. I'll put him on." In a loud whisper, he tells Miguel, "It's your lady friend," and hands him the phone.

"Fiona?" he says, cradling the receiver between his ear and shoulder. "No, it's no trouble at all. Really. Don't move—I'll be right there."

He hangs up, then grabs his keys from underneath the counter. I'm already on all fours, set to go wherever it is that Fiona and Amelia Mae are surely waiting, but he doesn't have my leash in hand. Since his own excitement has made him impervious to subtlety, I trot beside him. But when we reach the door, he finally realizes what I'm doing and shakes his head at me. "Sorry, Harold. Given the circumstances, I think it's best if you wait here."

Twenty-Six

Circumstances? What circumstances could possibly require me staying away from Amelia Mae? Why are they still in town? Or *are* they? Is their train stuck on the tracks farther afield? Or maybe the journey is making Fiona even more anxious, and she's decided to borrow a car and brave the highway, or . . . well, I've run out of scenarios. Now I'd just like an answer. Better yet, I'd like to see my friend.

"I don't know any more than you do, buddy," says Dane as I pace back and forth in front of the window. There are lots and lots of people walking down Main Street today, which means the weekend's either approaching or already here. Some of them are probably in from Chicago to spend some time on our beach, which I'm told is even better than the one they have (though I'm also told those are fighting words, so perhaps it's best that I can't say them). But I'm not looking for any old tourists.

I'm starting to get a mite dizzy from all my back-and-forthing when they finally part the throng. Miguel is carrying Fiona's bag, and she's clutching something that I can't make out; just behind them, Amelia Mae's skipping along with her backpack slung on a shoulder. She waves when she sees me through the window.

"Are you sure it's okay?" asks Fiona as Miguel holds the door open for her.

"Yes, of course. We're dog-friendly."

Well, obviously. But why does that matter?

"I just wasn't sure what else to do," Fiona says breathlessly to Miguel. "The conductor said we weren't allowed on the train, and I wasn't sure that would've been a good idea in the first place."

"Seriously, it's all right," he assures her. "You're always welcome here. I'm glad you called me."

I'm about to bound over to Amelia Mae when I hear it: *a yip*.

It's a weak squeak of a bark that some might even call pathetic. Which means they have a *puppy*.

Betrayal!

Fiona sits on the bench near the door, providing me with a better view of the beast she's cradling like it's a newborn human. What kind of yappy punter am I even *looking* at right now? It's no bigger than one of the jumbo bones Amelia used to get me for Christmas. If it has eyes, they're hidden under all that matted fur, which is various shades of dark and no doubt teeming with fleas. On instinct, I back away from it.

"Harry, don't be jealous," Amelia Mae says, kneeling beside me. She leans in close and whispers, "I was just starting to worry that it'd be too long before we saw each other again when this little critter poked his head out from under the dumpster outside the station. And who am I to look a gift stray in the mouth?"

His: So this mangy thing is a male. And while I see what she's saying, I can't bring myself to muster up the same enthusiasm she seems to have.

"Cute! You check for others?" asks Dane.

Heaven help me—there might be a whole *litter*?

"We searched around the area and couldn't find his mother or any other puppies. I think he's been abandoned." Fiona peers down at him. "Isn't he so sweet?"

Sweet is a freshly baked cruller. Sweet is anyone who stops to scratch behind my ears. The animal she's referring to is chock-full of parasites—and seriously encroaching on my territory.

Dane shoots her a quizzical look. "Thought you didn't like dogs?"

"I don't . . . dislike them," she says, petting his head. "It's more that I don't trust them. But this guy reminds me of my childhood dog."

"*You* had a dog?" says Miguel with the same incredulity that I'm feeling, too.

"When I was very young, yes," she says, not looking up. "A schnauzer mix called Lucy. We named her after the character in *The Lion, the Witch and the Wardrobe*. She was really my mother's, though—Jon and I barely existed in that dog's mind. And she was black and white. Not brown like this little bear," she coos.

Is she *baby-talking* this thing? That's not acceptable unless someone is doing it to me.

"Are you going to keep him?" Miguel asks.

"Well, that's impractical. But I just couldn't leave him there," she says, still staring at him.

"I understand." Miguel places a hand on her shoulder, but

he doesn't get it, not really. Fiona is being turned before our very eyes—not by me, despite my best efforts, but by some scrawny dumpster pup who's probably the descendant of a long line of rat-chasers.

"Do you have a vet I could call to see if I can get him an appointment?" Fiona asks.

"Yes, of course. The clinic that sees Harold is excellent and not all that expensive compared to the emergency clinic. I'll get you their number."

"Thank you," she says, looking at the dog again.

"You know this means we'll have to stay longer," Amelia Mae tells her. "And the bed-and-breakfast doesn't allow pets—remember the sign?" She turns and stares at Miguel.

I see what she's aiming for, and I don't mind it one bit. I'd love to cozy up next to her in the spare room. In fact, that might just ease the sting of how decrepit and repellent I'm feeling right now.

Miguel looks at me, then back at Fiona. "I can keep the dog for a night or two while you make arrangements for him. That is, if you think the inn will still have space."

Wait a second! That is *not* the solution. Though honestly, I should know better, and so should Amelia Mae. He hasn't even invited them to our house yet; of course he's not going to have them spend the night. He probably can't stand the thought of someone in his space so soon. Perhaps my ambitious ideas have outpaced his personal growth.

He adds, "I'll have to separate him and Harold in case he has something, but that should be okay."

As much as I don't want to cuddle up to this interloper, I *don't* want to be told what to do. Nor do I like the utter lack of control I have about all of this.

Fiona looks up at him. "I know you have your hands full; are you sure this isn't an imposition? I can see if we can get an appointment right away and rent a car this evening to head back to the city."

"Stay," he says quietly, and while I myself have never enjoyed that command, Fiona's glowing gaze says it's exactly what she was hoping to hear.

Twenty-Seven

The vet cannot see the tiny critter until early the following afternoon, and though Dane volunteers to watch it if Miguel would rather not, he insists that we will be fine to puppy-sit for a couple nights.

Fiona decides to walk over to the pet store to get "a few things," even though Miguel warns her that she's going to return with doggy doll clothes and cans of organic food that cost as much as a steak dinner for eight. While she's away, Dane locates a big cardboard box in the stockroom to serve as a temporary crate for the puppy, who rewards him by immediately peeing in a corner, then crying pitifully until Amelia Mae picks him up to comfort him.

"Eh, he's not awful," she says as he tries to chew off her arm. "But he's definitely not you, Harry."

I thank her by lying directly on top of her feet, and it's so good to be with her that having her toes under my belly and the nippy beast just over my head doesn't even bother me all that much.

Fiona returns a short while later, "sans dog clothing," she

informs Miguel, but with a whole bag full of other things that the puppy would need only if she intended to keep him. He gobbles down his fancy food so fast that I know it'll soon come right back out of all exits—but that's Fiona's problem, not mine. Except . . . if Fiona and Miguel decide to mate, as I intend for them to, it will be my problem.

Oh no. This was *not* the plan.

Dane, who's especially chipper about Fiona's return—probably because it's immediately improved Miguel's mood—orders pizza for dinner, which they eat in the reading nook after the puppy finally does his business on the sidewalk, then passes out in the very same box he peed in. Afterward, Dane tells Miguel that he and Natalie will close the store. "Go hang out," he says, raising his eyebrows in a way that's not as stealthy as he thinks it is. "Get the puppers settled."

"Will do. Thanks, Dane." Miguel sounds nonchalant, but I can smell panic setting in. He turns to Fiona, who's gathering their things. "Do you want me to take you to the bed-and-breakfast?"

She gives him another this-is-a-challenge stare. "It's your call. What's easiest for you?"

He hesitates, then says, "Why don't we go to my place first? The puppy's too small to go to the dog park and probably shouldn't be in the grass before he has all his shots. But I can take him on the patio and help him acclimate a little before you leave."

"If you're sure."

"I am."

We pile into the car and make the short drive to the house. "Oh, it's lovely," says Fiona as we pull into the driveway. "I thought it might be, but I just love cedar shakes, and all the hedges and vines are so charming."

"Thank you, though I can't really take credit," Miguel says. "That was all Amelia."

"Of course," she says knowingly.

When we reach the back porch, Miguel suggests that Fiona and Amelia Mae let the puppy check out the patio while he goes inside to make sure there isn't anything too embarrassing lying around. "I don't have people over very often," he explains apologetically.

"Don't go to any trouble for us. I promise we're easy," she assures him.

He and I have just gotten into the kitchen when it really and truly sinks in: They're coming inside! Into our house! With their smells and their selves and—well, yes, with the puppy, but beggars and choosers and all that. Without even thinking about it, I start zipping around in circles in front of the sink, waiting for Amelia Mae to join me. Oh, this is just so exciting! If to be together and have something to look forward to isn't the ultimate happiness, then I don't know what is.

"*Cálmate,* Harold," Miguel says, patting my back to get me to settle down. "You don't want to scare Fiona, remember? She may have fallen for that puppy, but she's still afraid of dogs."

I remember now, and while I manage to stop my yapping, I can't help but jump up on Amelia Mae the moment Miguel opens the door for her and the other two.

"Careful, love bug," warns Fiona, who's carrying the punter again. Before I can demonstrate some semblance of self-control, Miguel's taken my paws off Amelia Mae's shirt and is pushing my rear end down so I'm seated.

"Sorry, sorry. I think the puppy's got him especially worked up. I should've done a better job training him, but it's too late for that. Should I put his leash on?"

What is this, Westminster? Am I to be trotted around and have my remaining teeth examined as well? I might just have to slobber all over to remind him that I'm his pet—not a pageant animal.

"No, no, this is Harold's home," chirps Fiona. "Speaking of which, this is even more lovely than the exterior. Amelia had wonderful taste."

I have just decided that in spite of the puppy, I may actually like Fiona more than she likes me, because nothing about my Amelia seems to make her feel bad or intimidated. In fact, I think they might have even been friends if they'd had the chance.

Miguel glances around. "I haven't really had anyone over in a while, so I apologize that it's not super clean. But you're right—she did. Thank you for saying that. Come on in."

He gives them the tour and even lets Fiona poke her head inside his bedroom, which is by far the messiest spot in the house. Then we gather in the living room, where Amelia Mae lies beside me in front of the fireplace we never use anymore while Fiona and Miguel sit on opposite ends of our sofa. Fiona's got the puppy on her chest again, and just when I think he's asleep, he gives a little yip and licks her cheek.

"Oh, Walter," she says with a giggle.

"Walter?" exclaim Miguel and Amelia Mae at the same time.

"Doesn't he look like a Walter? I've been thinking that since we scooped him up, and it seems to be sticking. Something about the patch on his chin makes me think of a grumpy old man with a beard."

"And here I thought Harold was a strange thing to call a dog," Amelia Mae whispers to me. "Don't worry, I'm not about to refer to him as Wally."

Oh, thank goodness. She really is on my team.

"I . . . it's interesting to see you like this," Miguel says, tilting his head to one side as he regards her.

"Sorry," says Fiona with a sleepy smile.

"Don't be," he says.

In spite of his guilt and pain and hesitation, he's enamored of her. Amelia Mae, who gives me a triumphant grin, has sensed it, too.

If only I could say the same of myself and this ridiculously named puppy, who plays possum and pretends to be asleep until the moment Miguel drives Fiona and Amelia Mae back to the bed-and-breakfast. Then he cries and cries from the big plastic car crate Miguel dragged up from the basement, which I could not once be convinced to get into.

When Miguel returns, he relents and holds him. Walter finally falls asleep again, and Miguel returns him to the crate, which he's filled with old towels. He puts the crate in his bedroom, and the beast proceeds to keep us up half the night. In fact, his whining and constant needing to go out remind me exactly of what Amelia's friend Carly once said about having a newborn; it almost makes me glad I can't remember the first early months of my life. He exhausts himself just as the sun begins to poke over the horizon, and Miguel and I oversleep until the dog's whimpering rouses us yet again.

A few hours later, we meet Fiona and Amelia Mae at a small

plaza downtown. Miguel lies and says the puppy wasn't much trouble at all while Fiona coaxes the thing—ahem, *Walter*—into a harness, and I try not to gloat when he pulls this way and that, futilely trying to regain his freedom. Then they pick up lunch from Spoon and eat back at home on the deck while I introduce Walter to one of life's true pleasures, which is dozing in the sun on a not-too-hot day. We're just finishing up when Riley appears at the back gate. "Hello, all! Amelia Mae, you ready to go?"

"Go? Go where, exactly?" says Fiona.

"To the vet! I called Riley to see if she'd take me and Walter," Amelia Mae tells her mother.

"I'm going to have to lock up my phone," says Fiona, but she doesn't seem upset. "And why, exactly, did you want Riley to do my dirty work?"

"We wanted to give you two a chance to spend time together. Duh."

"It's no trouble at all," says Riley. "We had so many dogs when I was growing up that people thought we ran a kennel. This is routine for me."

"Are we being set up?" Fiona says with amusement to Miguel.

"It appears so."

"Don't worry, Harry will chaperone," Amelia Mae assures them, winking at me.

Fiona sighs, then rises and goes inside, shaking her head. When she returns, she hands Riley a small plastic rectangle, the oversized car crate, and Walter's tiny harness and leash.

"I suppose there are worse things than being the target of other people's plans," Miguel tells her as she watches them get into Riley's car. "You want to go for a walk?"

"I'd love to."

They leave me at home, and I'm so pooped from last night that I don't even complain. They're holding hands when they return, and I think I'd be less shocked to see snow falling from the summer sky—not because they're touching on purpose in a prolonged way, as it's clear that's what they've been wanting to do all along, but because . . . I guess I thought Miguel would be worried about what Raina or the other neighbors might think about him. He must be so focused on Fiona right now that it either hasn't occurred to him or doesn't matter. Either way, I'm winning.

"Do you want to read for a while before they get back?" he says after serving her a glass of ice water.

"That sounds great," she tells him. "I actually have a book in my bag."

They return to the sofa, stretching out so that their legs are on either side of each other. But instead of disappearing into their stories, she sets her paperback on her stomach. He never even cracked his open and is already looking at her when she looks at him. They both smile. Then she says, "So . . . what's it like to have a dog?"

He regards me momentarily. "Where to even start? It's incredibly mundane."

What?! How dare he, after all I've done for him?

"There are so many routines you have to follow every single day, and they get upset if you don't do things at the same time. You have to plan all your vacations around them, and basically all of your outings, as you've probably gathered. Really, your whole life revolves around this creature who may or may not realize it."

I realize it! How can he not see that? I'm starting to get

upset when he smiles at me and says, "And it's one of the best things that will ever happen to you, because that animal will just *love* you, even when you don't deserve it."

Oh, Miguel. How kind of you to notice.

"Sounds a lot like parenthood," she says, and unless I'm imagining it, her eyes are just a bit misty.

"I can't say for certain on that front, but I've always wanted to have a child. I suppose I did imagine it that way."

"Why didn't you?"

"Amelia didn't want to, and we made our decisions together. I always believed that's why our relationship was strong."

"Mm," she says, nodding.

"Unlike her, I wasn't worried I'd turn into my father—that would've been somewhat difficult, as he was never around enough for me to catch his habits. But I would've been lucky to turn into my mother. She was so joyful and endlessly thoughtful. My sister is, too. You'll like her."

"I bet I will," she says, and I myself like the certainty with which they're speaking about the future. "How lucky you are, to have had so many good women in your life."

"Truly," he says. Then, very quietly, he adds, "I . . . I do feel guilty."

She doesn't ask him why; they both know he's falling for her. And I'm pretty sure she's already fallen for him.

"Oh, Miguel. I understand," she says softly. "I don't know if it helps, but I do, too. And I'm trying not to rush this for that reason."

Instead of saying more, they look at each other and eventually go back to reading, or at least they pretend to; I somehow doubt either one is absorbing a single word on the pages they're flipping.

A few minutes later, Fiona's lids begin to flutter, then slowly close. The next thing I know, her mouth's hanging open, just a smidge, and her glasses are halfway down her nose.

Miguel watches her for a while. Then he carefully extricates himself from the sofa and gets a blanket from the armchair, which he drapes over her. I'm certain she's going to wake, but she just closes her mouth and curls to one side and doesn't wake again until Amelia Mae comes hollering through the back door. "Gotta pee!" she says, rushing past us. "Riley's on the patio with Walter trying to get him to go to the bathroom, too!"

"Oh!" exclaims Fiona, glancing around.

"You fell asleep," says Miguel from the armchair.

"But that never happens to me. Honestly, I barely sleep at night. And forget cars and planes and other people's living rooms," she says, blinking hard.

"Why not?" says Miguel.

"I don't really know. I'm usually just . . . *on*. Thinking about things, though Amelia Mae will tell you I'm worrying and she's probably not wrong. I have no idea what just happened."

I do. She feels safe with Miguel. She feels safe with *us*. Even me! So safe that her busy brain turned off for a while and let her rest.

And as for Miguel—there's color in his cheeks, a spring in his step, an *aliveness* that hasn't been there in a long time.

She rises and walks over to him. "Thank you for that."

"Thank *you*," he says quietly. They're almost the same height, so he doesn't have to reach far when he pushes a stray piece of hair behind her ear. She's standing very still, and so is he. Then he leans forward and—

I bark. Loudly.

I swear I didn't mean to, and I know I shouldn't have. But it's too late; Fiona has startled and stepped back, and Miguel's shifting awkwardly. "Sorry," he says gruffly. "It must be the puppy."

"It's fine," she twitters. "I think I'll get some water and check on Riley and Walter."

"Of course."

Miguel glances at me as she heads into the kitchen, but he doesn't look upset. Just sort of . . . confused.

Me, too, buddy. Why on dog's green earth would I sabotage my own mission?

Twenty-Eight

Fiona and Amelia Mae decide to have dinner on their own and leave the puppy, who's sleepy because of his shots, with us. Fiona tells Miguel she'll reach out later, and when the doorbell rings that evening, I jump from my bed and scramble down the stairs, certain it's them. After all, I know Amelia Mae wants to spend as much time with me as possible before they return to Chicago.

Except when Miguel throws the door open, it's not them at all; it's Miriam! She's on the stoop, wearing a bright blue dress and a smile that's painted a dark color. I bark and circle her. Just when I think things couldn't possibly get better, here she is!

"*Hola, perrito,*" she says, stooping to let me slobber kisses all over her. "I missed you."

"Miriam," Miguel sputters. "*¿Qué haces aquí?*"

"Happy to see you, too!" She stands and holds out her arms. "*Ahora, ven aquí.*"

His eyes are wet when he finally leaves her embrace. He rubs them quickly. "Why didn't you tell me you were coming to visit?"

"Tell you? You'd have to pick up the phone for me to do that," she says, reaching up to wipe off the smear of lipstick she's left on his cheek. "Besides, I knew you'd say you were fine and not to bother, just like always. So, I did what any good overbearing sister would do and got on a plane. I should've done it six months ago, but you know how work keeps me chained to my desk." Miriam went to school for way longer than most people do and now she has an important job at Puerto Rico's biggest university, helping students . . . well, I don't actually know what she helps them with, but Amelia said she was excellent at it. "*Lo siento,*" she adds.

"Are you apologizing for surprising me, or for breaking a world record for number of suitcases you got on a single flight?" he asks, reaching for one of the many bags on the stoop behind Miriam. "It looks like you're moving in."

"Watch it or I'll take you up on that."

He pushes his lips together in a thin line, but I can smell that he's as thrilled as I am that she's here.

Miriam hauls in a few bags, too, then kicks her shoes off beside the door and bends to scratch my ears. "Is it just me, or is Harold getting old?" she says, looking up at Miguel.

Is it just me, or does someone need to save the commentary for when I'm not around?

"He's been *un poco loco* lately," says Miguel, frowning at me. "I want to say it's age, but I feel like there's something else going on."

I glare at him. *You mean your ongoing protest against pants and your subsisting on cereal?* To be fair, that's been on the decline since Fiona showed up. Still.

"I don't know if he'll ever really recover from . . . *tú sabes,*" he says softly.

Oh. That.

The truth is, I don't *want* to recover from losing Amelia. But I'm not sure I should feel that way when I'm supposed to be helping him recover from the same thing.

"I bet he's lonely," says Miriam.

"Lonely! I talk to this dog all day long."

"At least you're talking to *someone*."

"I'm going to pretend you didn't say that and take your fourteen suitcases up to the guest room. By the way, we're puppy-sitting, so don't be surprised by the *perrito* in the living room. Though he's knocked out from his vaccines, so we may not hear from him for a bit."

She looks at him questioningly.

"I'll explain after I take your bags up." He disappears for a little longer than necessary, but eventually he joins us in the kitchen.

"*¡Por fin!*" Miriam's propped on one of the stools at the small counter between the kitchen and the dining room. She reaches into the pocket of her dress and pulls out a bright yellow orb. "I brought you something."

"*¡Una guayaba!*" he exclaims as she passes it to him. "*¿De dónde?*"

"My backyard, *claro*. You can't get them that fresh at the grocery store."

He looks up in amazement. "But how'd you sneak it past the goons at the airport? Last I heard, they were still screening for anything with seeds."

She grins. "I have ways."

He holds it up to his nose, closes his eyes, and inhales deeply. "Smells like home. Thank you."

"*De nada*. It should be ready to eat in the next day or two.

Remember when you used to make those little guava cakes Amelia and I both loved? With the powdered sugar on them?" She breathes in like they're on the counter in front of her. "Too bad I couldn't bring a suitcase full of *guayaba,* because those are the best."

Miguel hesitates. "I made them the other day. Though I had to substitute quince paste."

"You did not!" She examines him carefully. "For *who*?"

He looks away.

"You're well aware that I'm going to keep asking until you tell me."

"Um."

"Miguel," she commands.

He grimaces. "Jonathan's sister."

"Jonathan, as in JMB?" He nods. "I thought she lived in Chicago—and isn't he still missing?"

"He isn't anymore. Well, not to us, at least. It's more than I want to get into right now, but he's having some kind of not-quite-midlife crisis and is hiding out in Copenhagen. And yeah, Fiona does live in Chicago. But she's in town with her daughter for a couple days. The puppy's hers, or at least I think it's going to be. She found it when they were supposed to be taking the train back yesterday."

"Supposed to be?" She hoots. "Yet somehow she's still here—and please don't tell me it's just the puppy. No wonder you look better than I was expecting. Is this why you haven't been calling me back?"

Walter must have heard them talking about him because he has roused from his stupor and wandered into the kitchen. He gives Miguel a needy look, but Miguel's too busy grabbing glasses from the cupboard to notice him. I glance at the pup and sigh, because though I wish it were not, it is nonetheless my dog-given duty to show him the way.

First, I make eye contact with him—well, as much as I can, with all that fur hanging over his face. Once I'm sure he's paying attention, I clang my food bowl against the wall, hard, and the noise echoes through the room.

"You've already eaten, Harold," says Miguel, his back still to me.

I nose the bowl again, and then a third time for good measure, before staring pointedly at Walter.

"I see," he says. "You're taking care of your new pal. It's not time for him to eat, but that's very kind. You can both have a treat."

He fetches a Snausage for me and an even smaller, softer version for Walter, who is giving me grateful googly eyes. Then he addresses Miriam.

"As I was about to say, I call you back. And Fiona's just a friend."

She holds up a manicured hand. "I didn't say a thing about her being anything more. I'm glad to hear you have a friend. You could use one."

He twists a corkscrew into the bottle of wine he just plucked out of another cupboard and fills the glasses with dark liquid. "I have plenty of friends," he says, handing her a glass.

She takes a sip and murmurs her approval, then examines him. "Who? Ding-Dong Dane?"

"Against my will, but he's growing on me—like a fungus," he adds. "And, of course, Riley."

"They're great, Miguel, but those are your *employees*. Who else are you hanging out with outside of work?"

He wrinkles his nose and looks at me.

"*Exacto,*" she says with a laugh.

"I'll have you know that Harold happens to be the best company."

I reward him with a meaningful glance, and he pats my head. "How long are you staying?"

"Long enough to meet this Fiona person."

Miguel mutters something indecipherable into his glass.

"*En serio*. I want to meet her."

He lowers the glass. "She's leaving soon, so that's unlikely to happen."

"You know I'm not waiting for your approval, right?" says Miriam, taking another drink. "West Haven's not a big town. I'll find her."

"Don't threaten me. Besides, I'm not sure I'm ready for a relationship."

Miriam immediately softens. "*Lo sé*. But you really do look good, Miguelito. What if you are ready but it just feels scary?"

"And how would I ever know the difference between the two?"

She smiles. "I don't know that you can. You just do it anyway and trust your gut. Speaking of risks, I do have news."

"You dating someone?" he immediately asks.

I expect her to laugh, but she just shakes her head. "No, but I'm working on it with that therapist I told you about. I knew Mami dying when we were little messed me up—but turns out Papi taking off on us was maybe even worse. She thinks it's why I have such a bad picker. You really should go to therapy, Miguel. It's been life-changing."

"Why does everyone keep saying that to me?" he mutters.

"I can't imagine!" says Miriam before tipping her glass back.

"I moved in with Amelia three weeks after we met. Getting close to people isn't my issue."

She flares her nostrils and waits.

"What?" he eventually says.

"Oh, nothing. Just questioning your use of the plural there. You had no issue getting close to *Amelia*. The rest of us—" She presses her lips together and raises her brow, causing him to roll his eyes. "So, my big news is that I have an interview at the University of Michigan in two days. They're looking for a dean of students for the Residential College, and apparently the person they'd picked backed out at the last minute. If the job description is to be believed—and I'm not sure about that yet—it's a lot less paperwork and more face time with students."

"Terrifying."

"Ha-ha. You know I'm a people person. It just so happens I'm also a money person, and they'd pay me a lot better, and would cover my fee to relocate. They even flew me into Grand Rapids instead of Detroit, even though it's almost twice the price, and are covering my rental car, too. Gotta love that Big Ten budget." She examines him from across the counter. "Why don't you look happy about this? I'd be teaching at your alma mater. Even better, we'd actually be living in the same place again for the first time since we were teens."

"I *am* happy," he says, but his expression's pained, like someone's pressing a knife to his back and telling him to smile. "*Pero,* I have to tell you—you'll probably hate it here. It's freezing, and there are maybe ten *boricuas* in the entire state."

"Given that one of them is trying to recruit me and I'm sitting across from another, I'm going to assume your comment is a test of the emergency hyperbole alert system. As for the weather, I can handle it. There are worse things than being cold."

"Spoken by a woman who needs a sweater if it dips below eighty. Besides, there's a reason they're asking you to come in the summer instead of January. Trust me on this one."

"I do trust you, but I'm going to drive to Ann Arbor in two days to verify for myself." She flashes an enormous grin. "Which means you'll need to introduce me to Fiona before she leaves."

Twenty-Nine

"For the record, I feel I've been tricked," says Miguel.

"Tricked! You're the one who suggested brunch!" says Miriam, bumping her hip against his. They're standing side by side at the kitchen counter, arranging the feast they just spent the morning pulling together. Miguel's face is dusted with something—flour, maybe? He won't let me get close enough to sniff the individual ingredients, but the sweet, eggy smell makes me think he's made French toast. He used to make it for Amelia, who always tossed me her crusts because she understood what an injustice it is to dine on the same thing indefinitely.

"I was under duress," he grumbles.

"Yes, your evil younger sister, encouraging you to eat in the most terrifying way—*with other people,*" says Miriam, laughing. She wipes the powder off his cheek with her thumb. "This is just friends getting together for fun, remember?"

"Fun's for young people like Ding-Dong. Not forty-two-year-old dinosaurs like me."

"Hey, I represent that," says Dane, appearing in the doorway. "And you don't look a year over Paleolithic."

Miguel startles. "If you continue to refuse to use the doorbell, Dane, I'm going to get you a shock collar."

"It's called a lock, chief. Maybe I'm not the ding-dong here," says Dane. He turns to Miriam. "Hiya, Miriam—long time no see, but you look great. When'd you get in?"

"Last night, and not a moment too soon," she says, pushing her curls off her face with her forearm.

"I'll say." Dane opens the cupboard to grab a mug. "Want coffee, Riles?" he says to Riley, who must have come in right behind him.

"Thought you'd never ask."

"Me, too," says Brenna, appearing behind her.

"On it," says Dane.

"Thanks for having us over," Brenna says to Miguel. "It's nice to see you all outside of work."

"You don't mind coming by? I know you've been working a ton lately. Hanging out with your co-workers on your off day probably isn't much of a break."

"Miguel, you worry too much—I'm happy to be here. Besides, Natalie needs hours."

"You sure she's okay?" he asks.

"She'll be fine. And if she's not, she can call Riley," says Dane, grinning.

Riley pretends to be offended. "I'm off the clock until tomorrow. It's all you, Dane."

"I'm not sure if you remember, but I'm Miguel's sister," Miriam says to Riley and Brenna. It's the first time I've seen the two of them beside each other since . . . well, I can't recall when. She extends the hand she just wiped on her apron to Riley first. "Miriam. We met . . ."

Riley nods, knowing Miriam doesn't want to say "at the funeral" out loud. "I remember. It's good to see you again."

"You, too."

"Nice to see you," echoes Brenna, and Miriam smiles at her.

Dane hoists himself onto the counter next to where Miguel's standing. "Your lady friend here yet?"

"Is your police escort here yet, or should I call them to tell them you're waiting for your ride?"

Dane holds both hands up. "Just a question, chief! Just a question."

Where are Fiona and Amelia Mae, anyway? I've been excited since I heard Miguel invite them over last night. So excited, in fact, that I found myself roaming around the second floor half-asleep early this morning. Fortunately, I didn't rouse Miguel or Miriam or even the little yipper and went back to my bed when I realized what was happening.

I head to the living room to wait in front of the window. A big black Labrador pees in our yard, then Raina jogs by. A woman pushes a tiny dog in a stroller, even though I've seen that Chihuahua prancing past a million times and know for a fact that he doesn't need a ride. Finally, there's Amelia Mae, practically dragging Fiona behind her as they walk up the street. I start barking to herald their arrival, which sets off Walter, who comes scrambling over. I swear if he pees next to me I'm going to carry him back to the dumpster myself.

Fiona comes to the front door, which seems a bit odd, but it does give Miguel a chance to greet her alone. He hugs her, then hands her Walter.

"I'm sorry we're late—the rental place is even smaller than I thought, and they don't have our car ready yet. Has this little guy been much trouble?" she asks, holding him up to admire him.

"Not at all, and I'm glad you came. It's impossible to make a small brunch and have it be any good, so I might have cooked a little too much. I hope you're both hungry. And the coffee just finished brewing. Of course, I have tea, too . . ." Miguel's babbling like he's just been hit on the head by a bunch of black walnuts. He's probably nervous to introduce her to Miriam.

"Let's let them chat, Harry," Amelia Mae whispers to me. "It's a miracle we made it over—Mom was scribbling in her notebook all morning, which is why we were late to get the rental car. But between us, that's a good thing, 'cause she only does that when she actually cares, and she hasn't cared about anything other than me in way too long. Still, she talked to Uncle Jon last night, and they were arguing again. Something about cutting the tether, whatever that means. That whole mess has really turned her upside down. I don't want to tell her I'm worried because she's got enough to think about, but . . ." She pushes her face into a smile. "At least I'm here now."

I want to hear more about what made Fiona not care, but Amelia Mae is already directing me to the kitchen.

"Hello, everyone!" she announces, giving a big wave. She turns to Miriam, who's standing beside Dane at the counter, and says, "I'm Amelia Mae."

Miriam freezes.

"Take it your brother didn't tell you that the girl here shares a name with our Amelia," Dane says in an uncharacteristically low voice.

She shakes her head. "No, he certainly did not. Seems like a big thing not to mention."

"He's got a lot on his mind these days, what with the bookstore's budget issues and his new love and now being on puppy duty." He plucks a berry out of a bowl and pops it into his mouth, then holds the bowl out to her. "Want one?"

"I'll pass, but I'm going to need a second helping of what's been on my brother's mind."

Dane's eyes land on Fiona, who's just appeared in the doorway with Miguel. "Unlike some, I'm an open book. Maybe we can grab a drink after my shift."

Miriam raises an eyebrow at him. "I hope you're not asking me out."

"Since you told me no the last four times I asked, I wouldn't dream of it. But I do know a good place to get a cold beverage this evening if you're interested."

Dane asked Miriam out? Repeatedly? This is news to me—though admittedly, I used to pay a lot less attention to everyone else because I was so busy focusing on Amelia. Still, I thought he was all about Riley.

Miguel directs Fiona over to Miriam. "Miri, *esta es* Fiona," he says. "Fiona, this is my sister, Miriam."

Miriam starts to extend her hand, but Fiona has already decided they're going to hug and has wrapped her arms around her. "It's so nice to meet you. Miguel has been the best host, and incredibly understanding about my brother's crisis. I assume he told you about that."

"Oh, yes." Miriam's curls bounce as she nods. "I'm glad my

brother's gotten a friend out of this debacle. I just hope Lakeside's able to weather this."

Someone who'd never heard her speak before might miss it, but there's just the slightest threat to Miriam's tone. Miguel shoots her a warning look. "Why don't we eat? Please, pile your plates," he tells everyone. "We've made way too much food."

"Where's the Lucky Charms?" Dane says, surveying the counter.

Fiona looks from Dane to Miguel quizzically.

"Chief here has a cereal jones that some would say borders on the obsessive," Dane explains.

One of the corners of Fiona's mouth tilts up. "Is that so?"

"It's not a *jones,*" Miguel says. "Cereal's just easier than cooking when it's only me and Harold."

"If I'd known, I would have picked up a few boxes on the way over," teases Fiona.

"Then I would have eaten that, too. All breakfast's good," he says, inching closer to her.

"Best meal of the day," she says, and now they smile at each other.

Amelia Mae's loaded up a plate and has decided we're eating in the living room, away from the adults and Walter, whom they're passing around like a bread basket. "Don't tell your owner, but I got you a piece of French toast," she says, tearing off part of a slice to feed to me. "Try not to swallow it all at once."

That's a tall ask—the toast is even better than I remembered, although I guess that's what happens when you go without something for a while. I gobble it down. Amelia's busy spearing berries on her fork and dipping them in whipped cream, so I peek my head around the corner. Riley, Dane, and Miriam are seated around the kitchen table, but I hear Fiona and Miguel in the hallway and belly-crawl in their direction to find out what they're up to.

"I brought you something," says Fiona. "Just a tiny little gift to thank you for the past few days."

"Really? I got you something, too," says Miguel. "One second." He steps into the living room momentarily and grabs a book off the tall, built-in bookshelves.

"*Stoner!*" she exclaims, turning it over in her hands.

"It's actually my copy, but I've read it plenty of times, so I'm happy for it to find a new home," he says, watching her.

"I can't wait to read it and tell you what I think," she says, pressing it to her chest momentarily. My Amelia used to do that with books, too; I wish I could understand for myself what's so magical about a bunch of bound, scribbled-upon paper that makes a person want to hug it.

Fiona slips the paperback into her bag and hands him another book that she's just retrieved. "This is my favorite Laurie Colwin novel," she tells him. "Personally, I think she *does* get her male characters right, but you be the judge."

"I will."

Fiona glances at me momentarily. Then she leans in and presses her lips to Miguel's. It's a quick kiss—so fast, in fact, that he doesn't have a chance to close his eyes, nor do I have the opportunity to bark at her. I wouldn't've this time, though.

Because somehow, what just happened feels right.

She spins and saunters back into the kitchen. He follows her, and I follow him. Amelia Mae's left her hiding spot and is seated at the table now, whispering to Riley. "You remember what we discussed, don't you?" she says, and Riley laughs lightly and glances around. When she sees that Brenna's still in the bathroom, she whispers back, "I do, and I'll talk to her as soon as the timing is right. I promise."

"Good," says Amelia Mae. "Remember, when you find someone as good as she is, you do what you can to keep them in your life." When she spots me, she turns to her mother. "Speaking of friends, look how sad Harry is," she says, pointing at me. "He doesn't want us to leave."

"He looks perfectly doglike to me," says Fiona mildly. "Not sad and not happy. Somewhere in between."

By the time Walter has learned to do his business on the grass instead of her rugs, she'll have realized that I, like all of my kind, have a full range of humanlike emotions. I can't believe I'm admitting this, but maybe the puppy *is* a good idea, if strictly for educational purposes.

"No, I can tell he's broken up over us having to go back to Chicago," Amelia Mae insists.

"Dear heart, I like it here, too, but you really do need to get to drama camp sometime this week—I want to make sure you have time to practice your lines. You're going to want to be at your best for the play."

She blows at her hair, which has fallen in her dark eyes. "Why? They wouldn't miss me if I didn't show." She leans toward me and says, " 'Real isn't how you are made. It's a thing that happens to you.' "

I do love *The Velveteen Rabbit*! Beth reads it a few times a year, or at least she did before she left.

"That's from the play we're putting on for camp," she explains to the others. "But that's not even my line—I'm just a stupid chorus toy. Not that I care. The book's better, anyways."

"The book's always better," says Riley.

"Darn skippy," says Amelia Mae with a grin.

Sadly, my French toast has just told on me, and I've filled the air with what even I can identify as a highly unfortunate odor.

"Oh, Harry," she exclaims, pinching her nose. "I've *got* to get you outside."

I glance up guiltily.

"I'll walk him," says Miguel, starting for me.

"I'll take him out back," she volunteers.

"I'm sure Harold would love it if you ran him around outside for a few," he admits. "Try to get the devil out of him, or at least out of his gut."

Fiona smiles, which is when I realize Miriam's studying her. I don't think she dislikes her—but she doesn't *like* her, either. Strange. Like my Amelia, Miriam usually warms to almost everyone.

"Before you say it, I'll be careful. It'll be good practice for when Walter comes home with us," Amelia Mae tells her mother. She tugs me lightly by the collar. "Let's go, stinky friend."

I don't know about getting any devils out, but my stomach does sound like a pot of boiling potatoes. Once she lets me loose into the backyard, though, the gurgling sound disappears in the din of chirping birds and cicadas.

She plops down on the back stairs while I mosey around the perimeter. I stick my nose in some dandelions and sniff a soggy patch of mushrooms before finding a patch of grass to kill. I lift a leg, then scamper back over to her.

"I wish we didn't have to go home, Harry," she tells me. I sit beside her because even though my gut's still rumbling, it's rude to wander too far when someone's talking to you. Also,

I'm unusually tired for this early in the day, which is probably owing to the pup, who slept only slightly better than the night before. "Between us, I think Fiona and Miguel would be bananas together." Seeing my face, she adds, "I mean, really good. Don't you think?"

In fact, I do.

"Now listen, Harry, I'm the first to admit that my mom's weird. She has been since my dad left, or at least that's what Uncle Jon says. I was little, so I don't remember her back then. Uncle Jon says he's a good-for-nothing dirtbag. But I still wish I had a dad."

Amelia Mae wants a father? This never occurred to me. I rest my head on her leg to let her know I'm sorry. None of us should have to be without the people we need—yet this, somehow, is often exactly how life unfolds. If you ask me, it's incredibly unfair.

"I know everyone thinks I'm so clever and I have it all figured out, but sometimes I just feel really sad and lonely and it's like no one can tell. You know?"

I sigh, because do I *ever.*

"I swear you speak human, Harry," she says, patting my head.

I swear you speak dog, Amelia Mae.

She strokes my ears and says, "It's not all bad news. I know it's only been a couple days, but Fiona's happier than she's been in ages, and it's more than just Walter. Don't get me wrong: She's already freakishly perky—or at least she tries to be. But it would be nice if she could just stay regular happy. Trouble is, that would mean letting people really get to know her instead of making me and Uncle Jon her reason for everything. That derpy counselor I saw said you can't rush feelings, but I don't think I agree. Being around people you like makes it happen faster." She leans down and gives me a little hug. "And dogs. I wish that instead of bringing Walter home, you and I could be together all the time."

I do, too, though that wish makes me feel ever so slightly disloyal to my own Amelia. For now I try to memorize her big dark eyes and her perfect frown and this moment, just in case we don't get another one.

"Amelia Mae, please bring Harold inside!" calls Fiona from the back door. "We have to go back to the car rental place soon."

"Drat." Amelia Mae puts her head next to mine and makes a little humming sound. "You're the best, Harry," she says after a moment.

I don't know about *that,* but I do feel . . . strange. It's not the feeling I have when Miguel tolerates me warming his feet in the winter, or even when I manage to get him out of bed for more than a quick bathroom trip. Then this isn't me being in touch with my purpose.

I guess . . .

I guess it has been so long since I have felt like this that I didn't recognize it right away.

When we get inside, Fiona surprises me and squats down beside me. "Harry, I think you've helped me see the light about dogs," she says, looking at the space just over my head. "Thanks for being so sweet to Amelia Mae."

No, thank you, *Fiona Foster,* I think, as I lean against her legs. *Thank you and your daughter for reminding me and my Miguel of what regular happiness feels like.*

Thirty

Miguel and Miriam head over to Lakeside after brunch. They leave me behind, but that's okay; I have a feeling Amelia Mae won't be at the store, and since I'm still worn out from the pup, I'd rather save my energy for when she's around.

Miguel returns alone a few hours later. He doesn't say where Miriam is, but he's distracted—so much so that he trips on the runner rug in the hall. Then he serves kibble in my water bowl and doesn't even realize it until I repeatedly clang it against the wall to let him know I'm not interested in having soup for supper. At least he isn't grumbling at his computer, though. He even picks up the paperback Fiona gave him and flips through it. It's not real reading—he does that with his glasses on, prostrate on the sofa—but it's a welcome sign of life all the same.

It's cooler out than it's been in weeks, so after he puts Walter on a pee pad and somehow convinces him to do his business, he takes me for a long post-dinner walk. We loop past the school and the park where kids play their games, beyond the library and police station, both of which we share with the next town over, and finally to the top of the hill that looks out over Lake Michigan's horizon.

He doesn't speak as we walk—not to himself or to me—which makes me worry that something's amiss. But he's humming again, just beneath his breath, and the new if vaguely familiar tune tells me that he's thinking about Fiona. I wonder if not thinking about Amelia being gone all the time gives him the same kind of melancholy it brings me. Hopefully his heart knows that this is exactly what our Amelia wanted for him—to have someone else occupy his mind. After all, he won't forget Amelia or love her any less; that's not possible. But maybe Fiona can help him go on without her once I'm not here anymore.

We sit on the bench on top of the hill for a good while, staring out at the water as he absentmindedly strokes my head. When the sun starts to collapse in on itself, he stands and nods east, and having been given the signal, I point my nose and guide us home.

Only after we let ourselves inside the house does Miguel finally break the silence. "Miriam," he announces. "*¡Llegué!*"

There's no response, but there are a couple of wineglasses and a set of keys on the coffee table in the living room. Above us, I hear something—a drumming sound, maybe, or hammering. I can't really tell, but someone's here and making a whole lot of noise.

"Raccoons?" Miguel wonders aloud. "That's strange. They've never gotten inside before." He looks at me with raised eyebrows. "Maybe the squirrels have come for their revenge, Harold."

Har, har, I think, but then I realize this is the first time in ages he's cracked a joke about my misbehavior. *Okay, Miguel. You earned that one.*

Except he must be half-serious, because he grabs the broom from the door leading to the basement. I'm beyond pooped already, but curiosity gets the best of me, and I follow him upstairs.

"Miriam?" he calls as he ascends with the broom in hand. "Are you here?"

Now I hear scrambling sounds that are a lot like the kind I make when I'm caught dozing on the bed. Moments later, Miriam comes flying out of the guest room into the hall. She's smiling widely, and her curls are in every which direction. "*¡Estoy aquí!*" she announces. Spotting the broom, she adds, "Do we have more cleaning to do?"

"No—" Miguel begins, but before he can finish his sentence, Dane, shirtless, emerges behind Miriam and salutes him.

"*Ho-la,* chief!"

"What on earth?" says Miguel, glancing back and forth between them.

"Dane and I were just catching up," says Miriam.

"You can say that again," adds Dane, and they look at each other and giggle.

Well. *Well.* This is a development I did not see coming, but I can't help but like the idea of two people I love together.

Apparently, I'm alone in that sentiment, because Miguel is glaring at Dane like he's trying to set him ablaze. "I am going to need to speak with you privately," he growls.

"What are you, her chaperone?" says Dane, grinning even wider.

"Did I mention that I plan to murder you while we're speaking? Slowly? With my bare hands if need be?"

"Better your mitts than the broom. Besides, I already died the little death tonight, so I'm good."

Miguel groans. "What about Riley? Everyone from here to Lansing knows about your crush."

Miriam turns to Dane. "You were into Riley?"

"I used to be. Now I've seen the error of my ways. Big-time," he says, raising his eyebrows.

She laughs again.

"Besides, chief, Riley needs to fix her beef with Brenna. And I've known for a while that she and I are better off as friends."

"She and Brenna are still having issues?" Miguel's forehead's all scrunched up. "I should have picked up on that."

"I mean, Riley's working through some stuff in therapy." Dane claps a hand over his mouth. "Sorry—that wasn't mine to share."

"It's okay. Riley already told me about that," Miguel says, sighing. "It sounds like the right thing for her. So . . ." His gaze shifts from Dane to Miriam and back.

"I was a little surprised myself, but whatevs. I was *way* more surprised when a certain stunning sister made a move on me," he says, side-eyeing Miriam.

Miguel has pulled his head back and appears to be fighting his gag reflex.

"Don't be dramatic, Miguelito," says Miriam. "And Dane, we both know you made all the moves."

"Sure did. And for once, they worked!"

"I can't believe you two were getting it on in my house, of all places," mutters Miguel.

"My apartment's too trashed right now, though I'm totally going to fix that when I get home," says Dane, crossing his arms and leaning against the hallway wall. "But if you're upset because you were going to invite your lady friend back over, Miriam and I can skedaddle to give you some privacy."

"*Woman,* Dane," Miriam says, but she's smiling. "'Lady' makes her sound old. Which makes me sound old, because I'm pretty sure Fiona and I are about the same age."

"Roger that," he says, planting a kiss on the top of her head. "I will no longer use ye olde L-word. Unless we're talking about love, of course."

She giggles and loops her arm around his waist.

"Dane . . ." Miguel begins.

"I'm about to show myself out, chief—just gotta grab my shirt," says Dane. He lowers his voice and says to Miriam, "If you're still up for it, I'll see *you* tomorrow morning before you head to Ann Arbor."

"Maybe," she says, but then she kisses him on the lips.

"I'm going to need something much stronger to discuss this with you," Miguel says to her as Dane retrieves his shirt from the guest room and saunters down the stairs.

"Pour me one, too," says Miriam, who's just wrapped herself in the silky patterned robe Dane handed her on his way out. "I don't have to take off until ten tomorrow."

Downstairs, Miguel grabs a bottle from the bar cart in the corner of the dining room and serves them both a dark liquid that smells flammable. Then they sit on opposite sides of the sofa, legs stretched out, regarding each other like a couple of cats that haven't decided whether to cuddle or claw at each other.

"You first," says Miguel.

"*Bueno*. I'm a little concerned about Fiona."

"Wait a second—I thought we were going to discuss Dane."

"What's to discuss? He's a lovely distraction."

"The 'lovely' part is highly debatable. Are you sure you want to get involved with him? After all, you yourself said you have a bad picker."

Miriam sighs so heavily that her whole torso heaves. "For today? Maybe tomorrow, or even when I get back from Ann Arbor? Sure. Beyond that, I don't know that I want to be involved with anyone. But giving a nice guy a chance instead of waiting for some self-centered prick to give me the time of day—well, I'm sure my therapist would call that progress."

"Define 'nice.' "

She lifts her glass to him momentarily before taking a sip. "He pursued me. He complimented me more in three hours than that jerk from Caguas I dated did in two years. *Te prometo*, you don't want to hear the details beyond that," she says, and now he pretends to barf into his drink. "I'm much more concerned about you getting caught up with Fiona."

"Fiona? Why? You told me you wanted me to be happy."

"I *do*. You know that. And she seems great."

"But . . ."

"But as you yourself have pointed out, she lives in Chicago, and you live here. She has a kid with the same name as Amelia, which is probably not helping you on the guilt front. And frankly, I get the impression she's holding something back."

"Sure," he says cautiously. "She's been open about that."

She sputters a little. "You do hear the irony in that statement, no?"

Miguel's on the verge of glaring at her. "She's related to someone who's either in crisis or is a covert narcissist. I know you don't choose your siblings—" Miriam raises an eyebrow at him, but he continues. "But she's obviously protecting Jonathan. Which is something you and I, of all people, can relate to."

"Absolutely. But Miguelito, spoken as someone who's known you thirty-nine out of your forty-two years of existence, you're a serial monogamist who doesn't do casual. When you fall, it's hard. And I just don't want to see you wrapped up with someone who isn't in this for the long run. You know what that did to Mami."

"Fall? Who said anything about *falling*? I just met Fiona, and she's leaving tomorrow."

"When she could have easily left today, or even the day before—and don't tell me it's about the puppy," she adds, glancing at Walter, who's in a pile near the fireplace. "Because I'm not buying what you're selling. You're into her."

"Says who?" scoffs Miguel.

"You, every single time you talk about her," says Miriam. "Miguel, you've been through so much. First Papi leaving us, then Mami passing, and now . . ." Her voice trails off. "If you get serious about Fiona and she takes off . . . I just worry about what happens then."

He looks away. "Well, lucky for you, she's leaving, so we won't have a chance to find out. And lucky for me, you're flying back to Puerto Rico and aren't likely to entertain a relationship with Ding-Dong from two thousand miles away."

"You know I don't want you to be holed up here alone."

"I'm not alone. I have Harold."

"You do," she says, casting a grateful glance at me. "I can tell Fiona makes you happy."

"Happy's not my goal anymore, Miriam. I just don't want to be in pain."

Now she frowns. "I'm pretty sure one leads to the other—but maybe I shouldn't have said anything. Point is, I haven't seen you like this in a very long time. Just go slow, okay? The last thing you need is a broken heart."

"I appreciate that you're worried about me, Miri." Instead of meeting her eye, Miguel looks up at the ceiling. "But you don't have to be. Because when your heart's already been shattered into a million pieces, there's nothing left to break."

Thirty-One

"I'll call you the minute I'm done with my interviews," says Miriam, giving Miguel a hug. "If all goes well, Michigan's Puerto Rican population will rise to eleven," she adds, pulling back to wink at him. "So, wish me luck."

"Don't worry, cupcake. You've got this," says Dane, who stopped by with a paper bag full of baked goods this morning to see her off. "And we all know that your brother's geeked for you to move here."

"Dane," warns Miguel.

"Come on," he says, waving his muffin at Miguel as I hover, waiting to catch any chunks or crumbs that fall my way. "You know it feels amazeballs to live near your favorite people."

"Not *all* my favorite people," Miguel says gruffly.

Dane tugs at his hair with his free hand. "Oof. Sorry."

"Apology accepted, Ding-Dong, but only because you're not going with my sister." Miguel squints at Miriam, whose nose is wrinkled like a bunny's. Her bottom lip's trembling, too. "I didn't mean to make you upset, Miri," he quickly adds.

"Does that mean you hope I get the job?" she teases, but a tear's already trailing down her cheek. She wipes it away and adds, "Sorry, Miguelito. I've just missed you, and it's been so nice to be together."

"How can you miss me when I'm right here?" he says, enveloping her in his arms again. "And I hope whatever you want to happen is exactly what happens."

"Me, too." Then she murmurs something that I can't quite make out. When she lets him go, his eyes are welled with tears. Is he finally realizing how much better it is when he's surrounded by people he loves?

I hope so. And I know, deep within me, that I have Fiona to thank for that.

Miguel waves from the stairs while Dane walks Miriam to her rental car, then rides off on his bike. Once they're both gone, I expect Miguel to head to the kitchen table; while I nip at my belly and backside to calm myself, work is his preferred method of self-soothing. But he goes upstairs instead, and after a moment, I hear his bedroom door close.

I should probably follow him just in case he's gotten in the shower to finish the cry he started. I definitely should. That's my job, after all, and while he talks a good game, he's obviously sad to see his sister leave; she'll be back, of course, but once she returns, then she'll leave again.

Except . . . I'm terribly tired today. And not only do my paws and hips hurt, my torso's strangely sore, too, which is probably from attempting to evade Walter; after I demonstrated how to hop on the sofa when the humans aren't paying attention, he tried to keep the good times rolling by sinking his miniature fangs into my fur. I'll just rest a minute in the kitchen. Though, come to think of it, the small rug near the front door isn't *that* scratchy. Yes, that'll work just fine . . .

I don't know how much time has passed when Amelia Mae's voice startles me back to consciousness. "There you are! I thought you'd nap all day, Harry."

I look at her with wide eyes to make it clear that I'm awake. Wide-awake now, and ready to make the most of our time together before they go back to Chicago.

"I wanted to check in on the dog, but I also thought I'd tell you how moved I was," Fiona's saying to Miguel.

"That's an understatement," Amelia Mae whispers to me. To Miguel, she adds more loudly, "She just read *You Were Here*. She cried her face off."

He's visibly confused. "Wait—"

"John Williams is next on my list, but *You Were Here* was the only one of Amelia's novels I hadn't read, and it felt like the right time," says Fiona, glancing away. She seems to be considering something as she slowly turns her face back to him. "I picked it up from Lakeside yesterday afternoon. Natalie was very helpful. She found it for me right away."

"You read my Amelia's novels?" he blurts, still wearing that *what just happened* expression.

"Of course. Just like thousands of other people," says Fiona, but if anyone's asking me—which, sadly, they aren't—she sounds awfully careful in her response. "I saw one at the library back in the late nineties and did a double take because of her name. Naturally, I borrowed it immediately and loved it. I ended up reading through her entire backlist over the next few years. She was a true talent."

"You—your shelves—" Miguel's mouth and brain still

aren't working in tandem. "I thought you liked David Foster Wallace and . . ."

Fiona looks baffled, but now she's amused, too. "Remember the other day at the bookstore when I said I like love stories? I meant that; it's just that we've only discussed the type of books you and I both enjoy. Your Amelia's novels—well, they're wonderful. *Low Tide* is my personal favorite."

"So, I've been reading your brother's books, and you've been reading my partner's books . . ." Miguel looks like he's on the verge of overheating. "Sorry, I know it's a good problem to have. I just wasn't expecting it."

"No problems detected," says Amelia Mae, glancing back and forth between them. "Right, Harry?"

I wish I could agree, but I cannot. Not when Miguel has lowered his gaze and is staring at the door with the sort of concentration he normally reserves for his spreadsheets.

"You read her books, too . . . didn't you?" Fiona asks cautiously.

He opens his mouth, but no sound comes out.

She tilts her head. "Can I ask why not? I'm sure loads of people told you how fantastic they are."

"They did, and to be honest, I don't know," he says after a moment. "Maybe I was afraid I wouldn't like them. Or maybe I'm just a snob. Either way, I regret it every day. And now it's too late."

She places her hand on his forearm. "There's still time to read them."

He shakes his head sadly, and though I wish I didn't, I understand. The bookshelves in our living room hold a copy of every single one of Amelia's novels. But there's simply no point in him trying to right this wrong when she'll never know that he did.

"I guess," he says vaguely. "Maybe one day. But it wouldn't change anything."

Fiona's voice still sounds like flowing water, but there's something different about her now, even if I can't quite put my nose on it. "Well, when you do, I'd love to hear what you think. Speaking of books, there's something I wanted to tell you . . ."

"I'm listening," says Miguel.

Fiona's gaze has just landed on Amelia Mae, who's squatting beside me. And perhaps my senses have gone dull, but her face seems to change; the natural smile she had a second ago looks pasted on now, and behind her glasses, her eyes aren't crinkled at the corners. She reaches into her canvas bag, which is slung across her shoulder. "It's just that I brought you something."

Beside me, a dark cloud has passed over Amelia Mae's smile, too, but Fiona doesn't notice. She passes Miguel a stack of papers held together with a thick clip. "These are hot off the press from Jonathan—sent at my request. I'll tell you more once you've had a chance to read them."

"Really?" asks Miguel with an excitement I haven't heard since Jonathan's assistant, whom we now know to be Fiona, called to see if he could do an event at Lakeside. Okay, that's not true—since he shook Fiona's hand for the first time.

"Really," she says. "I told you I'd get him to come around, and he did. He's been working on this short story for eons, and although it took some doing, I've convinced him to sell it online, and maybe even in print if we can figure out distribution, and donate the profits to Lakeside Books."

Miguel is staring at the pages. "What a privilege. Are you positive?"

"It's not just my decision, but yes," she assures him. "I can't wait to hear what you think."

"How soon are you heading back to Chicago?" he asks.

Amelia Mae rolls her eyes. "We can stay until you're done reading. I'm not going to make it to drama camp today either way."

Miguel looks at Fiona, who nods. "Like Amelia Mae said, we're not in a rush. Why don't we take Walter on a walk to get him out of your hair, and you can give me a call when you're done?"

"Brilliant," murmurs Miguel. "Absolutely incredible." He peers at me over his reading glasses—the pair he spent nearly half an hour searching for and finally located under the sofa, because where *else* would they be? "It's almost impossible to believe that I'm the second person to read Jonathan's first work of fiction in several years. Oh, I can't wait to talk to Fiona about this."

He began reading the pages while they were still there, but she stopped him and said she didn't want to bias him. So, she and Amelia Mae left with the puppy so he could "digest in peace," as she described it.

I don't know about peace, but over the past hour, he's laughed. He's gasped. He's snorted. As he tore through the twenty-some pages that Fiona printed out at the local library, he has looked . . .

Like a man who's finally remembered who he is under all that pain.

My breathing slows as I watch him reading a second time, or maybe it's a third. I'm nearly as relaxed as I was with Amelia Mae on the beach, but this feels less temporary. No, he and Fiona haven't declared their love for each other yet. Still, I've waited six and a half seasons for him to be healed enough to enjoy himself without reservation, and I know that has everything to do with her.

He's so happy that I almost wish he'd read the story one more time. But after another glance at the ending, he abandons the pages on the coffee table and heads upstairs to take a shower. I follow him, but instead of sitting outside the bathroom door, I take the opportunity to rest. I'm not worried that he'll cry now. Also, I don't feel so hot. I'd like to fix that before we see Fiona and Amelia Mae again.

I've started to drift off beside Miguel's bed when he comes bounding out of the shower, as bare as the day he was born. He's dripping water all over the floor and flapping his arms around like he's trying to take flight.

"Harold!" he cries, and I leap to my feet. "It's like I've known the whole time, but it's been lurking beneath the surface. Something really hasn't been sitting right with me since page three, and I finally figured it out."

I watch him, trying to make sense of what he's saying, as he wraps a towel around himself. He's still blathering on when we head to the kitchen, where he grabs the phone off the wall and dials the number on the small card on the fridge.

"It's Miguel. Yes, it's stellar, just truly fantastic—that's what I'm calling about. I was wondering, can you come over? Maybe you could drop your daughter and the dog at the store so Riley can keep an eye on them, and we can pick them up afterward so she can say goodbye to Harold before you leave. No, no—nothing's wrong. It's just that there's something I want to speak with you about privately."

Thirty-Two

Fiona comes striding up the driveway to the deck, where Miguel and I are waiting.

"Hello, Harold," she says, and I give her a grin nearly as wide as the one Miguel's wearing.

"It's you, isn't it?" he says. His hair's still wet, but he's thrown on another linen shirt, this one in a darker hue, and he just brushed his teeth.

"What do you mean?" she asks.

"You're his secret weapon!" he says excitedly. "Jonathan wouldn't exist without you. Or at least his books wouldn't. I see it now."

"Yes." She lowers her eyes and raises a hand to her face, almost as though she's mortified by this admission. "I wondered if you knew. I'm sorry I didn't say something earlier—I wanted to, and believe me, I've been trying."

"There's no need to apologize. I'm dazzled by your genius," he says, and she looks at him again.

Then he steps forward, puts his hand gently behind her head, and puts his lips to hers.

This time, I don't even *want* to bark.

They're still kissing, and their bodies are pressed together; I'm getting a strong whiff of what my Amelia liked to call "the tingles." But Miguel and Fiona fit together differently than he did with her. And that's okay. In fact, it's just right.

At once, I'm overcome with the strangest, most melancholy joy—because I just realized that I have fulfilled my mission. I no longer need to worry if he'll be okay once I'm gone; he will be.

Our Amelia would be so proud of us.

"Was that too much?" he says breathily when they finally let each other go.

"No." Her voice is lower than usual. "I could've done that all day. But I'm dying to know: How did you figure it out?"

"It was the line about who the protagonist would have been if she'd been born in another era. I recognized that from our conversation at the park. You must've been up all night editing."

Her eyes flash with something; I don't know what it is, but it's no longer her mating instinct.

Miguel doesn't catch it, though. "No wonder we've had such a connection," he says in a husky tone. "I've spent years admiring your hard work, your influence."

"Influence," she repeats.

"How much do you edit? Do you start when he thinks of an idea?" he asks. "I want to hear everything."

She sits gingerly on one of the chairs on the deck and places her hands on her knees. "Miguel, I think you should sit down."

"What is it? Are you all right? Should I bring you something to drink?" he asks, taking the chair beside her.

"No, it's not that. I . . . think there's been a misunderstanding."

He leans toward her, concerned. "How so? What can I do to help?"

"I didn't edit the story you just read." In a near-whisper, she says, "I *wrote it*."

He pulls his head back almost violently. "I don't understand."

"When you just said you knew it was me, I thought you meant you knew I'd written the story, and *Missing Person*. Honestly, I assumed you'd known since we talked about literature at my house. It felt like you were peering right into my heart and were only waiting for me to find the courage to reveal it to you."

"No—I—I don't get it," he says haltingly. "*You* wrote *Missing Person*? Did you write *I, Edward,* too? And *The Way We Weren't*?"

"Yes. I mean, it's complicated." She's gripping her hands together tightly. "*Missing Person* is the book of my soul, but Jon has a remarkable memory, and he helped me with the details because I forgot a lot of what happened, probably from the trauma. In that way, he practically wrote it with me."

Miguel looks as though he's awoken from a deep sleep and is having trouble telling what's a dream and what's reality. I'm starting to feel a wee bit dizzy myself. What happened to the tingles, to their connection? They should be professing their love right now—not confessing that they've completely miscalculated each other.

He stands from his chair and takes a step away from her. "Who knows about this?"

"You're the first person I've told," she says. "Vik knew from the start—he'd pushed Jon to give up the charade so they could enjoy their life together without constantly being under a microscope. Yet I've never breathed a word of this to anyone. It's an incredible relief to say it aloud."

But she doesn't look relieved. And it's probably because his face is twisted up in pain.

He curses quietly in Spanish. "I always wondered how a twenty-two-year-old could have possibly written *Missing Person*. The answer is, he couldn't—and he didn't. Why didn't you tell me when I told you about my parents, and how much that story meant to me?"

"I tried to," she says, wincing. Why isn't he consoling her like he did when she told him she hadn't been taken seriously, or at least touching her to tell her it's going to be all right? "I've been trying to summon the courage nearly every time we've been together. I was just . . . afraid."

"The girl doesn't know, then," he says plainly.

Fiona lowers her head momentarily. "Amelia Mae is quite clever, as you've probably gathered. Now that she's older, it's clear she has her suspicions. Jon and I were going to tell her together, but then . . . he left."

"Is that why your brother ran off to Europe? Because he didn't want to fess up?" He rubs his forehead and doesn't wait for an answer. "And is that why you wanted to write the bookstore a check—because it's really *your* money? After all, you're the one who built JMB's entire legacy, and your brother's the front man. No wonder you read the article I wrote."

"Miguel, neither Jon nor I wanted to keep this up. We had no idea that it would come to this. But you don't know what it was like for us," she says with newfound urgency. "My ex-husband ran off the minute he found out I was pregnant with

Amelia Mae. A few months later, my employer pink-slipped me because they thought I couldn't do the type of reporting I'd been doing if I was expecting or worrying about childcare—they actually said that, though of course they didn't put it in writing, so I couldn't sue them. I had bills to pay and a young child to care for. Jon helped me with Amelia Mae when I could barely look after myself, let alone an infant. Really, he nearly saved our lives. But he was working at Burger King at night and studying during the day, and we desperately needed money. The manuscript I'd written a few years earlier was just sitting in a drawer, and even though it had been rejected by dozens of literary agents, I knew in my soul it was good. Really good. Except no one would give me the time of day."

Miguel exhales loudly, waiting for her to finish.

"So, I made the protagonist male and gave him a sister instead of a brother. Then I asked Jon if I could use his name, since it was really his story, too—after all, we'd lived through it together, and he'd supplied so many of the specifics that my mind refused to remember. When the first few queries didn't get a response, I mailed a photo of him with the next letters I sent to literary agents, knowing that his youth and good looks would be the foot in the door we needed to get someone to read the whole manuscript and see its potential. I doubt we could've gotten away with it now, but it worked then. Ten days later, he'd signed with Bunny, and a week after that, boom—a five-way auction for the manuscript that I'd repeatedly been told 'lacks imagination' and 'isn't salable,'" says Fiona, making little motions in the air with her fingers. "That's not even including the foreign rights and then all the film stuff and the prizes. *Now* do you get it? We were both broke and beaten down, and just hoping to survive and give Amelia Mae a good life, Miguel. But . . ."

"One book turned into three," he says quietly.

"Yes," she concedes. "I'd call it golden handcuffs, but after a while, I began to recover from my ex leaving and the depression I'd experienced over him and losing my job and what felt like everything else. I finally had the time and money to write fiction, as I'd always wanted to. Truly, I don't know if I could have stopped if I'd tried. But over the past couple years, Jon has been convinced we were on the verge of being found out because so much is on the internet. My poor brother, who wants nothing more than to be left alone, has entire AOL chat boards dedicated to him!"

Miguel grimaces, but he still doesn't go to her.

Fiona continues. "He panicked, and then *I* freaked out when I realized what this could cost us—which led to a year of writer's block. I haven't been able to write . . . until you showed up at his door. Then it was like the floodgates had opened back up. I can't tell you how much that means to me. I feel like myself again, when I haven't in the longest time. Was I incorrect in thinking that maybe you did, too?"

Miguel says nothing now.

"I'm truly sorry you feel deceived," she tells him. "That's the last thing I wanted."

"Thank you." He squeezes his lids closed. "But why did you call me and offer to have Jonathan do an event at Lakeside?"

"I was telling the truth about loving Amelia's work—and helping bookstores. I went to one of her readings in Chicago before she got ill, and we got to talking afterward. She mentioned how hard it was to run a bookstore, and she spoke so highly of you. She even told me we'd get along. And it turns out she was right."

Miguel's eyes are as wide as an owl's. "You knew who I was when we met? When you first called the store?"

"I did," she says simply. "I hadn't thought twice about my conversation with Amelia until I saw an article online about her passing and . . . I only wanted to help in some small way and had no idea so much was riding on that one event. I thought maybe she'd have mentioned me to you—I told her that she and my Amelia Mae shared a name, and she said it couldn't possibly be a coincidence. But then you were so surprised when I introduced myself, and things just . . . happened the way they did."

His face has gone pale. "Why didn't you tell me that? I would have wanted to know you'd met Amelia. But now that it's coming out like this . . ."

I start pacing between them, though I'm not sure what I'm trying to accomplish. I wish the other Amelia were here to help me. Because she was right: They've just made things unnecessarily complicated. And I don't know what to do about it.

"Have you ever been rejected for who you are? It wasn't just publishing that told me I wasn't enough, Miguel," rasps Fiona. "I wanted to be a mother more than anything, and my ex pretended like he wanted that for me, too—only to leave me in the lurch when that happened. Even now, I'll meet someone who becomes a friend, but as soon as we start getting close and I tell them about the losses I've encountered, they retreat because they're only interested in the sunny version of me. People say they want authenticity. The reality is, they want it in the smallest possible doses and exclusively when it's convenient for them." Fiona rises from her chair and stands in front of Miguel, so they're eye to eye. "I liked you from the get-go. And you liked me, too—no matter what you think now, I know I wasn't imagining the spark between us. And even though I felt terrible about the circumstances that led to us meeting, I've waited an awful long time to feel the way I feel when I'm around you. But now I can't help but wonder if you're just like everyone else."

"I'm not," he says, but his voice lacks conviction.

"No? It occurs to me that you didn't rush to compliment my genius once after I told you I wrote your favorite novel."

"Fiona—"

She cuts him off. "Nor are you embracing me right now and telling me it's all right that I couldn't tell you until I was ready. Because it's not all right, is it? You liked the illusion of me. Maybe even parts of me that fit your preexisting narrative. But you don't want the whole package—and you hate that you've just seen it."

"That's not true at all."

Except it must be, because he still hasn't put his arms back around her, and he's not comforting her, either. He's just standing there like he's frozen from tip to tail.

Fiona shakes her head sadly. "I'm going to go. We should have left this morning. Or maybe days ago."

His shoulders slump, and he stares across the yard instead of looking at her. "Okay."

What is he talking about? This is the opposite of okay! He's supposed to be *groveling* right now. "The hero, no matter how tortured, how racked by guilt and suffering he might be, has to fight for his love's love," Amelia said one time when she was helping another writer with her work. Really, if I learned anything from her reading her books aloud to me, it's that the hero must care; he has to *try*.

But Miguel must be all out of caring. Because when Fiona grabs her tote from the back of the chair then walks down the driveway and out of our lives, he lets her go.

Thirty-Three

Miguel doesn't get in the shower to cry. He doesn't slap and mutter at his computer, either, and he doesn't call Miriam or Dane. Instead, he sits on the sofa, staring at the papers on the coffee table and radiating pain. And no amount of my nosing him or sitting on his feet makes him speak. It's like Amelia's memorial all over again, except worse.

Because this time it doesn't have to be this way.

He's still silent the following morning. In fact, he doesn't even tell me we're going to the bookstore when he loads me into the car.

"Off to the stockroom," he grumbles to Riley when we arrive. "Keep an eye on Harold."

She gives him a curious look but doesn't try to engage him in conversation. Natalie's at the register, so Riley and I busy ourselves sorting and shelving. I feel terribly blue, but I'd rather be blue here, so at least there's that.

We've just approached the new and improved Romance section when she starts talking to herself. "It's working, but I doubt it'll be enough. We probably need months of solid romance sales to turn things around. I wish he'd listened to me sooner."

Oh, so she's speaking to me. *Go on,* I tell her.

"I asked Brenna, and she said we're already up eleven percent."

Riley spoke with Brenna? On purpose? But even that doesn't really lift my spirits.

She continues. "That's pretty good for a single week, but it's always busy at the beginning of August, so maybe it's nothing. I don't think so, though."

A few kids have just wandered in and they rush over to the graphic novel section. Once Riley makes sure they've found what they're looking for, she returns to me. "Oh, buddy," she says, squatting to scratch my back. "It'll be awful if I have to do it."

What's going to be awful? I lift my ears and wait for her to go on.

She gives me a quizzical look. "I swear you understand what I'm saying sometimes."

Not just sometimes, Riley! Now, tell me what you're talking about!

"It's just—well, what if another opportunity never comes?"

This is a very good question. Now I understand that sometimes there is no later, that the opportunity in front of you is the only one you're guaranteed. I rest my head on Riley's foot to let her know I'm still listening.

"I know it's a big bookstore chain, and that comes with a whole corporate culture that maybe isn't the best fit for me, but I feel like I might be able to make it work," she says softly. "I wouldn't be on the floor anymore, but it *is* a manager role . . . oh, Harold. I wish this could be easy." She stands and glances around. "Miguel told me I should look elsewhere, but I don't want to leave. I love this place, and I guess now that I might not have the option in the future, I feel like I need to make things right with Brenna. An apology's a start, but it really wasn't fair for me to break things off with her so abruptly without telling her how much I was suffering. So, I think that's what I want to do next. And doesn't what I want mean anything?"

Riley? Leaving? Absolutely *not.* I rise and press my torso against her, hoping to remind her that she's as much a part of Lakeside as any of us. What would the store even be without her?

It wouldn't. Forget JMB and the stupid event that should've been for Fiona all along. If Riley's not here to help our customers buy way more books than they ever intended to and be thrilled about doing that, we're truly doomed.

"It just sucks, Harold," she says. I don't look away when she gazes at me; her eyes remind me of my mother's, though it's more of a feeling than an actual memory. "At least I don't have to decide immediately. They said I can take my time. Hopefully Miguel will figure things out before then. I believe he can. I just hope he figures out how to believe that, too."

She stops talking because Miguel's just come trudging out of the stockroom.

"You good, Riley?" he asks. "You've got a look on your face."

"I'm fine," she says so flatly that it's like she hopes he hears she's lying.

His eyes follow her gaze to the Romance section, and I know—I just *know*—he's thinking about Fiona. "Take the job," he says flatly.

A nervous laugh escapes Riley's mouth. "Pardon me?"

"I'm aware that Borders offered you the manager position," he says, and her head whips back. "You should take it. I'm sure Brenna told you that they're good people over there. Or at least she would if you asked her, which you should."

"How on earth did you hear about that? I haven't told *anyone*. Even Dane."

He shrugs in an attempt to be casual, but I can tell it's taking him effort to even have this conversation. "It's not a big industry. Lamar and I went to school together, and he called to make sure I wouldn't be upset if they hired you."

Riley balks. "I didn't put you on my reference sheet for a reason."

"A good reason, no doubt. But you don't need to worry—I told him you'd be perfect for the gig."

"Why?" she asks, horrified. "You *want* me to leave? Do you even care whether I want to go?"

"Of course I do," says Miguel, slipping his hands into his pockets. "I'm telling you to go precisely because I care about you. Like we talked about last week, you could run this place in your sleep. And I'm never going to be able to compensate you for that, say nothing of your nonexistent job security."

Riley's rapid blinking tells me she's on the verge of crying. "You're saying I asked for too much?"

"No, Riley. If anything, you've never asked for enough. I owe you so much. We all do, but especially me—we wouldn't have survived without you while Amelia was sick, and then . . . after. But I'm afraid you'll regret it if you don't take the job."

"If I regret something, it's not pushing you on romance earlier." Her voice warbles. "Sales are up, Miguel. If you can find a way to get us through the next month or two, we could survive."

"Romance is *not* going to save us."

"It already is."

His expression shifts from empathy to irritation. "Maybe it's helping, but I don't know how to get us through the next couple months, and I've already tried every single thing I can think of. I've emptied my savings account and badgered banks from here to Marquette. I went on a ridiculous cat-and-mouse hunt in Chicago. I tried to make amends with Amelia's parents when I would have preferred to have someone stick a hot poker directly into my spleen. I'm not sure what more you want from me."

"I want you to keep trying!" she cries. "It's not over yet, so stop acting like it is!"

He rubs his forehead for a moment, then says, "I understand how you feel. I really do. But this is in your best interest. You'll make more money and have a better life if you go work at Borders."

A single tear escapes the corner of her eye. I whimper and rub myself against her leg, but for once, she doesn't reach down for me. "That's it?" she asks him quietly. "After all I've put into this place?"

"Riley, I'm incredibly grateful for everything you've done. But you have a bright future ahead of you—you'll probably run your own store someday or do something even better, like get out of here and go see the world."

"And if I don't want to?" she says, wiping her cheek with the back of her hand. "I've seen a lot of the world, Miguel. What I want to see now are the people and places I already love. You should understand that more than anyone."

He closes his eyes. He's swaying a little, and for a second, I wonder if he's feeling faint, like I am. "I'm truly sorry to disappoint you, but I'm out of steam and almost positive that Lakeside will close this year. I don't want that to negatively impact you more than it has to."

Riley's always been as ferocious as a golden retriever. But now—well, if I were Miguel, I'd be a bit worried, because her glare says she might just bite. "Then stop and let someone else try," she says sharply. "Respectfully, this isn't just about you, or even your and Amelia's dream. You have four employees, and I speak for all of us when I say we don't want to work somewhere else. Plus, this place means something to our town—to our community. How many groups meet here? How many kids learn to read right on our rug, beneath our rainbow? Remember what Amelia always said? Stories save lives. How many lives have been saved because someone bought a book from this bookstore? So yeah, Miguel. I've been holding back because you're hurting, and I don't want to add to that. But you're going to have to stop acting like a lone wolf and let other people in."

Miguel takes an unsteady breath. "I tried that, Riley. And all I got was false hope and the discovery that there's no limit on the number of times a heart can be broken."

Thirty-Four

My Amelia always got blue after she finished writing a novel. She hid it well, so most times I was the only one who could tell. She still saw her friends and went to Lakeside and helped Miguel cook for whomever she'd invited over to brunch or dinner. Yet between one story and the next, she smelled less like ink and more like rain. She didn't talk as much, either, even to me. Instead, we'd go on long, quiet walks. We'd plop down in the sand at the lakeshore and watch the sailboats glide by in the distance. Sometimes she'd hold me close and take these deep, shuddering breaths. "I'm okay, Harold," she'd assure me because—well, because she was Amelia, and she felt my worry in her own heart. "I gave it everything I had, and now the world looks a little different."

But her stories lived on—and in those days, she still had new beginnings up ahead. So, her sadness never lasted too long.

I hover near Miguel when we get home, but I do not try to comfort him. Nor do I devise some harebrained strategy that may appear to work at first, only to backfire spectacularly. I, too, have given it everything I have—and Miguel has rejected love anyway. My beloved bookstore is still going to close, and I will probably never see Amelia Mae again.

The world looks a lot different now.

I sleep at the foot of Amelia and Miguel's bed that night, rather than in my own. The ground is cold and hard, and somehow that feels right, too—or at least it does until I awake in the middle of the night in pain.

In spite of the little lightning bolts coursing through me, I need to move my legs, or I fear they won't work come morning. The sliver of moon is behind a cloud, so the second floor is enveloped in darkness. But I know every inch of this house, and surely, I don't need light to make it into the hallway and down the stairs.

Wait, is that my Amelia?

It couldn't be.

But I swear I hear her voice in the kitchen, or maybe it's the attic, calling me. Where is she, though? It's so dark, and everywhere I turn there's more nothingness. And pain—so much pain.

"Harold!"

It's not Amelia this time; it's Miguel, and I must have done something wrong. Is he shaking me? That's not like him. Or are we bouncing? I'm all turned around.

"Oh no," I hear him say. Who is he talking to? It smells like we're in the car, but I can't get my eyes to open. "Harold, buddy, come on. You're all I have, Harold. We're almost at the hospital. Stay with me."

What? No. The animal hospital is expensive and scary. I just took a tiny tumble—can't he see that?

Miguel's hand is on me, so I must be in the passenger seat.

He's touching my head, and my belly, and—ow. *Ow.* "Tell me you'll be okay, dog. *Please.*"

I can't tell him anything, obviously. But he's just stopped the car, and he's getting out, and now he's lifting me out of the seat.

"You took a bad fall," he says to me. It's not comfortable, having his thick forearms around my tender torso. I imagine it's uncomfortable for him, too, and I feel bad about that. "Oh, Harold. I'm sorry. I've been pushing you past your limits. I should have known you needed to rest, not be in the middle of all this excitement. And then letting that puppy stay with us—it was too much."

He hasn't pushed me at all. I've wanted this excitement, with new and old people to love. Even Walter wasn't as bothersome as I thought he'd be. Up until Fiona walked off and took Amelia Mae with her, I have been . . . happy.

But of course, that's exactly the problem. I've been so busy thinking about myself that I have forgotten all about what's truly important.

Don't worry, Miguel, I think, gazing up at him as he rushes me into the animal hospital. *It won't happen again.*

Thirty-Five

"There you are. Oh, thank goodness, Harold. Is he okay?" Miguel asks, talking to someone else now.

"He's stable. It's a start."

Who is that? With much effort, I manage to pry my lids open. The buzzing fluorescent lights overhead make it blindingly bright, and the room reeks of bleach and fear. After a moment, I make out a man in pale blue pajamas standing beside me. I've never seen him before. Oh, wait—we're at the hospital, and they gave me some sort of shot, and . . . that's all I remember about that.

"But he's all right now?" Miguel sounds frantic.

"I'd like to get his blood panel back, but based on the ultrasound, it appears that Harold's heart is failing. I'm very sorry that I don't have better news."

I'm still woozy, but I can see that Miguel's on the verge of either cursing or crying. Maybe both.

Amelia's murmur turned out to be a lot more than that. Funny that the person who knew the human heart so well had one that went and quit on her. Now mine is, too. Maybe it's the drugs they've given me, but there's a strange sort of comfort in this.

"Is there something he can take?" asks Miguel. "Medication? A special diet?"

"I'll definitely be sending you home with meds and a long list of diet and exercise modifications. Even so, he's fourteen. That's past the average lifespan for a Brittany-setter mix. It's honestly a wonder he's made it this far without an incident. Judging from the echocardiogram, this is a chronic issue that's gotten worse over time."

Miguel's face is twisted up, and he sniffles. "He's been sort of off for at least a month. I've even caught him wandering around at night."

Wandering? How am I just now hearing about this? I remember that one time, but I had no idea this had become a habit. I'm mortified.

"I didn't bring him in—" A sob catches in his throat. "Because I was preoccupied. I'm so stupid. I should've made an appointment."

"It's okay," the man assures him, and I take back every sassy thing I've ever thought about vets. What a kind person he is, handing Miguel a tissue and directing him to the plastic chair against the wall of this tiny, terrible-smelling room. "A month probably wouldn't have made a difference. I don't know if several would've, either. Besides, if he wasn't having symptoms, we wouldn't have tested for it. He's old, and sadly, this is often what happens when dogs get old. What's important is that you know now, and there's a lot you can do to make him comfortable."

I try to twist to look at him, assure him I'm okay, but my body feels so, so heavy, and I can barely lift my head.

"Easy, Harold." Miguel's at my side again and using the voice he used with Amelia when she was sick. "The drugs in your system are confusing you. Just lie down. I'm supposed to take care of you, remember?"

No, Miguel. You're *confused. That was not the deal I made with Amelia.*

"Keep talking to him," says the vet. "They understand more than we can possibly imagine."

You don't say.

"It's going to be okay. You took a tumble down the stairs and got banged up pretty badly. We think you passed out." Miguel sniffles again. "I know you don't like this place, but it's a good thing we got here as fast as we did."

I whimper because my throat and mouth refuse to work the way I want them to.

His voice catches. "When I saw you at the bottom of the stairs, I thought I'd lost you. I'm so sorry, buddy. I promised Amelia I'd take care of you, and I haven't done the best job of that."

Yes, he has! But why, when that's what *I* promised her?

"I know you're old, and that you can't live forever. But dog, I need you a little bit longer," he whispers. "I'm not ready to say goodbye just yet. Okay?"

My lids are growing heavy again, and I'm so very tired, but I force myself to stare into his eyes.

I'm still here, Miguel, I tell him. *And that's where I'll be until I figure out how to get you to the other side of this.*

When we get home, Miguel tells me I can have whatever I want, so long as it's not chocolate or poop. This is a lovely offer that I would be pleased to take him up on, were it any other time.

Right now, however, I have few desires. Of course, I'd like to return to Lakeside as soon as I'm able. I want to roam among the shelves and sniff all the wonderful not-brand-new books and, in a perfect world, happen upon Amelia Mae reading stabby stories in the yellow chair. And naturally, I long to curl up on the braided rug that I still remember my Amelia hauling in and placing in four different areas before realizing it was always supposed to be beneath the window, where the sun can warm it—and me. I will never not relish those pleasures.

But all that's dimmed by my overwhelming need to sleep.

Miguel sets my bed up in the living room near the bookshelves and brings me some mashed chicken soaked in broth. I can't manage more than a few bites, but it's delicious and almost makes me forget how terrible I feel. The vet gave him a gate that he's placed at the bottom of the stairs, like I'm some sort of toddler. Then again, I mistook the second floor for a buffalo jump, so maybe it's for the best.

I'm groggy. Whatever pain medication they have me on makes me feel like I'm crawling my way through the hours—not that I'm moving all that much. When it's time to use the bathroom, Miguel has to hold me up with this shameful sling contraption. "It's that or doggy diapers," he tells me as he props me over the grass and waits for me to pee. "I think we both know this is the more dignified choice. You'll be able to hobble around soon, but not yet, dog. Not yet."

And indeed, when I arise the next morning, I'm already doing better. My head's not so fuzzy, and I'm even able to get up on my paws. I'm excited to show Miguel how much I've improved, and that he really doesn't need to worry about caring for me. I'm good.

There he is now! He stoops to examine me. "I'm relieved to see you're on the mend, Harold," he says, ruffling the fur on top of my head oh so gently. "You were my wake-up call, so I owe you."

Is that so? This wouldn't be the silver lining I would have selected, but I'm in no position to be picky.

A shadow crosses his face as he stands. "It's time to accept reality," he says.

Maybe, but the only thing the man's facing right now is our bookshelves. He scans them momentarily, then plucks out three hardcovers. Jonathan's super serious author photo is staring at me from the back of the bottom copy.

I do not like this one bit.

"There was a reason Miriam was worried." He laughs bitterly. "Here I was, so caught up in a mirage disguised as love that I forgot all about making money and keeping the store alive."

Did he just say "love"?

But he keeps jabbering as he walks into the kitchen. I limp behind him, trying not to draw too much attention to myself.

He opens the trash. "If I hadn't gone to Chicago in the first place—if I'd said no to going back to her house—" One by one, the books thud as he drops them into the bin. "If I'd just stayed home, I might be in the same position, but I wouldn't be this miserable. Ignorance may be for willful idiots, but it sure beats the truth. And the worst part?"

I thought he'd already unpeeled that, but it appears there are multiple layers to this odorous onion.

He turns and startles slightly as he sees me. "Harold, if I hadn't dragged you to Chicago, you probably wouldn't have passed out, and you certainly wouldn't be as sick as you are right now. I had no business letting you run around with a tweenager. I failed you."

He's as wrong as he's ever been. I'm clear that my happiness isn't the objective here, but Amelia Mae is the best thing that's happened to me since my Amelia passed. And as much as I fault myself for overfocusing on her, that made it easier for Miguel to spend time with Fiona. No, he didn't fail me; I failed *him*. I should have figured out how to explain to him that love isn't just the answer.

It's the whole point.

He slides down the back of the cupboard so he's sitting next to me. His entire body radiates pain, and not the kind I'm in. "I wasted all that time," he says.

He puts his fists to his eyes and clenches his jaw, and instead of letting the tears out, he's fighting to keep them in. "I blew it. Year after year, I blew it. Amelia told me to branch out, to read other things. I acted like she was telling me to go binge pulp, but she was talking about her own books. I *knew* she was, even if she didn't come out and say it. But I was too afraid that I wouldn't like them, that they would somehow impact the way I felt about her, so I just avoided them altogether. I'm as awful as her parents."

You're not. You're nothing like those horrible people. You made a mistake; their harm was on purpose.

I rub my head against his leg, and he places his hand on my back. And at last, a sob escapes his mouth.

Then he says the thing that finally—*finally*—makes me understand why he's so distraught.

"All that time, I could have been reading Amelia's novels instead of JMB's or Fiona's or whatever they are. It didn't matter if they were good or not, or if it turned out I hated romance. Those books, they were *hers;* they were part of her heart. I'm a fool, Harold, the very worst kind. I prioritized a stranger's words over the woman right in front of me, who I loved more than everything in the whole world times a million. Now I can't do a thing about it because it's too late. And I will have to live with that for the rest of my lonely life."

He watches me for a moment, then pushes himself onto his feet. "Come on, dog. It's time to get some sleep," he says, lifting me from the kitchen floor. He walks me to the living room and gently places me back in my bed. "Rest up. I'm going to clean myself up, then start making calls to get the bookstore ready to close. I'll call Dane to give him a heads-up, and he can tell Riley, since I highly doubt that she wants to hear from me. Then I'll let the others know, and give Kathy notice in the next day or two."

Not that I can protest, but I don't want to sleep. I need to help him see that he's got this all wrong; the rest of his life doesn't have to be lonely, and in fact, it's not supposed to be. I'm here, at least for now. So is Fiona, if only he'd call her and apologize. He has Riley and Dane and Miriam and their family in Puerto Rico. Yes, Amelia was his reason, but she would have wanted him to find a new one. To do all the living and loving he can while he has a chance.

But he's already stepping over the stupid baby gate and heading upstairs without me.

What will I do? What *can* I do when I'm in such sorry shape? Just as Miguel claims to be, I'm truly out of ideas.

So, I close my eyes and ask for help, in any form it decides to arrive.

Thirty-Six

I swear I'm not trying to mope, but I also don't know how to mask how I'm feeling, the way so many humans seem to be able to. It's not just my sorry state; now that Miguel has decided the store is closing and he's destined to be alone, everything seems unappealing. I couldn't even bring myself to finish my special food this morning.

Really, I don't think Amelia understood what she was asking for. Maybe she overestimated his capacity for love, to say nothing of my intelligence.

"*¿Y tú también,* Harold?" Miguel says, throwing himself on the sofa. He's stripped down to his underwear, although I'm not sure if this is a sustained cry for help or the result of his decision to barely use air-conditioning to save cash.

Me, too, I think, lifting my head momentarily to acknowledge I've heard him.

"Come on up here, dog. You look miserable down there."

I eye him from my bed. Surely this is a trap; I'm never allowed on the sofa.

"Come on," he says, patting the spot beside him. "I'll give

you a lift. Besides, it's not like we're expecting company. Miriam won't be back for a few days."

Yes, and that's part of the problem—she's possibly the only person who could talk sense into him right now! Still, I rise cautiously and let him lift me onto the cushion. Then I circle for a moment, trying to find the right angle, before curling up just far enough away that he and I aren't touching.

"You sure you're okay?" he says, reaching out to pet my head. "I hope those medications are doing what they're supposed to."

I don't mean to sigh, but the sound escapes all the same. "Is it the girl?" he asks. "You really liked her, didn't you?"

You think?

"I'm sorry about what happened with her mom, but I promise it's better this way. The minute you begin a relationship, you've just invited loss into your life. I mean, if you really think about it, there's no such thing as a happy ending—not if you really follow the story all the way to its true conclusion. And we don't need any more loss. Do we, boy?"

Just days earlier, I did agree with him. I don't anymore. I'm ready to accept the inevitable loss, however painful, if it means more love. Besides, Amelia said she knew what was best for him, and I have to believe her; I just have to.

Miguel's computer's open on the coffee table. He reaches forward and flips it closed. "Maybe that's why Jonathan hightailed it to Europe. He may not have written those books, but he's still wiser than I've given him credit for. I have to wonder what it would be like to just . . . just *disappear,* maybe move through the world anonymously. I mean, I'd still want to reach out to Miriam, let her know I'm okay. And she can let the cousins know, since Titi Ceci doesn't remember me anymore."

This time, my sigh's on purpose, but Miguel's so lost in his delusions that he doesn't even hear me. "Honestly, Harold, the fact that disappearing sounds idyllic means it really is time for me to close the store. Or maybe I could sell the business, and Dane, Brenna, and Riley could run it without me. We all know they'd be better off that way. The only one who really needs me is you."

"Like hell we'd be better without you," says a voice from behind us, and Miguel springs straight into the air like a cat who's spotted a cucumber.

Dane's standing in the doorway to the living room. His sunglasses are perched atop the bird's nest on his head, and he's carrying a paper bag. "Sup, Harold?" he says, tilting his chin at me as I rise to greet him. "I heard you had a gnarly fall, so stay put."

"*¡Ay, Virgen,* Dane!" exclaims Miguel. "Are you trying to kill me? How'd you even get in here?"

"Opposite of killing, chief. I came to check on you." Dane squints at him. "Gotta say, I took you for a tighty-whitie guy. Kind of happy to see you in boxers."

Miguel glances down but makes no attempt to cover himself. "Have you not heard of knocking?"

"I totally knocked. You didn't answer, but I saw your car was here, and the back door was unlocked."

Dane knocked? I missed that, which is weird—there are few things I enjoy more than barking at the door. I didn't hear him walk in, either. Oh, I really am on the decline.

"Why would I answer?" scoffs Miguel. "I don't need to be sold on salvation, and I'm sure as hell not buying a set of encyclopedias."

"I'm agnostic, and the interwebs have rendered encyclopedias irrelevant." Dane lifts the paper bag. "I brought us breakfast, but I'm gonna need you to put some pants on so I can actually eat. Mm-kay?"

Remarkably, Miguel trudges upstairs and throws on the clothes he was wearing the day before. Then he pours a couple of mugs of coffee, hands one to Dane, and sits next to him on the sofa.

"Don't know why you're here," Miguel says, his mouth full of the enormous muffin Dane just passed him.

"Come on, dude. I could tell when you called last night that you're in a bad way. Fiona's gone, you're talking about closing the store, and I hear you told Riles to accept another gig. I'll take 'crisis' for five hundred, Alex."

"I am not in crisis, Dane." He sighs. "Okay, maybe I'm not doing so hot. How upset is Riley?"

Dane licks a crumb off his finger, then points the digit at Miguel. "She's not great, but in classic form, she's more worried about you than herself. Why don't you let us help you figure out how to bring in some cash, fast, so you don't have to choose the nuclear option? The beginning of September is just weeks away. That's time for us to come up with *something.*"

"I own a calendar."

"Hmm." Dane sinks his teeth into his muffin, then glances around as he chews. "Listen, chief, I meant what I said. I can totally work for free for a while to help you save money. This is a sweet little place. I could move into your basement or something to make sure it's fair. No offense to Harold, but you could probably use the company."

He's not wrong about that, but Miguel glowers at him. "After seeing you pop out of my spare bedroom, that is literally my worst nightmare."

"I know you speak two languages better than I can manage one, but I'm pretty sure you're misusing the word 'literally.' "

"Stop while you're ahead."

"Roger that—though my offer stands. Also, if you really do close the store and need a new gig, my aunt runs a marketing firm in Grand Rapids. Says she's always looking for warm bodies. You could probably write press releases and stuff."

Miguel freezes. "A desk job?"

Dane takes a sip of his coffee. "Yepperdo."

"Surrounded by dozens of employees, too many of whom will stop at my cubicle countless times a day to talk about asinine television shows I've never heard of? And ask if I want to eat lunch with them and a bunch of other cogs I have nothing in common with?"

"That's usually how that works." Dane nods to himself. "Though it's probably more like hundreds of employees."

Miguel shudders. "I take back what I said about you living in my basement. *That* is my worst nightmare. Literally."

"See? You're not selling the bookstore. You can't."

"You're not half as clever as you think you are."

"Debatable." Dane drains the last of his coffee, then walks off with his mug. "Hey," he calls from the kitchen. "You going to call Fiona and make things right, or what?"

"Or what," he mutters. When Dane returns, he adds, "I regret having mentioned that to you."

"You willingly volunteered those deets for a reason, chief. It's not good to keep it all bottled up inside. And like I said, I'm not going to tell anyone that Fiona's the real Oz. The more

I think about it, the more I get why she waited to say anything. She's in a tricky situation. Who knows how her agent and publisher will react if they find out she's been writing the books all along? And you know some of JMB's fans are completely bonkers. I'm sure it stings, but she had good reasons."

Miguel glances toward the window. "Maybe she did. Maybe I should have been kinder to her. But the fact remains that I still feel like a fool. I wasted time with Fiona when I should have been finding a real solution to keep the bookstore open and paying more attention to Harold's health. I've failed Amelia, nearly murdered her beloved pet, and squandered our dream. It's over, Dane. Everything good is over."

Dane puts his mug on the mantel and strides over to where Miguel's seated. He puts his hands on his shoulders and squats in front of him. To my surprise, Miguel doesn't move or tell him to scram.

"I know it feels like that, chief, and that sucks," Dane says quietly. "But it just so happens that you're still here. Yeah, your literary idol isn't who you thought they were—but don't you think you were into Fiona because that beautiful brain of hers wrote the very same book that made you feel seen? Heck, it doesn't even matter whether you decide to keep the bookstore open. Just stop telling yourself you don't want love and everything good is over. Because I knew Amelia, and although I never told you this before, I read most of her books."

"You *did*?"

"Focus, my dude—that's not where I'm going with this." Dane presses his forehead against Miguel's. "What I'm trying to say is, the story you're telling these days? As your friend and hers, I need you to hear me when I say: It's not the one Amelia would've written for you."

Thirty-Seven

The silence startles me awake.

Normally, the air's abuzz; it's subtle, but the sound's always there if you listen for it. But now an eerie quiet has fallen over the house. The fridge isn't humming, the electrical outlets aren't vibrating, and the cool air has stopped whooshing from the vents. The lights are off, too. Unless those pills from the vet have *really* thrown me for a loop, I'm pretty sure it's only been a few hours since Dane left. What happened between then and now?

I hear Miguel in the kitchen and, with some effort, rise to go see what's happening.

"Hello?" He's sitting at the table, staring at the phone. "Kathy, are you there? Did you hear what I said about—" He presses some buttons, lifts it to his ear again, and then sets it on the counter. "That's odd. Did something trip a breaker?"

He tells me to stay put while he wanders around the house, flipping switches and messing with the metal box on the wall in the basement. "Anything?" he calls, but then he seems to remember that I am a dog and cannot tell him that no, nothing has turned back on. He looks utterly perplexed when he trudges back up the stairs.

He steps outside onto the deck. Raina's on her back porch, too. She's sipping a glass of wine, and for once, she doesn't seem apprehensive about seeing Miguel. "Hi there," she calls.

"Hi," he says hesitantly. "Is your power out?"

"It is. Just having the last sip of chardonnay before it gets warm," she says, raising her glass.

"I'm sure we'll be back up and running soon."

She shakes her head. "Most of the state's out, and most of the Northeast. Part of Canada, too. They're saying it's a major blackout."

His eyes widen. "How'd you know that?"

"I just got done with my shift at the hospital—I was finishing up when the news came through, and fortunately, we have a generator. It's some kind of utility failure. If I were you, I'd probably eat anything especially tasty in your fridge, because we're going to be in the dark for a while."

"Oh, jeez—I hope not."

Raina shrugs. "Kind of nice to have some downtime, be mostly unreachable for a bit. And it's not as hot as it's been, thank goodness." She pauses, examines him for a moment. "Hey, you doing all right? I know you've been through a lot, and I'm really sorry I haven't said anything. I guess better late than never. Or at least I hope it is."

He squints in the late afternoon sun. "It's okay. And yeah, I'm hanging in there. Thanks for asking."

"Good. You have my number, right? If you need anything? I mean, it won't work now, but when the power's on, you can call anytime. Or just come knock."

He blinks. "Thanks, Raina."

"Course," she says, then finishes the rest of her wine.

Miguel looks around the backyard, then down at me. "Well, Harold, what the heck are we going to do now? I can't even call Miriam to see if she's okay."

As it happens, I have an idea.

I don't wait for him as I head back inside. "Where are you going?" he calls after me. "You're supposed to be taking it easy."

I'm sure there *are* easier ways to do this, but I don't have thumbs, so I stick my face in the bookshelf. It's tight in there—so many books all crammed together—and my neck and back hurt. Honestly, even my snout's sore.

"Harold!" he hollers when he spots me. "What are you doing?"

What does it look *like I'm doing, Miguel? I am trying to save you!*

He's striding toward me as I finally free a book with my paw. I grab it between my teeth, trying hard not to slobber too much on the pages, and place it at his feet.

"What in the . . ." He takes the book from me, and I whimper weakly. He glances down at the cover, then frowns at me. "That's not nice. Of all the things to bring me, you had to pick one of Amelia's novels. Come on. I'm already hurting here."

My dog, is he dense.

Miguel turns and surveys the bookshelf. "You're not as smart as the average pig, Harold, but you do have a point. It's time to pack up her books—they're too painful to look at. I'll get a box from the garage. That'll give us something to do."

That is *not* what I was aiming for! The man may be determined to self-destruct—but not on my watch.

Oh, you lesser primate, I think when he returns with a weathered old box that smells of mold. *Don't you do it.* I growl—just a tiny bit, but I need to warn him. I lift my head and make direct eye contact, daring him to challenge me.

With narrowed, unblinking eyes, he reaches for the novel he's never read and grabs it with his stupid bendy digits.

Suddenly Miguel's hand is not his hand. It's that meaty mutt Amelia and I encountered that one evening, baring its fangs on the darkened street. And the novels are no longer the product of their author but rather my Amelia herself, on the verge of being attacked. Except this time, I will be the one saving her rather than the other way around.

I snap.

I'm already back to myself by the time Miguel yanks his hand away. He's shaking it like he's been burned, though it appears that's also what a person does upon finding their flesh between a set of teeth. "What is going *on* with you, dog?" he asks, staring at me with bewilderment. "Haven't you ever been told not to bite the hand that feeds you? It's a good thing you didn't break the skin," he says, examining his palm. "That medication must be messing you up. Please remember I'm the one keeping you alive."

I will myself not to cower, as I normally would, and attempt to raise my upper lip enough to tell Miguel that boxing up Amelia's books will not be tolerated. Unfortunately, I've always had a bit of an underbite, so my attempt fails. I know this because he snort-laughs, then says, "You look deranged, Harold. That's a mug only an orthodontist could love."

I examine his grungy T-shirt and the smudge of dirt across his cheek, which he must have gotten when he was rooting around in the garage. *I* am the deranged one in this situation?

"Okay, I didn't mean that," he says. "But I don't get it. What is this about?"

I don't know that I could explain it to him even if I could talk. Instead, I let out the sort of sigh I typically reserve for sunny spring days when I'm splayed out on the deck, knowing summer's just around the bend.

And then I realize that I, too, must keep going. I must show him what needs to be done. I put my face back into the bookshelf and pull another novel out. It falls to the floor.

Miguel does not react. So, I do it again with the next book. Thud. Finally, he squats down beside me. "Careful," he says, reaching into the pile. "I'm just taking one copy."

Good choice, I think as he picks up a paperback; on its cover, a woman stares out at the water. Of course, there are no bad choices here, but that one speaks to me.

He's still squatting beside me, and he thumbs through the book for a second before standing. As he begins to walk away, I'm conflicted. I don't want to leave this spot, but I need to make sure he doesn't take these copies anywhere near the trash or do something else he shouldn't.

"It's okay, Harold," he calls over his shoulder. "I get what you're trying to make me do. Now lie back down and relax. I'll be right back."

Something in his tone makes me believe him. Or at least I want to, and for now that will have to do.

He returns a few minutes later with his reading glasses. Then he drops his pants in the middle of the floor and plops down on the sofa. While I wish he'd stay clothed in case anyone swings by, at least I can keep an eye on him there. He lies longways and props himself up with some pillows. Then he opens the book and begins to read.

At once, his whole face is a frown.

This is *not* what I was hoping for.

I watch and I wait. This is exhausting in its own way, so I lower my head for a little bit, and when I lift it again a while later, he's still frowning . . . but not as much.

"Hmm," he says, because the man is a loud reader in the same way that Amelia was a loud writer. "Huh. Isn't that something. Oh."

It's rather monotonous, his muttering, and I fall asleep at some point. When I wake, he calls to me. "I haven't left, Harold. I'm sure they've closed up the store, so I'm still here."

And then, after a few minutes, I hear the craziest sound.

Miguel is . . . *laughing*.

Not that strange little grunt-laugh thing he does, or the "ha-ha-ha" that he uses when he feels the need to be polite (admittedly, I haven't heard that one in the longest). No, this comes from deep in his belly. From my bed, I can see that his whole torso's shaking as he turns the page. "Ohh," he says to himself, pausing for a moment to wipe the corners of his eyes. "He's a real dolt, this Giles, but Stephanie knows what to do with him. Oh, that bit with the dinghy was funny. I bet she got that from one of the first trips we took to Puerto Rico, when I insisted on taking my cousin Luis's boat out and nearly got us stuck."

He's talking about the story where the woman goes looking for her missing father but ends up finding love with an eccentric sailor whom she hires to help her track him down. Like in most of Amelia's novels, things really go south once the ill-suited duo team up—in this case, to head to the tiny island where her father's hiding out. Only for a while, though. The heroine stops trying to do everything herself, the sailor gets over his fear of commitment and declares his love, and after a few more missteps that make them prove their devotion to each other, they sail away to happily ever after.

"Couple more pages," he calls to me.

He doesn't need to assure me; I've already vowed not to prioritize my own comfort over his ever again. Except . . . what if I'm wrong and he's right and it really *is* too late? After all, Amelia will never know that he's read her work, let alone enjoyed it.

It's another hour before he gets off the sofa. After taking me outside to pee, he serves me more special food, then makes himself a bowl of cereal. "Have to use this milk before it turns," he says, taking the bowl back to the sofa. He shovels the cereal into his mouth absentmindedly as he keeps reading.

"Giles is being so stubborn, Harold," he says to me. "I don't know how he's ever going to redeem himself at this point." The sun's starting to set, and he'll need a flashlight soon if he wants to continue. He places the paperback on the coffee table.

I wait for him to say or do something, but it's back to being creepily quiet. I belly-crawl over to the sofa, where Miguel's still splayed out, and see that his torso's shaking again. This time, though, he's not laughing. He pulls his hand from his face, and beneath his reading glasses, all the tears he hasn't shed yet are finally running rivers down his cheeks. "Oh, Harold," he sobs. "I miss her so, so much."

My heart hurt before, but now the ache is unbearable.

What have I done?

Miguel weeps and weeps, and the longer it continues, the worse I feel. Yes, I wanted him to read Amelia's books. But Giles and Stephanie's happily ever after must have seemed cruel. And reading his name in the acknowledgments—which was always her favorite part of the book to write—was probably rock salt in his gaping wounds.

I messed it all up, and I have no idea how to fix it. I get right next to him on the sofa and attempt to put my head on his lap, but he just curls into himself, armadillo-style, and continues to cry.

Even after he finally stops weeping, he refuses to budge. I try whimpering, then pawing at him. "It's nearly dark. Go to sleep, Harold," he mumbles. "You need to heal."

That makes two of us, friend.

I don't go back to my bed, though. I have to keep an ear out for Miguel in case he needs me.

The crying must have exhausted him because he passes out on the sofa with his mouth hanging open and his T-shirt hitched up past the odd crater in his stomach. The house is hot and stuffy, but it still doesn't seem right, seeing his nearly hairless body all uncovered like that.

It's a fitful night. I keep waking abruptly, forgetting where I am, then having to relive the entire fiasco all over as I remember why Miguel and I are both in the dark in the living room.

The sun's just begun to rise when he finally stirs. He rubs his eyes and glances around with confusion, like he's forgotten how he got there. "Morning, Harold," he mumbles at me.

Morning? That's all he has to say? How about, *Don't worry, I'll never read another one of these novels again, so you don't have to lie awake fretting about me,* or, *Sorry I gave you such a scare. How about we put this book back where it belongs and pretend this never happened?*

He glances down at himself and wrinkles his nose. "Good thing the water's still on. I'll need a shower after I feed us."

Thankfully, he pulls on his shorts before he grabs the newspaper from the front stoop. Then he strolls past the rest of Amelia's novels, which are still in a pile on the living room floor, and into the kitchen, where he serves me my medicine and what's left of the special food, and himself a bowl of dry cereal.

A return to normalcy! Granted, it's not my preferred variety of normal, but it's a step up from last night. Dare I trust it?

"Evsclsd," he says, peering at the paper he's just unfolded.

I stop eating and stare at him. Say what?

He swallows his mouthful, then says, "Everything's closed—whole state's basically shut down and it'll probably stay that way for another day or so. No idea how they printed the paper, but at least we know not to get too excited about air-conditioning." He motions to the back door. "Come on. I'll let you out."

I do have to pee, so I amble over to him. "Take it easy," he tells me, helping me down the deck stairs to the patio, then onto the grass. Hard isn't an option; my right hip aches something awful today, and my chest feels like fire ants are setting up shop. It takes a long time for me to relieve myself, and I nearly wet my own leg in the process. Thank goodness Miguel's the only one to witness my infirmity.

The dread from last night creeps back when he heads upstairs to bathe. I should've skipped breakfast and attempted to hide Amelia's novels while he was eating. I don't know if he can handle more crying. And what if he boxes them all up and throws them out like he did JMB and Fiona's books?

He returns wearing clean clothes and smelling like a new man. Still, I can't help but feel nervous when he takes up residence on the sofa again. He's picked a different paperback to read this time, and he's on his back, holding the book over his head. It doesn't look comfortable to me, but he's humming as he reads.

I must be staring because he turns to acknowledge me. "Harold, did you know this is a series?" He gestures to the bright yellow cover. "Stephanie has two sisters, Lucy and Sophia. This is Lucy's story."

He doesn't have to tell *me* that, but I'm not upset when he continues.

"She loathes Adrian. She has since they were kids because he used to ignore her, or so she thought. And now that they're adults, he's acting like he's got a mouth full of rocks instead of speaking up for her at the town council meeting. He didn't mean to—he's just so stunned by how beautiful and funny she is, and kids used to tease him about his accent. But now she thinks he's the same aloof kid she knew and hated," he says, shaking his head. "Harold, I swear Adrian is based on me; I didn't ignore Amelia, but she knows I used to be self-conscious about my voice when I was younger. Regardless, I have *no* idea how he's going to prove her wrong. He may have a killer career and those V-shaped stomach muscles—but as of right now, this guy's got work to do."

He sure does.

He continues. "I mean, why can't he figure this out without putting Lucy through all of that first?"

Sometimes humans really make me question the validity of the entire food chain.

Then he holds the book in front of his eyes again. "More soon," he murmurs. "See you on the other side of this chapter."

By "chapter," he apparently meant "book," because he's still reading at lunchtime. But I don't want to bother him because at least he's not crying or talking about closing the store. And honestly, though I need to pee again, it's kind of fun to see him turning the pages like his life depends on it—and maybe it does.

At some point he shifts into a seated position. Watching him is like witnessing a storm pass through: First come clouds, then rain—he's already cried twice—followed by a hint of light. And then he breaks into the sunniest smile I've seen on him since Before.

When he finally closes the paperback, he places it on his chest, sighs deeply, and says, "Ohhh, that was satisfying. He *needed* to go through all that, and so did she. That's the point, isn't it? They had to work and change to find each other. To find love."

I hope he's listening to himself right now.

After feeding me and taking me out back, he clears out the bookshelves at his eye level, moving his thick hardcovers to the bottom shelves where Amelia's books were stored. Then he places all her paperbacks on the empty shelves, wedging a large, polished agate in the gap at the end of the second stack. I remember that rock; he bought it for Amelia when we were in the Upper Peninsula.

He regards the shelves for a while, moves a few copies around, then retrieves another novel in a color I can't make out. "Let's see what you've got, Sophia," he says before throwing himself on the sofa yet again.

And this is what we do for the rest of the daylight, with neither of us leaving the living room except to tend to our basic needs. While he reads, I laze in my bed or lie beside him on the sofa and listen to him tell me about the story. I wonder if he realizes that I was there for most of those novels, though a handful were written before my time. And when he reads me lines aloud, it's almost like Amelia's here with us. "'I am done with people. The only one I can rely on is my dog,'" he quotes, laughing. "Wonder where she got that one from, huh, Harold?"

Speak for yourself, Miguel, I think, even though I do adore that passage. *I love people.*

Then again, if he keeps reading, there's a slim but real possibility that at some point he'll remember that he does, too.

"Trust issues!" he declares when he's nearly finished. "They *both* have them! So did the characters in the last novel. It's like a weird theme she keeps returning to. Maybe it's because I'm not great about relying on others." He frowns. "That's probably why I'm up a creek with the store right now."

Ding ding ding! The question is, what's he going to do about that?

Instead of elaborating, he finishes the novel, then grabs another from the shelf. He waves it at me. "I'm going to read the last one she wrote next. Then I'll work my way through the rest of her backlist."

Even as he's telling me this, the house begins to buzz. We both startle. "Power's back," he says, but he doesn't sound as pleased as you'd expect for someone who's sweated through several shirts. He looks down at the book and thumbs through the pages. "It's hard not to skip ahead. But also, I wish it could go on forever. This has been . . . really nice."

It has. It might be the best time he and I have ever had together without Amelia, even compared to Chicago. And while he has cried nearly enough to make up for all the crying he didn't do in front of me before, he looks—I won't say good, as there are still dark circles under his eyes, and he needs a haircut if he wants to avoid morphing into an unshorn alpaca. He looks better, though; less haunted and more alive.

"Actually, I'm going to save this one," he tells me, his eyes skimming the copy on the back of the paperback.

But I wanted to hear his thoughts on Adam's proposal!

"I'm pretty sure Amelia wrote this, or at least finished writing it, when she was already sick, Harold." He smiles faintly. "I'm glad you're a dog, because I'm not sure I could say this to anyone else, but I have a sneaking suspicion this one's about us, even more than the others. Now, I know she wasn't an academic and I didn't inherit a grocery chain, but . . . well, I'll have to find out later. Since the electricity's back on, I've got things to do. Things I can't do alone," he says solemnly, answering the question I could not ask. "But I'm going to have to make a whole lot of apologies before anyone even *considers* helping me."

He seems to have forgotten that the four most endearing words in the English language are "I need your help." "People love to be useful and to be valued," Amelia informed Miguel one time when he was hemming and hawing about asking Derrell, a neighbor a few houses over, to figure out why our lawnmower wouldn't start. "Think about it," she told him. "You might prefer to take care of things yourself, but you never actually mind when someone else asks you for a favor." Miguel got over his pride and went to Derrell's, and the next thing I knew, he was back to terrorizing the neighborhood with that awful machine, and Derrell grinned and waved whenever he drove by in his truck.

"If that's what it takes, that's what it takes," says Miguel, placing the paperback on the table beside the sofa. He turns to me. "Harold, it's time to make things right."

Thirty-Nine

Miguel decides he's going to Amelia's office the next morning. "Do you want to come with?" he asks me.

Neither of us has been up there since she passed; I haven't wanted to. Still, I know I should visit at least once more while I'm able. So, I rise to my feet to indicate that I'm game if he is, since I have a feeling this has something to do with him making things right.

He hoists me into his arms and carries me up the first set of stairs, and then up the narrower stairway leading to the attic. When we reach the top, he gingerly sets me on the carpet.

Amelia's office is a cozy space with a low, vaulted ceiling and exposed wooden beams. The windows at either end are small, but there's a skylight on the south side that helped keep her plants alive. This used to be the happiest place in the world other than the bookstore.

No longer. Amelia's not here—and now that I'm looking around, I'm realizing her plants aren't, either. The monstrous monstera, the heartleaf philodendron, the orchids: They're all gone. Of course, there's no way they would have survived all that time without water and attention. But even their *pots* are missing. Miguel must have cleaned them out when I wasn't watching, and while I'm certain he meant well, I don't like his sneaking around, nor the strange and sterile feel of the room now.

But then he gets on one knee in front of her desk and gingerly picks up a carved wood vessel in the center. I remember that container, which looks sort of like a vase with a lid, from the memorial, and that somehow, some part of Amelia is in there.

"I know it's weird that I leave her urn up here," he says to me. "But up until now, it felt like she belonged here. Maybe she did or maybe she didn't. Either way, I don't want her so far from me anymore."

Now he sits cross-legged on the rug and puts the urn just in front of him. I lie beside him, close enough that he can touch me if he needs to. "Hi," he says softly to the urn. "I'm really sorry I haven't gotten here sooner. Honestly, I think leaving you in your office was just one more way I've been shutting people out, thinking that somehow it would ease the pain." He puts his hand on top of the urn. "Of course, you already know it never did. But I did do something that might surprise you." He's started to cry, but he's smiling, too, and it reminds me of a rainstorm on a sunny day. "I read your books. A whole bunch of them. And it made me realize how wrong I've been about not relying on other people."

And, ahem, the dog who loves them, I think, scooching closer to him.

"Amelia, you were the most trusting woman I'd ever met, and for some strange reason, you decided to pick *me,* the weirdo who's always struggled to trust people. I'd say I hope you didn't regret it—spending your too-short life with me, I mean—but every one of those stories told me that you didn't." He sniffs and wipes his eyes. "You believed in our love, and maybe just as important, you believed that I could change. Of course, I *did* change because of you, always for the better. But I'm not done changing, Amelia, and that's mostly because of you, too. I see now that you wouldn't have wanted me to be alone. You would have wanted me to love again, and not to push that away. It might be too late, but at least I understand. And if I get the opportunity to let love in, I will."

He cries for a minute or two, then dries his face on his T-shirt and rises. "Harold, I'm going to go put this on the bookshelf where it belongs," he says, picking up the urn. "I'll be right back."

He returns a few minutes later and walks to the extra copies of Amelia's novels, which are piled along the low attic walls and in stacks beside her desk; paper was the only clutter she allowed, but on that front, she was a true collector. "You know what I noticed?" he says to me, regarding the books. "Things never work out the way Amelia's characters expect them to. Not in a single story. They start thinking they want one thing, and she gives them something else entirely—and it's always what they need."

Then he begins to pull copies from the piles. "Don't freak out and nip me," he instructs as he stacks them in his arms. "I hope Becky and Bob will find the courage to read these, or at least skim them. But I guess even if they send them straight to the dumpster, I'll know I've done the right thing."

Her parents? Those warped weasels don't deserve to be in

the same house as my Amelia's novels, let alone receive their own copies.

"Believe me, Harold, I have my reservations, too," he says, frowning at the books he's holding. "But if I can come around, who knows what's possible? Remember, her mom did slip her a copy of *Sense and Sensibility* in high school. Knowing Becky, she was trying to warn her about romance and did it in a misguided way. Even if she did," he says, surveying the space, "it backfired. *Y gracias a Dios por eso*. Maybe she'll read the books and see how great it was that her daughter wrote love stories."

He totes his armful downstairs, then gathers another, and still a third. Finally, he returns for me.

"I got clean boxes," he tells me as I watch him place the sets into the cardboard containers in the kitchen. "We have ours—now it's time for Amelia's books to find new readers. Anyway, she always said her stories only belonged to her until she published them. The minute they were out in the world, they took on a life of their own."

Miguel fills a bunch of boxes, which he tapes up and hauls to his car. "Oof, these are heavy," he says on his way out the door the first time. "Probably should have called Dane to see if he could help me. Live and learn."

"Come on, Harold!" he calls, and I startle from my spot in the kitchen; I must have dozed off while he was in the driveway. "Don't want to be late!"

Late for what, he doesn't say. Instead, he picks me up again and places me on the seat. "Stay, okay? We're not going far," he tells me. "I'll drive very slowly so you don't hurt yourself."

Raina's on her front porch emptying her mailbox when we back out. I expect Miguel to drive past quickly, but he rolls down the window and calls, "Thanks for the other day!" He laughs nervously. "The news about the blackout, I mean."

She smiles. "I know what you mean, Miguel. You end up tossing a lot of food?"

"Didn't have much to lose. Though it was good to have to throw out all the freezer casseroles people brought over after Amelia died. It was time for them to go."

"Sounds like it was. I'm glad you're okay."

"Me, too," he says.

"Don't be a stranger," she says, then waves as he drives away.

We turn onto the big road, and that's when I realize we're heading to the bookstore. Even though I'm sore and he told me not to, I still get on all fours and press my mouth against the window.

"Oh, Harold, I wish you'd listen. I hate driving fifteen miles an hour," Miguel grouses, but he doesn't really seem upset. When we reach the parking lot, he pulls into his usual spot. "Can you walk?" he asks, gently setting me on the asphalt. I can, so he grabs a box from the trunk. "I'll have to get the rest of these after the staff meeting," he tells me. I must look confused because he says, "They had to push it back because of the blackout. And you and I, dog, should have been here ten minutes ago."

Sure enough, when we get inside, everyone's already gathered in the reading nook. It doesn't look like it normally does in here, and it's not just because of the Romance section. Wait—is that the missing monstera, right beside the sofa? The philodendron's over near the register, and the fern that I've always longed to pee on is in the corner in front of the window. I thought Miguel never went to the attic, but he must have been sneaking up there to water Amelia's plants this whole time. And here I thought I was hearing sounds of an old home settling, when it was his devotion all along.

Oh, Miguel, I think, spotting an orchid at the register, and although its flowers are gone, I can tell it'll bloom again soon. *What a good job you did—Amelia would have loved it.*

Riley, who's seated in the yellow chair, clears her throat when she sees him. "Sorry, we just got started," she says, and I wonder if she's really apologizing about sitting in Amelia's spot.

"You're good," Miguel assures her.

"I thought when you dropped the plants off after-hours, it meant you weren't going to show."

So *that's* why he was missing when I woke up from yet another nap yesterday evening.

"I understand why you'd think that, and I'm sorry I didn't communicate better. But I'm here now," he says, dropping the box on the floor.

Brenna's tie has little fish on it today. "Moving supplies?" she asks.

"We were talking about the store possibly closing," says Riley, exchanging a quick glance with her.

"Nothing like that," says Miguel. "I'll explain in a minute."

"Uh, boss, can I say something?" says Dane. His eyes are bright, and he's grinning like he's got a whole flock of canaries in his gut.

"Absolutely, but first, would you let me say something? It's important." Miguel kneels on one knee beside me. Then he looks at each of them for a beat longer than most humans find socially acceptable. "I want to begin by apologizing to each of you. I've had some time to think—and read. I've come to realize that if I'd listened to you all a long time ago, Lakeside probably wouldn't be in this position."

Brenna leans toward him, but Riley just frowns. Maybe that's why he addresses her first. "You called it—I did need help. I still do. I was drowning in my grief, and holing up on my own only made it worse, for both me *and* the store. That cost all of you a lot, but especially you, Riley. I'm sorry."

"It's okay," she says quietly.

"It's not, but I appreciate that," he tells her. "Also, I gave your therapist a call this morning. She's not taking new clients, but I'm seeing her colleague next week."

Her eyes widen. "Really?"

"Really."

"That's amazing, Miguel," says Brenna.

"Thank you. It doesn't feel amazing yet, but I bet it will in time." He looks around the nook. "Natalie, you've been asking for more hours, and I haven't given them to you because, well—" He points at Riley. "Because I wasn't listening to our new manager here. That changes here and now."

"Are you serious?" Riley exclaims. "You're making me manager? I thought we were closing?"

"We might, but not yet. And yes, I should have named you manager a long time ago. I owe you an even bigger apology for that, and I hope we'll be able to talk privately later. For now, will you forgive me?"

She bounds over to him but then stops short. "Is it okay if I hug you?"

He nods and stands, and she throws her arms around him. "Thanks, Miguel."

"Thank *you*, Riley," he says gruffly.

He turns back to the rest of the staff. "We're not closing in September. Riley's right—romance *is* selling, and I asked Kathy to give us one more month before she raises the rent. Believe it or not, she agreed. I don't know if I'm being unrealistic, but if you're all on board, I'd like to try to find a smaller and less expensive building for us by January so that we don't have to close then. Or at least not close anytime soon. I'm willing to sell my home if that's what it takes."

Dane holds up his hand like one of the kids at Story Hour.

"I promise, just a few more things and I'll give you the floor," Miguel says to him. He takes a deep breath. "So . . ."

"What is it?" says Brenna, and Natalie's jiggling her leg so vigorously that her chair's rattling.

"This place was our vision, Amelia's and mine," he says, turning to regard the rest of the store. "I've been thinking of the bookstore as her legacy, but thanks to Harold, I finally started reading through her backlist, and I realize that no four walls could ever truly serve that purpose. Amelia's *stories* are her legacy."

They all nod in agreement, and Riley wipes the corner of her eye.

"You four kept the shop open while I pretended to, and that was nothing if not a labor of love. As Riley recently reminded me, there's no other place like this around here, where people can stop by with their dogs or their kids or just themselves and know that they're welcome—no exceptions. Even those who are down on their luck can read a book that they can't afford to buy here, and we will open our doors for them again and again. Lakeside is so much more than a bookstore. But I can't keep it up and running by myself."

"You don't have to, chief," says Dane. "We've got you."

"I know that you do." Miguel clears his throat. "That's why I'd like to propose something . . . a bit unconventional."

Riley cocks her head, waiting, but Dane looks like he's ready to jump out of his chair.

"Fiona approached me about becoming an investor. In the store, I mean."

Brenna arches an eyebrow at Riley, who purses her lips knowingly. They've made up! I knew they would. And something tells me Amelia Mae's behind that, too.

He continues. "That isn't right for us, but it got me thinking about my business model. I want to make you all co-owners. The bookstore should be a cooperative, not a company. Technically, it already is, but I haven't been giving you credit for that. We'll share the decisions *and* the profits—and we'll also figure out how to increase them so that everyone is compensated as they should be."

No one says anything. And for once, I cannot interpret their body language.

Natalie's the first to break the silence. "Are you sure? I'm only here in the summers. That might not be fair for everyone else."

"I'm sure, though I understand why you might feel that way," he tells her, nodding thoughtfully. "But I also remember you had another job lined up and chose to work here instead. I want to reward you for that. To be clear, company shares would be based on seniority and tenure. And in the interest of fairness, that buy-in would adjust each year or whenever a person begins working here or decides to leave. I acknowledge that this model may not be right for everyone, and I get that, too." He looks at Riley. "Some of you have other options that may prove to be more attractive."

Riley, who has been jotting down notes on her clipboard, lifts her pencil and regards him. "Come on, Miguel. I just accepted the manager position. Now are you going to finally let me sell e-books or what?"

He laughs. "Don't expect me to like or understand it—but as I said, that decision's no longer mine alone to make. Speaking of decisions, I've been meaning to ask: Do we have Zara Aboah's event on the books?"

"I was waiting to find out if we were closing, but we have a tentative date for the first Tuesday in October."

"Fantastic, thank you. Can you tell her I'm excited she'll be here?" He stops and shakes his head. "You know what? Just send me her contact info. I'll call her myself."

She beams at him. "Done."

"I do have one more suggestion to run past you all while I have you," he says, oblivious to Dane's squirming.

"Is the JMB event back on?" asks Natalie.

"I think that ship has sailed. In fact, I'd like to recommend that we head in a different direction . . . and truly make this store a romance destination. Amelia designed this to be a place where readers who adore love stories are celebrated, not shamed, and Riley's right—instead of that being a feature, it could be *the* feature. We'll sell all kinds of books, of course, but the majority will be romance. We can even do a big event if Riley's still interested in throwing it."

She's blinking back tears. "Did you have a personality transplant?" she asks with a clipped laugh.

"Even better. I read a bunch of Amelia's novels during the

blackout and realized the power of a love story. I want to celebrate that, not hide it at the back of the store."

Brenna beams while Natalie claps. And Riley—well, she's officially crying now. "I'm so happy," she tells him.

"I was hoping you'd be on board since it was your idea. I'd like to have a big reopening event next Friday to mark the occasion. Now, that's soon, and it'll be a lot of work."

"Not if we all chip in," says Natalie.

"You don't—" He catches himself. "I'd love your help. Thank you."

Dane's got his hand up in the air again. "Uh, chief?"

"I'm sorry," says Miguel. "You've been waiting all this time to tell us something. What's up?"

His mouth is half grin, half grimace. "Can you and I go somewhere to talk?"

Forty

Miguel asks Dane if he'll meet him for lunch at an Italian restaurant in the next town over. The place is so-so, he explains, but they have outdoor dining with big fans everywhere, so I can tag along. I'm not in as much pain as I was before, but he bought me a humiliating if effective cooling vest and a portable water bowl, just to be on the safe side. Admittedly, I can't really feel insulted by his trying to take care of me—not when I can no longer pretend that I don't need help. I guess that's one more thing Miguel and I have in common.

"Over here," says Dane, waving at us from a table in the corner. He stands when he sees us, and I lick his palm by way of a greeting. "Hey, Harold."

"Hi, Dane," says Miguel. He starts to reach out a hand to Dane, but then he suddenly changes his mind and puts his arms around him.

"Chief, are you *hugging* me? On purpose?" Dane's joking, but the catch in his voice says this is a big deal for him. "Riley really got to you, huh?"

Miguel laughs lightly as he lets Dane go. "That's what friends do, right?"

"*And* you just called me a friend? I might just keel over."

Miguel sits across from him and takes a deep breath. "Dane, you've been a friend to me for a while now. I'm sorry it took me so long to realize and appreciate that."

Dane blinks hard. "It's nothing."

"No, it's everything." Miguel swallows hard, and his eyes are moist. How far he's come, from hiding in the shower to practically crying in public! "You've gone out of your way to make sure I'm okay—and when I'm not, you've been the first one to step in and support me. Riley and Miriam have supported me, too, of course," he adds quickly. "Still, you've been there for me when anyone else would have thrown their hands up and run in the other direction. And while I still wish you'd master the fine art of knocking, you have an uncanny ability to show up at the times when I really shouldn't be alone, no matter how much I want to be."

Dane is practically glowing. "You're welcome, chief."

"Honestly, thank you. I won't ever forget it. Even if you did behave inappropriately with my sister."

"Nice deflection." Dane reaches across the table and squeezes his upper arm. "I know you'll remember. And I bet you'll do the same thing for someone else one day."

"I hope you're right, Dane."

"I always am, chief. I always am."

A waiter appears and takes their order. The minute he disappears, Miguel asks Dane what he wanted to talk to him about.

"Soo . . ." he drawls.

Miguel narrows his eyes. "Is this about Miriam? Because

I'm willing to take back every nice thing I just said about you."

"Nah, but we'll get back to that in a hot second. So, here's the dealio: I called the bank the other day and said, hey, I want to withdraw part of my trust fund so I can give it to Riley's Aunt Kathy, 'cause she needs to buy more caftans so she can do it up properly in her retirement."

"What are you even saying right now?" says Miguel, leaning in over the table.

"I'm saying I bought the building."

"I'm sorry—*what* building?"

"Lakeside, dude. It wasn't complicated. In fact, I'm happy to say our little bookstore co-op will get a sweet break on rent now that a partial owner also owns the building."

"*Dude,* I'm on the verge of passing out," says Miguel, and Dane cackles with delight. "You're serious?"

"As a heart attack." He winces. "Sorry."

"Amelia had an aortic dissection, Dane—not a heart attack. That was my mom, remember? Either way, it's okay. But seriously, you live like a . . ." He raises his eyebrows at Dane's T-shirt, which is fraying at the edges.

"Person who doesn't spend his cash on stuff he doesn't care about?" he volunteers. "Yep, I do. I'm lucky to come from money, but that doesn't mean I want my parents' lifestyle. Yacht clubs and black tie? Hard pass. My dad's always telling me to get into real estate, though, and he'll be stoked I finally took his advice."

"Is this final?"

"Will be tomorrow. Should have been final a couple days ago, but the power going out threw a wrench in my plans, and I didn't want to tell you until it was as good as done. Got the funds, just gotta sign on the dotted line and pass Kathy a bottle of champers. So, that's what I was trying to explain earlier. We don't *need* a new building. You've already got one for as long as you want. That should help a lot with the short-term situation. And actually, the long game, too."

"Dane, seriously—I don't know how to thank you." He pushes his lips together for a moment, then grins. "But if you tell me the answer's you moving in with me, I'm selling my shares to Riley and escaping to Mexico."

Now Dane blushes. "Uh, no. I've got other plans. And lo and behold—there she is now."

"Miguelito!" says Miriam, striding across the patio toward us in a pair of heels that could double as ice picks.

I leap up, even though it pains me, and Miguel gasps and stands. "Miriam!"

"*Soy yo,*" she says, leaning in to kiss his cheek.

"Why didn't you tell me you were on your way back?"

"I wanted to surprise you. Guess what?" she says, eyes shining.

He examines her, then breaks into a huge smile. "I'm the brother of the new dean of students at the University of Michigan, aren't I?"

"*¡Ya tú sabes!*" she says, and now he picks her up and spins her around. "Even a blackout couldn't stop me from nabbing the gig."

"I'm so proud of you that I won't even give you a hard time for not calling me the second you got the offer. Tell me everything—including why Dane knew you'd be in town before I did," he says as he pulls out a chair for her.

"I promise I will, but first, do you mind if I stay at Dane's tonight?"

Miguel frowns, but he quickly recovers. "Of course not."

"I have to return to Ann Arbor to find a place to rent, but I'll be back in time for the reopening before I fly to Puerto Rico."

"You told her about the reopening?" Miguel says to Dane.

"I pick up my cellphone when people call," Miriam says pointedly.

"There's something else we want to talk to you about, though," says Dane, looking at Miriam.

"Please tell me this isn't some sort of intervention."

"Nope," says Miriam. She turns to Dane. "You tell him."

He swallows hard. "So, you know how I bought the building?"

"Yes . . ." says Miguel nervously.

"Don't sweat—I'm still all in. But I'm gonna try to spend some time in Ann Arbor, too. Just a couple days a week."

"With my sister, I take it," says Miguel, but he doesn't sound upset.

"We'd like to get to know each other better, see where this thing might go," Miriam says shyly, and Dane nods.

"Beth's ready to come back, so you can give her some of my hours, and my shares. 'Cause I'll need to cut back on my workload—if it's okay. I want to be there for you."

Miguel blinks hard. "Like I said, you have been this whole time. It's okay for you to take care of yourself, too."

Dane beams. "You're still my BFF, and I hope you know I've got your back for life. It's just that I'm ready for something a little different. So, sometimes you're gonna need to pick up the phone when you want to talk 'cause I can't barge in on you from Ann Arbor."

Miguel looks back and forth between them; I can tell that

overactive brain of his is working hard to process all of this. And then he starts to cry.

"Oh no—are you okay?" says Miriam, reaching across the table for his hand. "We didn't want to upset you. You've been through so much, and this probably seems so sudden."

"No, that's not it," says Miguel, wiping his eyes. "Even if it is sudden, Amelia always said that when you know, you know. I'm not upset at all." He wipes his cheeks with the back of his palm. "I'm . . . really happy. It just hit me that you're going to be here—well, not *here* here, but only a couple hours away, in the same state as me. I'll get to see you all the time." He sniffs, then regards Dane. "Provided this guy doesn't keep you too occupied."

Dane tugs at his hair, which looks like Miguel just ran the vacuum over it. "I would never."

Miriam's dabbing at her eyes now, too. "The offer was good, but more than anything, I wanted us to be together, Miguelito. We can see each other on the weekends and celebrate birthdays and Thanksgiving at your house. We could even go to Puerto Rico for Christmas and teach *gringo* here how to make *coquito,*" she says, tilting her head toward Dane.

He grimaces. "Is that made of frogs?"

"*Dios mío,*" Miguel groans. "We've got our work cut out for us. So . . . you two are serious about each other."

Miriam smiles at Dane. "We'll see."

"*Yo soy loco* for this beautiful *borinqueña*!" Dane kisses her neck, and she giggles.

"It's '*estoy,' querido,*" she says, still grinning.

Tears are running down Miguel's cheeks, but he's smiling, too. "Two of my favorite people together. I don't know what could be better than that."

As it happens, I do—and so does Miriam. "¿*Y* Fiona?" she questions. "You haven't mentioned her once, and you're not wearing that loved-up look on your face. ¿*Qué pasó?*"

"I messed up," he says miserably, then tells her what happened.

"So fix it," she says simply when he's finished.

"You say that like it's easy."

"There's nothing easier than love," she says, smiling at Dane, who leans over and kisses the tip of her nose.

"I don't know that she feels the same."

Miriam rolls her eyes. "Fiona? She's wild about you. You just need to apologize."

"And not do it again," Dane pipes in.

"Oh, I don't think we need to worry about that," says Miriam, examining Miguel. "If she gives him another chance—and I think she just might—something tells me he'll fight for love this time."

Forty-One

We spend the next day at the store. Miguel orders falafel sandwiches for everyone for lunch, just like he used to. And Riley sells even more novels than usual while Natalie helps Dane move the table full of books with serious businessmen on the covers to the back of the store to make room for more bare-chested men with lustrous locks. Meanwhile, Brenna's been glued to the computer, getting everything set up for the grand reopening. As for me, I take four naps but still manage to mooch a bellyful of handouts.

It's almost like old times . . . except, of course, Amelia's not here.

"You two good to lock up?" Miguel asks Riley and Dane at the end of the day. They nod. "That's our cue, dog," he tells me. "You need to take some meds and get to sleep."

I sure do. At home, he hovers like the best dog dad he is, and once he's convinced that he hasn't made a mistake having me out all day, he tucks me into my bed. I'm about to doze off when I hear him in the kitchen.

"Hi. It's Miguel. Right, obviously you know that because

you have caller ID. So, you know that I, uh. Well, I tried calling a few times earlier on break, so I guess I'll leave another voicemail. Harold, um, he had an accident right before the blackout and it turns out his heart's failing. We're home now. He's okay, but as you can probably imagine, he's pretty miserable, and . . . I'm just wondering if you might let Amelia Mae come visit him, sometime before fall? Harold's especially attached to her, and I thought she might lift his spirits. The vet said he probably doesn't have a lot of time left. No pressure, though. Oh, and again—I really am sorry about how I behaved, Fiona. You're right, I have no idea what you went through, and you deserve better. Also—oops, I guess that means I've run out of time. Okay, bye. I guess you can't hear that, either. Oh well. I really care about you, and I'd like us to be together, no matter how complicated that is. I wish I'd told you that when I had the chance."

Well, I'll be doggone. For my next trick, I am going to talk him into admitting he loves her. Unfortunately, I don't expect Fiona to let Amelia Mae come back to Michigan; I'm not even sure I would, if I were her. But I would very much like to see her again.

I wonder if she misses me.

I know she does.

But the medicine Miguel put in my food is making me groggy, so I close my eyes and let it take me under.

"Harold, can you hear her? Harold, buddy, wake up."

Huh? Where am I? The bright light streaming through the

living room windows means it's no longer night. But . . . why is Miguel holding the phone receiver out in front of me?

"Harry? Are you there?" says a voice, and I nearly pee myself in excitement when I realize it's Amelia Mae.

"He hears you!" Miguel tells her.

"Thank goodness—oh, Harry!" she cries. "You poor thing, how terrible for you! Are you okay? Are you bored out of your gourd?"

I whimper a bit.

"Aww, Har," she says. "I know, and I love you, too. We're going to figure something out so we can see each other again."

"Does your mom know you're calling?" Miguel asks tentatively.

"Of *course* she doesn't!" she scoffs. "I saw your name on her phone and helped myself to her voicemail before she had a chance to delete your messages."

"She deleted my messages?" says Miguel. "Actually, never mind, that's not the point. I don't want to get you in trouble."

"I'm perfectly capable of doing that on my own. And yes, she's being a dunderhead, but I'm on it."

He frowns. "I'm not sure you should be involved in our, um, affairs."

"I wasn't asking for your permission, Miguel. Is Harry still with you?"

"Yes," he says cautiously.

"Great. Make sure you put the phone near his ear, but not too close."

He follows her instructions, then says, "All right. He's listening."

"Harry, it's me again. Are you in pain? Do you want me to

tell you a story?" she asks, and I cock my head at the phone in anticipation.

"Stupid question," she says. "So, I've got a *great* one for you today. Let me tell you the tale of two otherwise intelligent adults who were so fearful of letting other people in that an almost-twelve-year-old girl and a—how old are you again?"

"He's fourteen," Miguel tells her, shaking his head in amusement.

"Right, a not-young dog and the girl had to intervene so the adults would stop beating around the bush and do what they really wanted to do, which was spend time together. *Ahem,*" she says loudly, and I smile because she really is something else. "I'm sure you're wondering, didn't all that give the lonely girl a chance to get to know the world's best dog? Don't tell Walter I said that. The answer is, yes, it did, so we can't totally blame the adults. But exactly when things were swimming right along for them, they had some sort of conversation in which they both said a bunch of things they probably didn't mean."

"*Ahem,*" says Miguel.

Amelia Mae ignores him and continues. "To be fair, they've both loved and lost before, so of *course* they're afraid to let on how much they like each other. And yes, there's a lake the size of a small sea between them—but the train ride's only an hour, and honestly, one of them is the most fretful city mouse in all of Cook County and should move to Michigan like her daughter keeps telling her to. And I guarantee her new best friend would love a bigger yard now that he's finally old enough to frolic in the grass."

Miguel's chuckling anxiously.

"Harry," she says solemnly, "I know this all sounds like a speculative soap opera, but I swear on my grandmother's knickers it's a true story. We just need to come up with a better ending."

"I presume you're talking about me," Miguel says.

"Ya think?" she drones. "You messed up."

"I did," he agrees. "But I'm going to make it right."

"Good. How are you going to do that?"

"I'm not sure, but I think it begins with the novels I've been reading."

"And what do *those* have to do with the price of printing in China?"

He laughs. "Everything. I'm finally reading Amelia's books. The other Amelia, I mean."

"Ohhhh. Well, that's a start. And boy, do you have a type or *what*? She told me, you know."

His brows inch closer together. "Who told you what?"

"Sorry—I mean Fiona told me the truth about *her* books. She and Uncle Jon sat me down the other night when the power was out. We had candles lit, and it was all shadowy and creepy and just *perfect* for revealing the big twist! Course, I'm pretty sure I knew all along, deep down. He spent so little time at his computer, and she spent so much on hers, not to mention all that scribbling in her notebooks. Really, it never made sense."

"Wait—your uncle's home from Europe?"

"Why? You wanna kidnap him?" she teases, and he snorts.

"Believe me, I do not. But I was thinking I could come to Chicago to see your mom. Except it sounds like the timing isn't good."

"Yeah, the rest of this week's crap. My play got pushed back because of the power thingy and I have rehearsals. But next week's wide open. I don't think you should come here, though. Not with Harry being all banged up."

He glances down at me. "That's a good point."

"I'm full of sharp thoughts."

"Also, we have the reopening," he says, more to himself than to her. "Though that's not until Friday."

"I don't know what a reopening is, but it sounds like a party."

"In this case, it means we're doing the opposite of closing," he says, smiling to himself. "The event is for our community—it's sort of a surprise. So yes, I guess it's a party. We're announcing that the store is going to focus on romance novels. Don't worry, we'll still have Stabby Peeps and the other books. It's just that Romance will take up the most space."

"Nice. You going to call it 'Happy Endings' now?"

He laughs nervously. "I'm not sure that's appropriate."

"Why not? I mean, I get that you adults make all kinds of great things sound naughty when they really aren't. But happy endings are why people buy books, after all—especially the ones with love in them."

Miguel is silent.

"So, are we invited?"

"Well, yes, of course. But I don't think there's any way to convince your mother to come."

"You leave that to me, Miguel. She talks a tough game, and she's *all* worked up about you, but I'm her only child, and if I really, really, *really* want to be there," she says in an exaggerated whine, "then that's where we're going to be. Pinky promise."

"Incredible."

"I am. What time?"

"Six o'clock, but we'll be open all day." He takes a deep breath. "Hey, Amelia Mae? Can I ask you something?"

I startle. This is the first time he's called her by her full name.

"Course," she tells him.

"Do you know why you're named Amelia Mae?"

"Yepperdo. I'm named after my mom's grandmother, who was the most important person in her life before me. Even before her and Uncle Jon's parents died, Grandma Amy—that's what she called her—was the one who mostly raised them," she tells him. "You know Mom was browsing at the library one day and saw a whole table dedicated to *your* Amelia May. And that's how she started reading her books, and, well—the rest is herstory."

Beside me, Miguel is very still, and I myself am so stunned I can't even whimper.

Oblivious to this, she keeps talking. "She says the stories are fantastic, but I need to wait until I'm at least fourteen to read them because of the sexy parts."

Miguel starts laughing, and once he gets going, he can barely stop. "So let me get this straight," he says when he's able to speak again. "Stephen King's okay, but not romance."

"Not *all* romance. I'm good with it. Men are disgusting, anyways."

"Agreed," he says, still laughing.

"I've gotta—actually, I won't tell you what I'm up to, because that would make you an accomplice. But before I go . . ."

Miguel looks at the receiver curiously. I do, too.

"No offense, but you really need to figure out how to use technology. Your message kept playing after you thought it stopped recording. I told Mom she'd better listen to it, or I'd cry." I can practically hear her smiling from Chicago. "You're welcome."

Forty-Two

"Just one more chapter, Harry."

It's the day before the big reopening, and Miguel has taken the morning off—but only after clearing it with Riley, who's finally in charge of staff schedules. I wasn't sure what he was up to when he lifted me onto the sofa. Then I spotted the paperback he was clutching when he plopped down next to me, and I understood.

It was time for him to read Amelia's last novel.

That was several hours ago. Now he's sniffling again and petting me softly because he's about to finish it. Fortunately, his tears don't worry me anymore.

And neither does the end.

"Oh, Amelia," he murmurs, closing the book and gazing at her photo on the back. "You pulled it off. I don't know how, but you brought Adam around and made me believe he could change in the ways he needed to. That he *had* changed for Carmen. You showed me it was possible, and I loved it—every single page."

He shuts his eyes and stays that way for so long that I wonder if he's fallen asleep. But then he sits up suddenly, and darned if the man doesn't look straight into my eyes like I'm human, too. "Harold," he says decisively, "you were spot-on."

Well, *I* know *that.* The question is, which part is he talking about?

"Not thinking about Amelia being gone all the time made me feel like I was betraying her, so I pushed Fiona away." He shakes his head. "And every time I put distance between us or insisted on making myself more miserable, your overbite would pop out, and I couldn't figure out what that was for—it was like you were mocking me or something. I understand you now, though, dog, and I'm sorry it took so long. You just wanted me to be happy and find love, because you knew that's what Amelia would have wanted for me. And now I see that I can love and be happy again without ever letting go of what she and I had together." He glances around. "I have the home she made for us. The friends I have, my community, my life—those are because of her. And of course you, Harold. She gave me you, too, and you made our little family complete." He wraps his arm around my back and presses his head to my fur.

Then he murmurs, "Thank you for helping me see she's still everywhere. That she'll always be with me."

Things are changing. And although I can't be certain, I don't think I feel that way because of my heart or what's happening at the store. One season is soon to become another, and there will be even less time than there is now.

I somehow sense that Amelia Mae knows this, too. Which is why I'm not surprised when she knocks on the back door the morning of the reopening.

Oh, hello, I think, peering at her through the glass as she grins and waves at me. *I definitely conjured you.*

Miguel, who has just walked into the kitchen behind me, hasn't heard her. Because when he spots her out of the corner of his eye, he immediately folds into himself, even though he's got a perfectly acceptable amount of clothing on. Then he remembers that he's dressed, stands back up, and throws open the door.

"Um, hi there," he says.

"Land ho!" She's wearing a pair of sunglasses that are too big for her face, and she lifts them to look up at him. "We have arrived."

"I see that," he says, squinting. "Or at least I see you. Where's your mother?"

She points in the direction of the street. "In the car. Can you believe I got her to drive here? And I convinced Uncle Jon to watch Walter, too, and he's *really* not a dog person. Though he swears Walter is a cat in a tiny dog's body."

I can believe it. She could've told me she got Fiona to sprout wings to fly them here and I wouldn't have been shocked.

"She did great," she assures Miguel. "I'm *very* proud of her. I'm sure she'll show in a minute, but I needed to see Harry as soon as possible. Is it okay if I come in?" she asks, already charging toward me.

"Don't get him too excited!" Miguel calls as I bark and rub myself all over her.

"We've got to be careful with you, Harry," she says, getting down on the floor, but I jump on her because I can't not. What is pain, anyway, when you're in love?

It's worth it, I think, licking her cheek as she giggles. *It's always worth it.*

On the deck, I can hear Miguel greet Fiona. Amelia and I immediately stop pouncing on each other, and she holds a finger to her lips and leans toward the door.

"I understand," he says. "I really appreciate you being here."

"It's for Amelia Mae. And for Harry."

"Thank you. This is the happiest I've seen him in—well, to be honest, since the last time they were together."

Amelia Mae grins at me.

"I'm glad," says Fiona. "Is he doing okay?"

"Better than I expected. Thanks for asking. How's Walter?"

"He's great. Well, except for his preternatural ability to steal our food if we so much as glance away for a second."

That dog is a far better student than I've given him credit for.

"He'll learn." He pauses, then says, "Do you want to come in?"

"I think I'll just wait here, if that's all right with you."

"Of course."

But instead of waiting, she goes to the doorway and gives Amelia Mae a little wave.

Then she walks inside, toward where we're sitting in the living room.

Her eyes rove around, taking in the photos and the throw pillows and the two shelves of colorful books written by the other person with the best name in the world. Her gaze lands on the paperback that's still in the center of the coffee table where Miguel left it yesterday.

And I see her smile ever so faintly, and I am reminded that maybe not now, or even right away, but at some point, everything will line up as it's supposed to.

Miguel appears behind her. "Hi," he says softly, as though he's greeting her again for the first time.

"Hi yourself," she says. "We told Amelia Mae the truth about the books."

"Yes, she told me when she called. What will you do next?"

Fiona pushes her glasses up on her nose and appears to be considering what she's going to say. "We're not quite sure . . . but we've discussed letting readers know that the books were a collaboration of sorts. After all, that much is true. We thought about announcing that I wrote them, but Jon is concerned that my ex might come after my finances or do something else that would be bad for Amelia Mae. So, we're treading lightly."

"That sounds wise."

"I hope so. I do know one thing."

"What's that?"

"Actually, two things."

He's closer to her now, very close, but she hasn't moved away. "I'm listening."

"I'm going to keep writing, but I'm going to truly focus on women's stories this time. And I'm going to publish under my own name. My married name, not Middleton-Biggs—I'm sure people will find out the connection, but I'm not going to start there. We're lucky, Jon and I, that money isn't a concern anymore. And I'm willing to fight to be taken seriously if I need to, for as long as it takes."

"I'm thrilled to hear that. The world needs your work—and to know that you're the genius behind it."

She bites her lip, then says, "Thank you. That means a lot to me, especially from you."

"What's the second thing?" he asks.

She gives him what my Amelia used to call *the look*. "John Williams has no idea how to write women."

He erupts into laughter.

"Oh, there's one more thing," she says, touching his hand.

"I await with bated breath."

"I'm still upset with you, but believe it or not, I'm still somehow happier when you're around. In fact, I've been miserable since I left Michigan."

He takes her hands in his. "Would you give me a chance to make it up to you?"

She smiles. "I'll consider it. Why don't we start with tonight's event and see how it goes?"

"That sounds wonderful."

"I should give them some privacy, Harry, just in case they want to smooch," Amelia Mae whispers to me. "I'll go grab your squeaky toy from the hallway. Be back in a few."

As I watch her lope over there, I'm overcome by a memory.

Not long before she died, my Amelia went to Chicago for some sort of author event—maybe even the one where she met Fiona, come to think of it—and left me home with Miguel. Back then, I didn't mind letting him sleep in because it was just for a few days, and I was rewarded with leftover cereal, which used to be a treat (oh, to be young and inexperienced again).

Maybe it was because she'd already had her first surgery,

but I was so worried about her, even though everyone said she'd be fine. Still, when Amelia finally returned home, I jumped on her legs like she'd just rescued me from the kennel all over again, and my eyes got all wet.

"Why, Harold, are you *crying*?" she said, letting me lick her face. "I missed you so much, too. I'm here now, though. I'm here."

"Dogs don't cry," Miguel told her, but she pulled a book off the shelf and showed him some passage that proves that we do. We cry when we're happy, and we cry when we're sad, though we also howl when we're really upset. Just like humans.

So, I let myself cry a little now, and it feels like happiness and sadness and remembering, all mixed together. And I don't mind, even though I know Amelia Mae might not understand it. I hope she does one day, though. Because it's the kind of feeling you can have only after you've loved so much that you know in your bones that moving on will never, ever be the same thing as letting go.

Forty-Three

It's time.

And we're ready. There are balloons and banners throughout the store, and right in front of the enormous Romance section, Brenna and Dane have loaded long tables with cold drinks and food that I'm forbidden to eat. There's only one thing left to do.

"Here we go," calls Miguel, wheeling the dolly toward the table that's in front of the braided rug and under the rainbow painting.

"What's in there?" asks Brenna, watching Miguel pull a box cutter out of his back pocket.

"Amelia's books," he says proudly. "She had dozens of extras she planned to use at events, but they've just been sitting in her office all this time," he tells her. "Think you can add them to the inventory before we get started?"

"You know I can."

"You're the best. Well, other than Riley," he says, and they laugh. "Technically she's the best, too. Are you two back on good terms?"

Brenna smiles sheepishly. "Then you knew?"

He nods. "About your cold war? Kind of hard to miss."

"Ugh, sorry. But yeah, she apologized, and I . . . well, of course I forgave her. I wish she'd have told me everything earlier, but it is what it is. I don't think we're right for each other, but I'm really happy to call her a friend again."

"I cannot tell you how glad I am to hear that," he says, patting her arm. "A friend like that is hard to find."

I watch from the front counter as Riley strides over to him. "Hey, boss?"

"Yes, manager?" he says, and she grins.

"How would you feel about a sign for this table that says, 'Read Amelia's Rainbow'? I'll keep brainstorming if you want," she adds quickly. "Still, I feel like we should do something extra special with the display—something that really brings attention to the author who started this place. What do you think?"

"I think . . ." he says, pivoting slowly to look around the store. He smiles when he reaches Riley again. "I think that would be the exact right thing."

Then he carefully cuts through the tape and pulls back the box flaps. "These are ready to find a good home."

Riley plucks a paperback from the box. Then she turns toward the rainbow, presses the book to her heart for a moment, and says, "They already have."

The bookstore is packed.

People are standing shoulder to shoulder. Riley and Brenna

have set up chairs in front of the podium for those who cannot stand, and those are all taken, too. There are even a few stragglers out front on the sidewalk. But this time, they're not here for Jonathan Middleton-Biggs.

They're here for our store . . . and for Amelia.

Because Riley and Brenna have accomplished a true feat and have called all of Amelia's author friends, even the one who upset Miguel by rearranging Amelia's books at her memorial. And though it was short notice, many have driven in and even flown in from across the country to celebrate Amelia and bring attention to the store with the help of a bunch of strangers on the internet, whatever that is.

"You're sure you're okay, Harold?" Miguel asks, bending down to scratch my ears.

I'm near the register, in the plastic wagon that Amelia Mae once used when she was young. She made Fiona bring it in from Chicago because she didn't want anyone stepping on me.

Me? I tell him. *I'm fine. Are you?*

"I'm nervous," he whispers.

Oh, Miguel, I say, licking his cheek. *It's going to be okay. Ask for help if you need it.*

"You're right, Harold," he says, and he doesn't even wipe his face. "We've got this."

We do—but deep down, I'm nervous, too. I see Dane, who has his arm around Miriam. She's back from Ann Arbor, and as Dane told Riley, they're having the world's longest one-night stand. Judging from the way they're gazing at each other, it might just last forever. I see the fellow with the cat backpack, on his butt in the middle of the crowd so everyone can *ooh* and *aah* at his companion up close. I see Brenna with

Riley and her Aunt Kathy at the front of the bookstore. And is that Becky slinking through the door? Bob isn't with her. Still, whatever Miguel scribbled on the note he included in the box of Amelia's books must have thawed her icy heart.

But Fiona and Amelia Mae still haven't arrived.

Miguel's been waiting for them. Despite the snacks and good company, the crowd's getting restless as they wait for him to speak. Riley says something to Brenna, then goes over to Miguel to tell him it's time to start.

He scans the room yet again and, with some reluctance, heads to the front of the store, pulling me behind him in the wagon. Dane's set up the podium with a microphone, which Miguel taps, and it sends a terrible screeching sound through the crowd. However, it does get everyone to stop talking.

"Hello," he says.

"Can't hear you," someone calls.

He tries again. "Thank you for being here tonight." He sounds better, though he's a bit warbly. "A few of you are new to our little bookstore. If that's you, welcome. Most of you are regulars, and we appreciate you so much. I also want to welcome our novelists—I'm told we have authors here from as far as Cincinnati and Seattle."

Someone hoots, and a woman yells, "Fresno in the house!"

Miguel waves. "*Hola,* Fresno. I so wish Amelia May were here to see you all. As most of you know, she was my partner and the cofounder of this bookstore. She died nineteen months ago."

People murmur, and some lower their eyes.

"Thank you," he tells them. "This event and your presence would've meant the world to her—"

A voice carries from the back of the store.

"Excuse us. Pardon us. Coming through," says Amelia Mae, who is using snake hands to weave through the crowd. Fiona, who's wearing my favorite yellow dress, is following on her heels.

I prop myself up on my front paws, and Amelia Mae runs to me as Fiona slides next to Miriam and Dane.

Miguel breaks into a grin. Fiona grins back, and the next thing I know, they're staring at each other like a couple of fools.

Of course, fool, Amelia always said, is just another word for a human in love.

"You know, I'm going to go off script here," says Miguel, still looking at Fiona. "There are no coincidences—that's what Amelia told me. I loved her terribly, but I never did agree with that."

Someone makes a surprised sound, but he continues.

"That's only because I thought she was telling me I had to embrace the crap that life slung my way—and there's been a lot of crap since she got sick and passed. But now I get it. That's not what she ever meant. Which I should have known, because she was the first to stomp her foot and speak up when things weren't fair. But she also knew that if you stop pushing so hard and let life happen the way it was always going to happen all along, the good will find you. The good *people*," he clarifies, and the lightest strands of Fiona's hair sparkle as she shakes her head.

He points a finger at the banner. "Now, for our big announcement. I believe most of you know that our store's next great adventure is dedicating this space to romance. We'll still carry other books, but this is a destination for people who love love."

The crowd erupts into cheering and clapping, and Dane kisses Miriam.

"Thank you," says Miguel, overwhelmed by their reaction. "There's more, though. My amazing co-owners and I—Riley, Brenna, Dane, and Natalie, who I'm honored to call friends as well—are pleased to announce that we are renaming Lakeside. Brenna?" he says, and she pulls the cloth off the new sign over the big picture window.

" 'Happy Endings!' " squeals Amelia Mae.

"That's right," Miguel tells her. He looks out at the crowd again. "That wonderful suggestion came from a budding writer who happens to share a name with my Amelia May. Something tells me that's no coincidence, either."

Oh, Miguel, you really get it. Keep it up and you might just come back as a dog in your next life.

He pauses and turns to Fiona, who's beaming. "As I learned reading Amelia's novels, love isn't just the point of our existence; it's the greatest gift you can give another person. I'm proud to be a part of a place that honors that."

Miguel finishes his speech, and people cheer again before wandering off to eat and drink and buy books. Then he goes to get glasses of champagne for himself and Fiona, but when he returns to the place where she and Amelia Mae were standing, she's missing.

He turns around in a circle. He's just starting to look worried when he spots her weaving through the throng with two men. It takes me a moment, but I realize one is Vik, and the other is—why, yes, it *is* Jonathan, but he's wearing a T-shirt and doesn't have his glasses on, and his hair's cut short. I'm just a dog, of course, but if anyone's asking me, he barely looks like the man on the books he was supposed to have written.

"Miguel," she says, accepting the glass from him. "This is my brother, Jonathan."

Miguel breaks into a smile, then shakes Jonathan's hand. "It's good to finally meet you. I hope you didn't fly back from Copenhagen for this."

Jonathan smiles, then slips his arm around Vik. "No, I flew back from Copenhagen for love. So, if anyone can appreciate what you've done with the store, it's me. I just wish I'd come in sooner. I really am sorry."

"Apology accepted. Besides, if you hadn't gone rogue, I never would have met Fiona," he says, smiling at her. "At any rate, there's no time like the present. Please, be our guests."

"We appreciate that," says Vik, and then they disappear into the crowd.

Fiona winks at Miguel and clinks her glass against his. "To love."

"To me loving you," he says quietly.

Her eyes widen.

"I should've said it when you came over to tell me about you and Jonathan," he tells her. "I understand now that it wasn't the truth that drove me away. I've been afraid of being happy—and of the possibility I could lose another person I cared about. But I promise you that I'll never let my fear of losing you get the best of me again. Will you give me another chance to show you how much you mean to me?"

"I already did, you fool," she says, then kisses him.

"I suspect Amelia knew exactly what she was doing when

she told you about this store," Miguel says when they finally pull apart from each other.

"I do, too," she says, glancing around. "And maybe she knew I'd end up loving you, too."

"I like that thought." He puts his arm around her waist and pulls her close. "Does that mean I get to be an early reader of whatever you write next?"

"You'll be the very first."

"I can't wait. In the meantime . . ." He dashes over to the register, where a long line has formed, and reaches behind the counter. When he returns, he's carrying a fresh copy of *Missing Person*. "Would you sign this for me?"

She regards it. "As JMB?"

"No, as yourself—the woman who wrote the book," he says in a low voice. "I know it's complicated, but this story will always have a special place in my heart, so it'd mean the world to me if you'd consider it."

Fiona hesitates before pulling a pen from the pocket of her dress. Then she squats down, balances the book on the edge of my wagon, and opens to one of the first pages. "It means more to me," she tells him, and beside the scribble that I assume is her name, there's a little wet dot where a tear has fallen. She stands, but instead of handing the book to him, she plants her lips on his and sinks into his arms.

"Harry, he did it!" whispers Amelia Mae, who's just appeared behind me. "He fixed it!"

Yes, the man has finally learned to grovel—and my heart feels so, so full.

A dog's only as happy as his owner, after all.

"Come on," says Amelia Mae, who has already started tugging the wagon away from them. "Let's leave these lovebirds to it and do a quick spin before we have to go."

"Don't wander too far," calls Fiona.

Amelia Mae smiles sweetly at her. "Have we met?"

"Yes, love, we have—and you have an alarming tendency to act out *Missing Person*. Which is exactly why I'm asking you not to wind up in Alaska."

"I won't," she responds in a singsong voice before winking at me and adding in a whisper, "Don't tell my mom, but I actually don't want to worry her any more than I already have."

"Harold, are you good?" Miguel asks me.

I raise my head to tell him I am for now, and that's enough.

"Well, you know I'm here if you need me," he says.

I do.

Amelia Mae pulls the wagon to the front of the store to what's left of the rainbow of love stories; thanks to Riley's display, nearly all the paperbacks have gone to good homes.

I didn't see it earlier, but someone, probably Miguel, has placed a framed photo of my Amelia in the center of the table. I know this shot; Dane took it years ago, not long after he started working here. In it, Amelia's seated on the yellow velvet chair, with me at her feet, and Miguel's smiling down at her. She's so joyful—and of course she is. Her favorite place, she always said, was wherever we were.

As I stare at the photo, I finally understand that Amelia may have asked me to take care of Miguel, but she never meant for me to give up my own happiness. She wanted me to create more of it for both of us.

I look across the store at Miguel, who's standing with his arm around Fiona, listening to Dane and Miriam banter back and forth. Brenna and Riley are hip to hip at the register, selling book after book after book. Beside me, Amelia Mae's yapping my ear off about the story she wants me to help her write tomorrow.

And I think to myself, *What a very good dog I've been.*

EPILOGUE

I am a summer creature, as that's when I was born, and nearly a year later, Amelia found me and made me hers. But fall, she always said, is the superior season, and I know I'm lucky to have lived long enough to spend this one with Miguel and Amelia Mae.

She, Fiona, and Walter have rented a small house on the other side of town, which she claims is just the right amount of creepy. It's also down the street from her new friend Ruby, who happens to be quite clever herself and doesn't think Amelia Mae talks too much. They're over here all the time. At Miguel's encouragement, Amelia Mae even goes up to my Amelia's office sometimes to work on her stories. Walter follows me around like I'm his hero, and while I won't say he's made me a dog's dog, I have relented and taught him a few new tricks.

Our house feels like a home again when they're in it. And something tells me that one day soon, they'll stay for good.

The medicine doesn't work, not the way Miguel's hoping it will. I'm not in terrible pain, but my hips stick at their hinges and my chest is heavy and I'm tired all the time. That's all right because Amelia Mae pulls me around in her old plastic wagon. I raise my head to the sun and close my eyes as we roll along. I smell the crisp air and the earth preparing to go dormant before it begins again. I hear leaves crackling beneath the wagon's wheels.

And, of course, I listen to Amelia Mae.

She tells me all about *Carrie* as well as her own stories but skips *Pet Sematary*—a mite too dark, she declares. Her tales are gory, but no one ever dies, even if they deserve it. As she explains, it's actually best if they just live on and suffer. "I'm going to call *my* bookstore 'Unhappy Endings,'" she says with a devilish grin as we pull up in front of the rainbow window one chilly October afternoon. "The whole store's gonna be filled with Stabby Peeps. Isn't that perfect, Harry?"

Oh, but it is. I suspect my other Amelia will be very famous one day.

At home, my bed is still beside the bookshelves, and Miguel has moved the urn and all the rainbow books back to the bottom shelf so I can rest my head near them. He helps me outside to use the bathroom and brings me bowls of the special food he cooks himself, and all of it is magically delicious. Amelia would be so very proud of him.

Fiona regularly goes to the bookstore with Miguel, and she's spent the night a few times when Jonathan's been in town and could watch Walter and Amelia Mae, because even she can admit that being alone overnight is an unreasonable amount of time. Miguel's different with Fiona than he was with my Amelia—and yet he loves her all the way. They are content, which means I am, too.

The days are slow; the days are fast. Some are as clear as a blue September sky, while others are so foggy, I'm not sure I was really there. But every day is the best day other than the ones I had with my Amelia, because we are together.

Then one morning I awake, and I know, just as she must have, that it's time.

I don't want to go. I'd like to keep watching Miguel be alive in the truest sense of that word. And sunny Fiona and cloudy Amelia Mae: I've barely begun to enjoy them. I want to see who Dane and Miriam become as a couple—although I imagine it is who they already are, yet somehow even better. There are so many tomorrows that I won't be a part of. I've been here a good long while, and that's a gift. But I understand now why my Amelia said it's never, ever enough.

Miguel seems to know, too, because he rises early and remains at my side, leaving only to bring me some water and my food, which I can't manage to eat more than a bite of. He asks Fiona to bring Amelia Mae to our house, and she lies beside me and tells me the story of how we used our magic to help her mom and my Miguel see that there's nothing less complicated than being with the one you love.

And then Miguel takes her place and tells me the story of everything.

Of a sparkling woman he spotted in a bookstore and instantly fell in love with, even though he thought that only happened in books—and how, miraculously, she loved him back, despite the fact that he wasn't the kind of man she wrote about. But as he would later learn, he was part of every story she'd ever written.

Of the dog she discovered at the shelter one summer day and how nothing—not his relentless leash-pulling or barfing on the rugs or repeatedly running away and making her cry—could keep him from being her very best friend.

Of her dream to fill the world with books, which made *their* dream into a real place where readers could find their own happy endings.

Of the adventures and heartaches and triumphs of their life, which they shared with me and each other for as long as they could.

Miguel's stopped talking now and is resting his hand gently on my head.

And I know that I am safe, and I am loved, so I let my eyes close once more.

Suddenly, there she is—my person, my love, my Amelia. She is standing across a grassy field that stretches forever, and she is calling me.

"Harold!" she says, and her smile's as brilliant as the sun itself. "Come on, boy. Run to me!"

How can I not, when I've waited so long to see her again? And finally, she's here. Right on time.

"Amelia!" I bark, tearing through the grass. "I love you I love you I love you!"

"I love you, too, you nutty dog!"

Even from here, I can feel her warmth on my fur, and I blink and blink as my eyes fill with tears.

"Aww, Harold. It's okay," she tells me. "I know you've been through so much. You've been such a good boy."

Yes, yes, I have.

"And you still are. I'm so incredibly happy to see you."

I am, too, and my tail nub's wagging, wagging, wagging. Oh, how wrong I was about ever after!

"I've been waiting for you, Harold," says Amelia as she kneels and opens her arms. "So, come here so I can scratch your ears and rub your belly and give you the absolute biggest dog hug of your life. Then we'll go run and play and spend the rest of time together."

"Harold?" I can hear Miguel now. He's farther away, and that old familiar tug to help him almost makes me open my eyes again. He must sense that I am caught between duty and desire, because his voice drops to a murmur. "It's okay," he assures me. "It's okay. Thank you. You saved my life day after day, Harold, and I'll never forget that. I love you."

I love him, too.

Of course, Miguel's already aware of that. And now we both know that he'll be fine. That he *is* fine. I've done my job; I've fulfilled my purpose, which is the most any of us can wish for.

So, I say goodbye—but only for now. Because one day in the far-off future, Amelia and I will greet him in the field that stretches forever.

Then I begin to run as fast as my legs will take me.

For my person is calling—

And she is my happy ending.

ACKNOWLEDGMENTS

Elisabeth Weed, you believed in this story from the start—and I'm so grateful, because I never would've gotten here without you. Thank you for all you've done to support me and my fiction career.

Alicia Clancy, working with you has been an absolute joy. I can't thank you enough for your brilliant editorial guidance and for expanding my vision for Harold (with help from Whiskey and Memphis, of course!). Likewise, my deep gratitude goes to the entire team at Delacorte and Penguin Random House for championing this novel.

Michelle Weiner, thank you and your team at CAA for helping my fiction find an audience beyond the page. Jenny Meyer and team (especially Heidi Gall), thank you for bringing *Dog Person* to more readers across the globe. Suzy Leopold, I owe you for helping spread the word about my work all these years. And I would be remiss not to mention Danielle Marshall, Jodi Warshaw, and Maria Gomez, who helped me become a far stronger storyteller and connect with so many readers.

Everyone says writing is a lonely business, but I honestly never feel that way—and that's because of my amazing community of writers. Emily Bleeker, Kerry Lonsdale, and Rochelle Weinstein, I'm lucky to have you in my corner. Likewise,

Chris Bailey, Anne Bogel, Katherine Chen, Lauren Faulkenberry, Katie Rose Guest Pryal, Alison Hammer, Kelly Harms, Sarah Jio, Orly Konig, Sara Reistad-Long, Jane Stinson, Darci Swisher, Laura Vanderkam, and all of my Career Novelist community, thank you for continually inspiring me.

Lauren Bauser, Shannon Callahan, and Pam Sullivan: I love you girls to the moon and back. Stefanie and Craig Galban, Stevany and Tim Peters, and Michelle and Mike Stone, kindergarten soccer is the gift that just keeps on giving; you all are the best. Jessie Katz, thank you for your guidance during one of the hardest times of my life.

Laurel Lambert, Janette Sunadhar, and the Lambert, Lizarribar, Noe, Pagán, and Sunadhar families, your love and support means the world to me. I wish two of my very favorite dog people, Patricia Pietrzak and Bill Pietrzak, were here to read this book because they'd see themselves on every page. Joyce Nelson, I'll never forget you and Bill telling me, on a bridge in Woodstock, Vermont, that I actually could be a novelist one day. Thank you for helping me make that dream come true.

JP, Indira, and Xavi, you're the heart of every story I tell.

Above all, thank you to my readers. You are the reason I write.

ABOUT THE AUTHOR

Camille Pagán is the bestselling author of numerous novels that have been translated into nearly two dozen languages, including *Dog Person, Good for You,* and *Life and Other Near-Death Experiences.* She has written for *The New York Times, O: The Oprah Magazine, Parade, Real Simple, Time,* and many other publications. When she's not working on her next story, you'll find Pagán talking shop with writers, hanging out with her two kids, or trying to convince her husband they should adopt yet another animal. She and her family live in Ann Arbor, Michigan, and spend as much time in Puerto Rico as possible.

camillepagan.com

ABOUT THE TYPE

This book was set in Scala, a typeface designed by Martin Majoor in 1991. It was originally designed for a music company in the Netherlands and then was published by the international type house FSI FontShop. Its distinctive extended serifs add to the articulation of the letterforms to make it a very readable typeface.